PRAISE FOR **squish**!

"Even the mildest young boy will see something of himself in Squish. *Super Amoeba* is an energetic, good-hearted escapade, one that young readers will enjoy."
　　　　　　　　　　　　　　　—*The New York Times*

★"The hilarious misadventures of a hapless young everylad who happens to be an amoeba. If ever a new series deserved to go viral, this one does."
　　　　　　　　　　　　　　—*Kirkus Reviews*, Starred

"The Holms strike a breezy, goofy tone right out of the gate."　　　　　　　　　　—*Publishers Weekly*

"A perfect mix of writing that is simple enough for early readers but still remarkably snarky, clever, and entertaining. . . . Kids themselves will soak up the humor, tidbits of science instruction, and adventure."
　　—*The Bulletin of the Center for Children's Books*

"A new graphic novel series that will have readers everywhere clapping their pseudopods in glee. There's some real science worked in here too and even directions for a kid-friendly experiment."
　　　　　　　　　　　　　—*Bookends* (*Booklist* blog)

Read ALL the SQUISH books!

#1 SQUISH: Super Amoeba
#2 SQUISH: Brave New Pond
#3 SQUISH: The Power of the Parasite
#4 SQUISH: Captain Disaster

squish
CAPTAIN DISASTER

BY JENNIFER L. HOLM & MATTHEW HOLM

RANDOM HOUSE 🏠 NEW YORK

Copyright © 2012 by Jennifer Holm and Matthew Holm

All rights reserved. Published in the United States
by Random House Children's Books,
a division of Random House, Inc., New York.

Random House and the colophon are registered trademarks
of Random House, Inc.

Visit us on the Web! randomhouse.com/kids

Educators and librarians, for a variety of teaching tools,
visit us at RHTeachersLibrarians.com

Library of Congress Cataloging-in-Publication Data
Holm, Jennifer L.
Captain Disaster / by Jennifer L. Holm & Matthew Holm. —
1st ed.   p.   cm. — (Squish ; #4)
Summary: Squish, comic book fan and grade school amoeba,
is made captain of his soccer team and following the example
of his favorite superhero, must figure out how to turn a
losing streak around without losing his friends.
ISBN 978-0-375-84392-1 (trade pbk.) —
ISBN 978-0-375-93786-6 (lib. bdg.)
1. Graphic novels. [1. Graphic novels. 2. Amoeba—Fiction.
3. Soccer—Fiction. 4. Teamwork (Sports)—Fiction.
5. Superheroes—Fiction.] I. Holm, Matthew. II. Title.
PZ7.7.H65Cap 2012   741.5'973—dc23   2011041155

MANUFACTURED IN MALAYSIA 10 9 8 7 6 5 4 3 2
First Edition

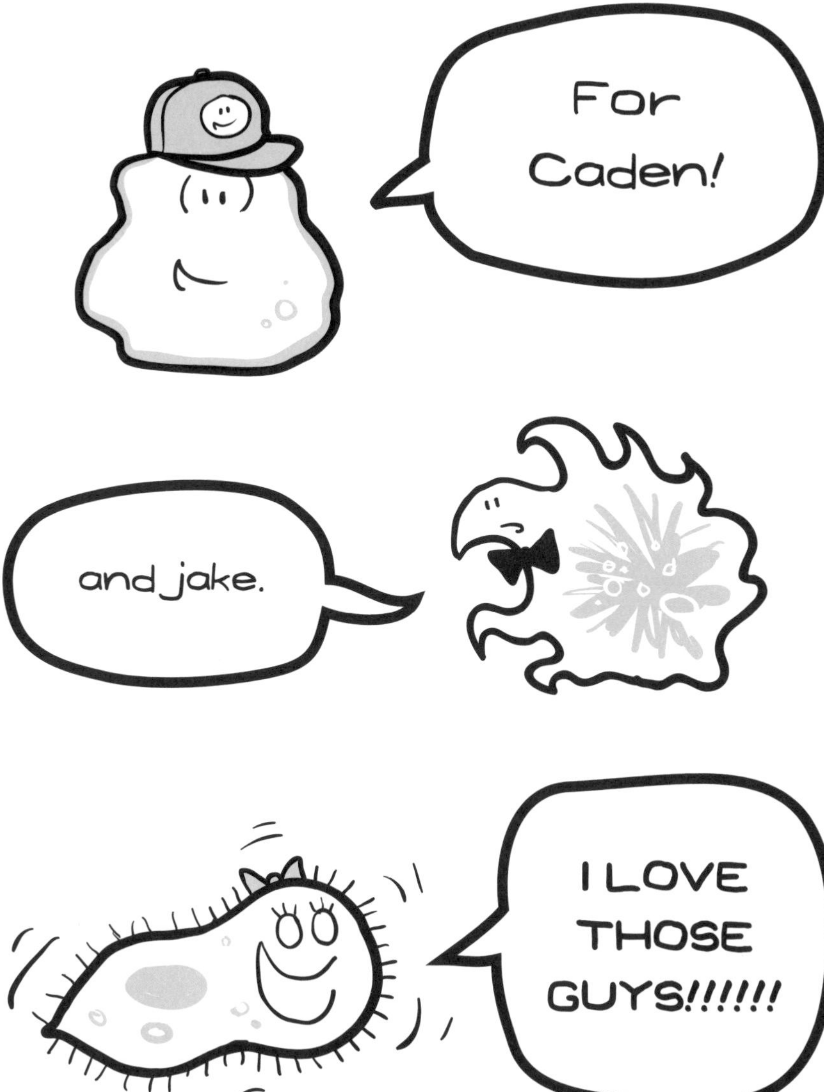
For Caden!
and jake.
I LOVE THOSE GUYS!!!!!!

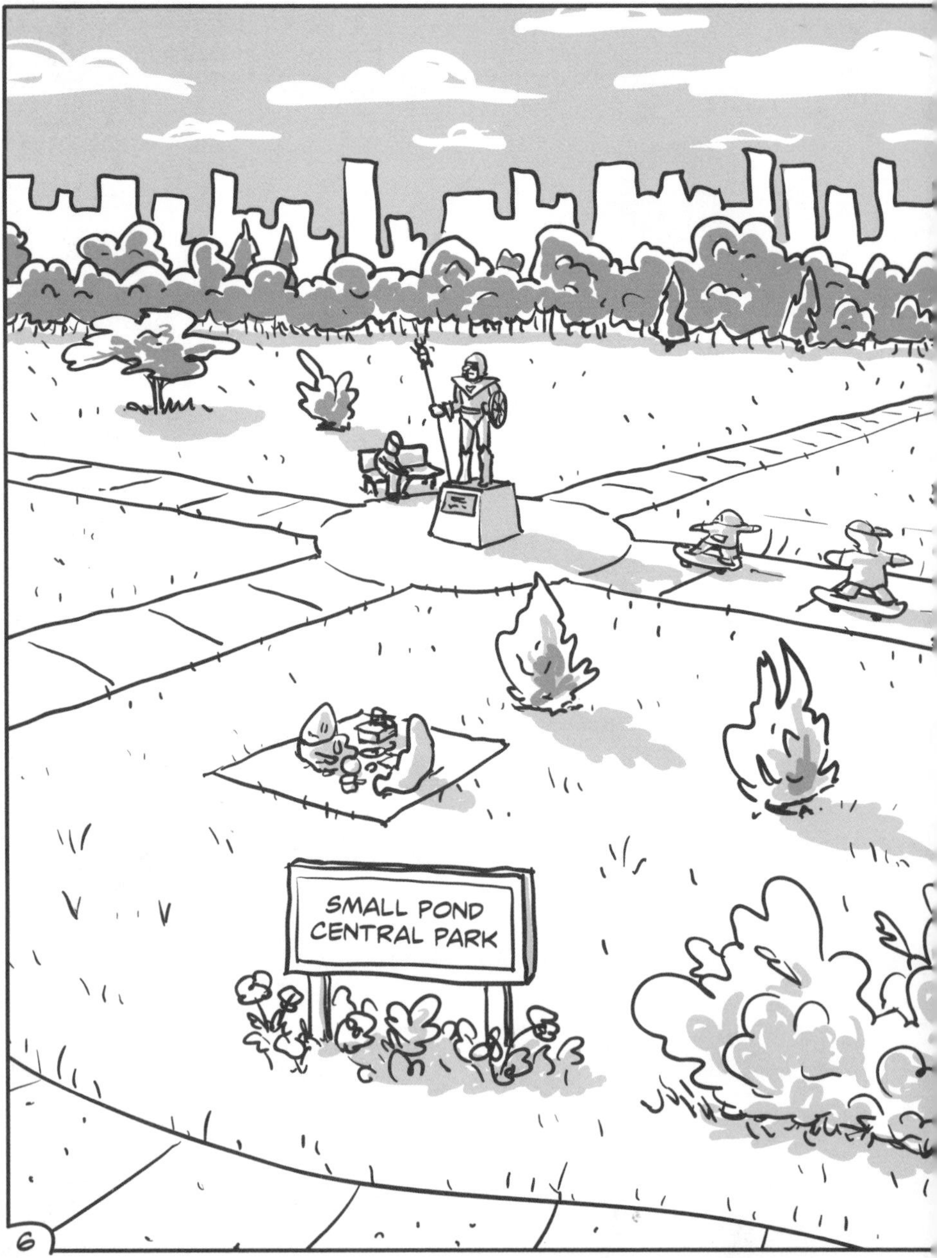
SMALL POND
CENTRAL PARK

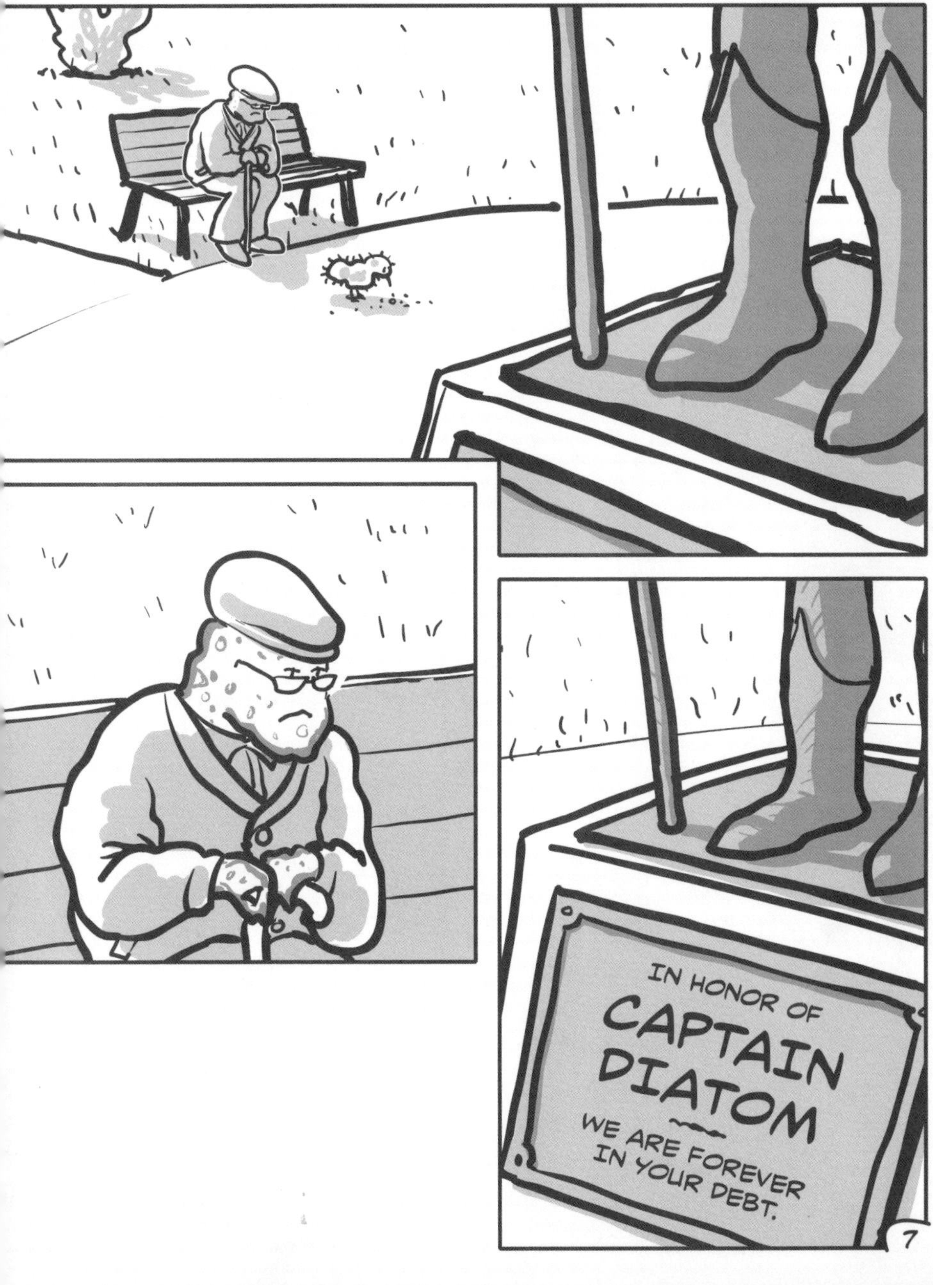
IN HONOR OF
CAPTAIN DIATOM
WE ARE FOREVER IN YOUR DEBT.

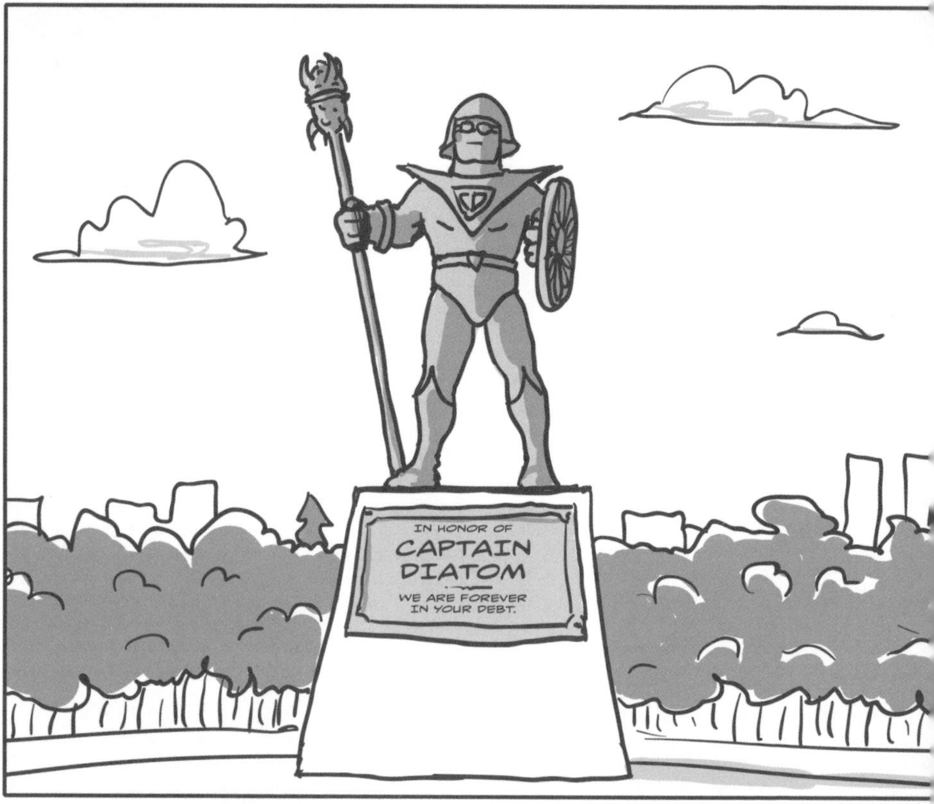
IN HONOR OF
CAPTAIN DIATOM
WE ARE FOREVER IN YOUR DEBT.

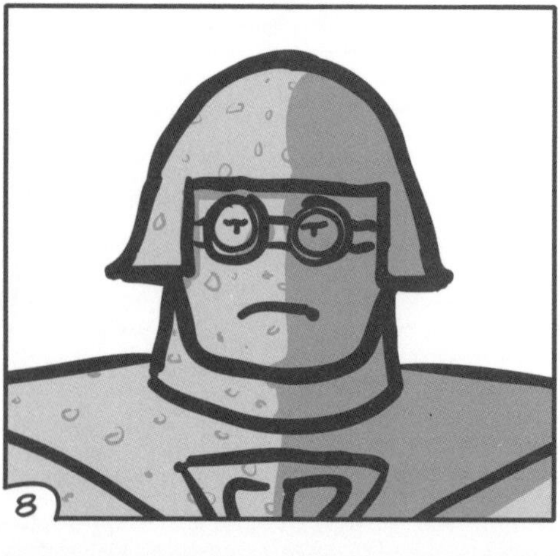

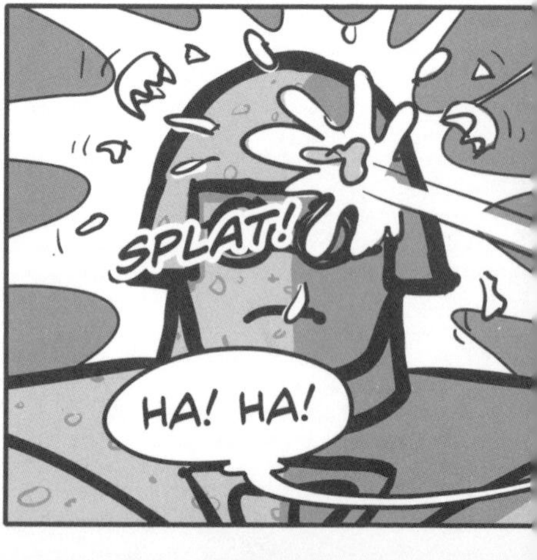
SPLAT!
HA! HA!

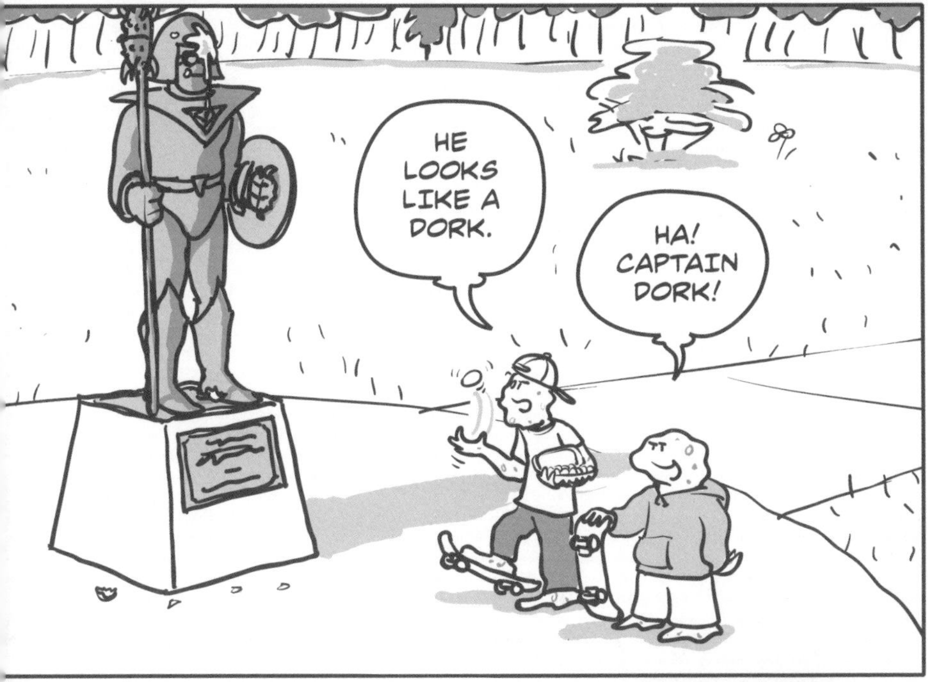
HE LOOKS LIKE A DORK.
HA! CAPTAIN DORK!

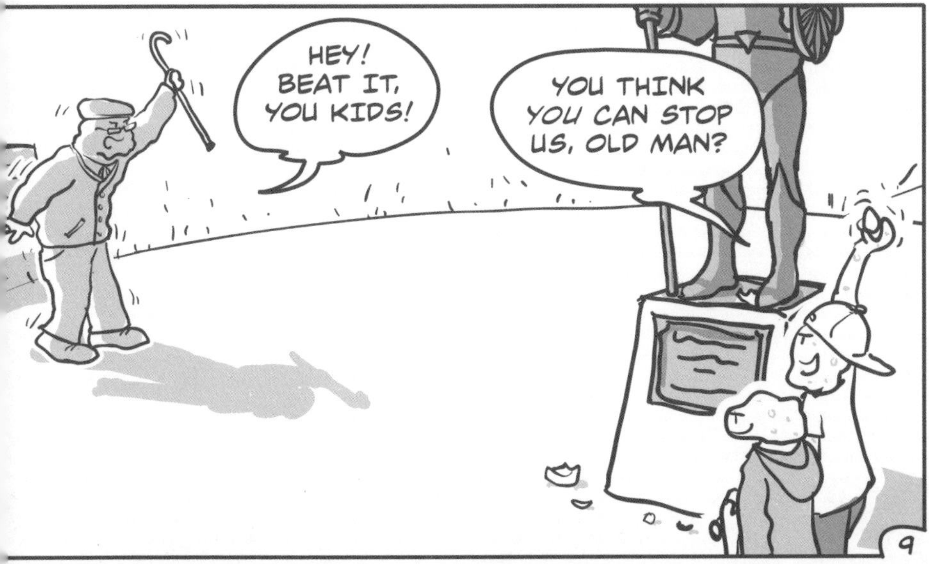
HEY! BEAT IT, YOU KIDS!
YOU THINK YOU CAN STOP US, OLD MAN?

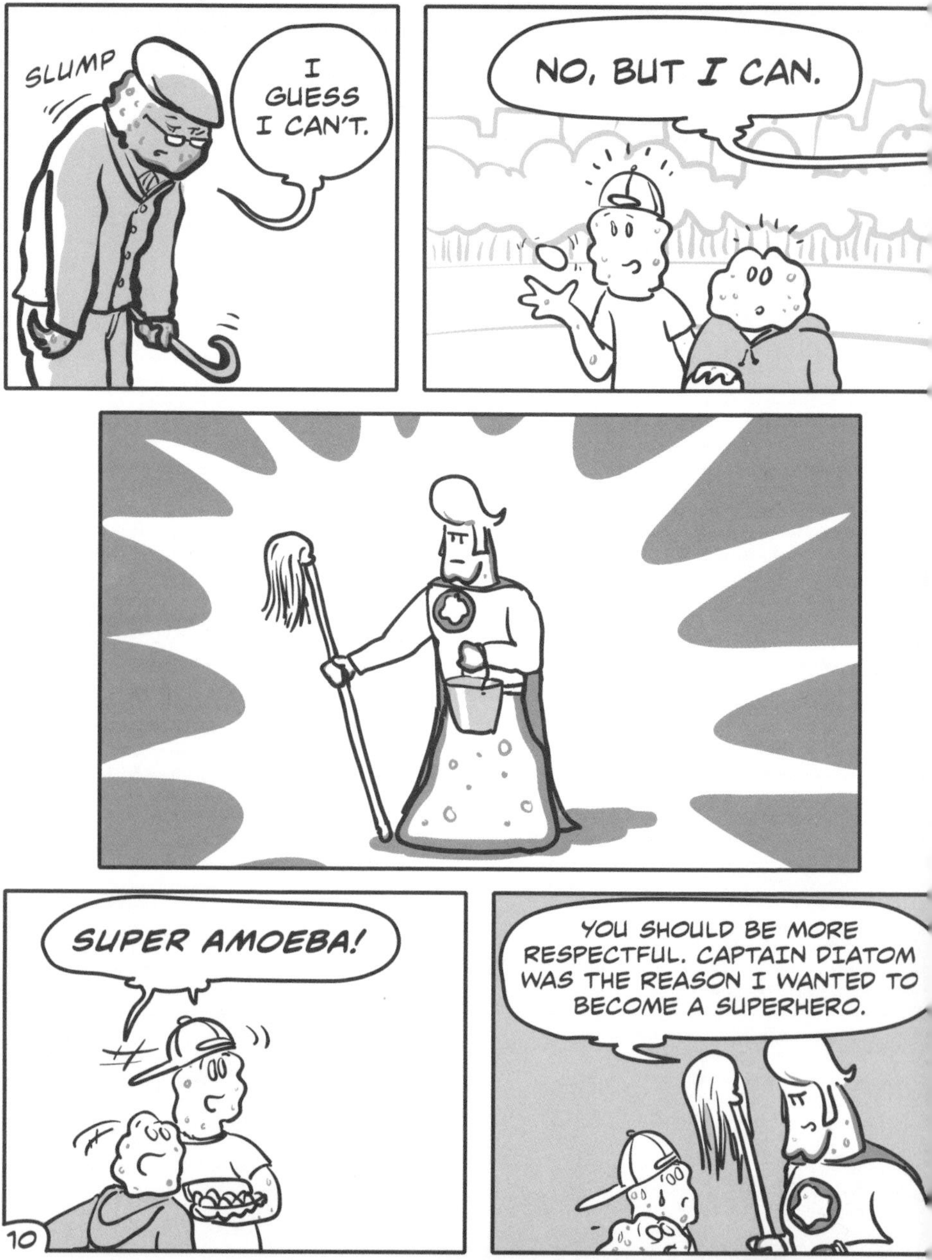
SLUMP
I GUESS I CAN'T.
NO, BUT I CAN.
SUPER AMOEBA!
YOU SHOULD BE MORE RESPECTFUL. CAPTAIN DIATOM WAS THE REASON I WANTED TO BECOME A SUPERHERO.

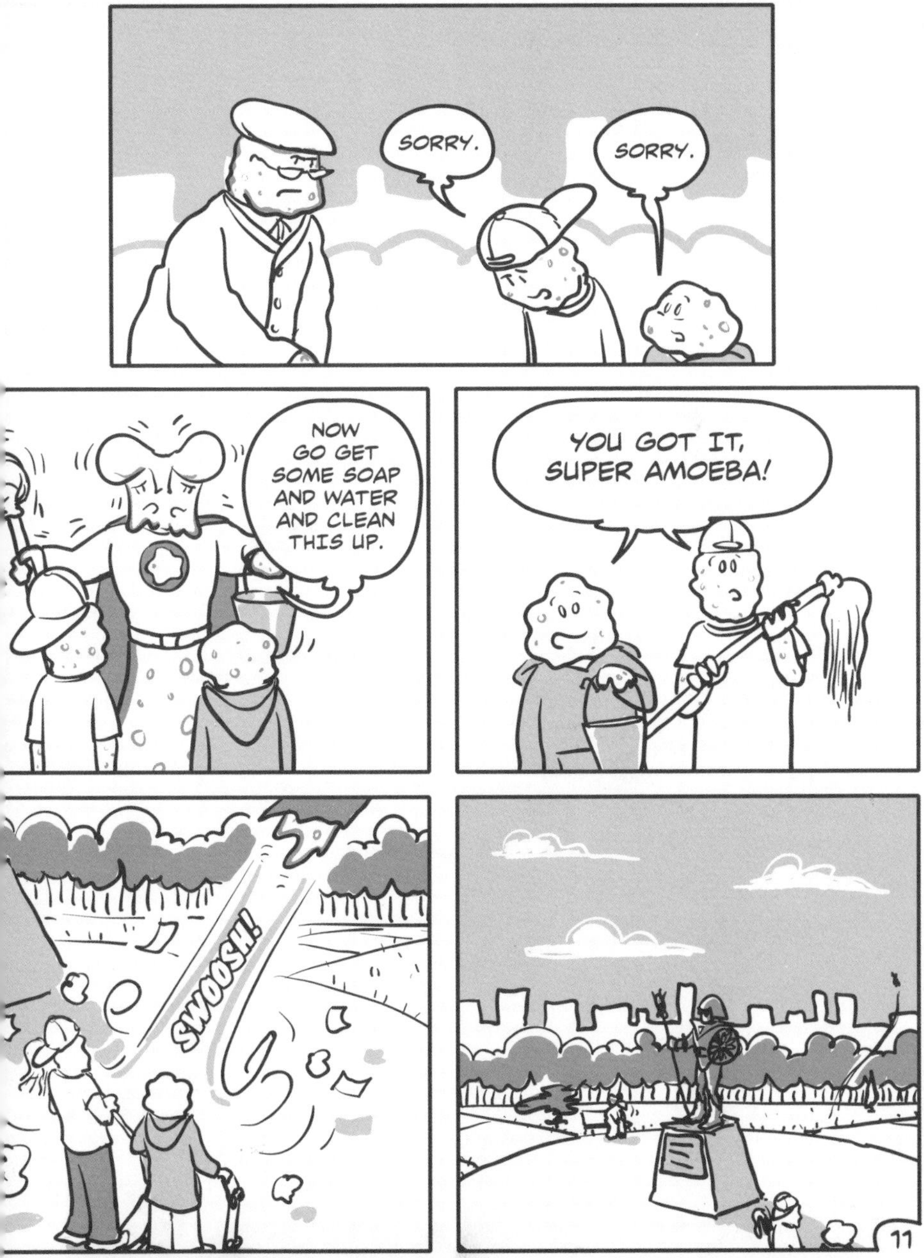
SORRY.
SORRY.
NOW GO GET SOME SOAP AND WATER AND CLEAN THIS UP.
YOU GOT IT, SUPER AMOEBA!
SWOOSH!

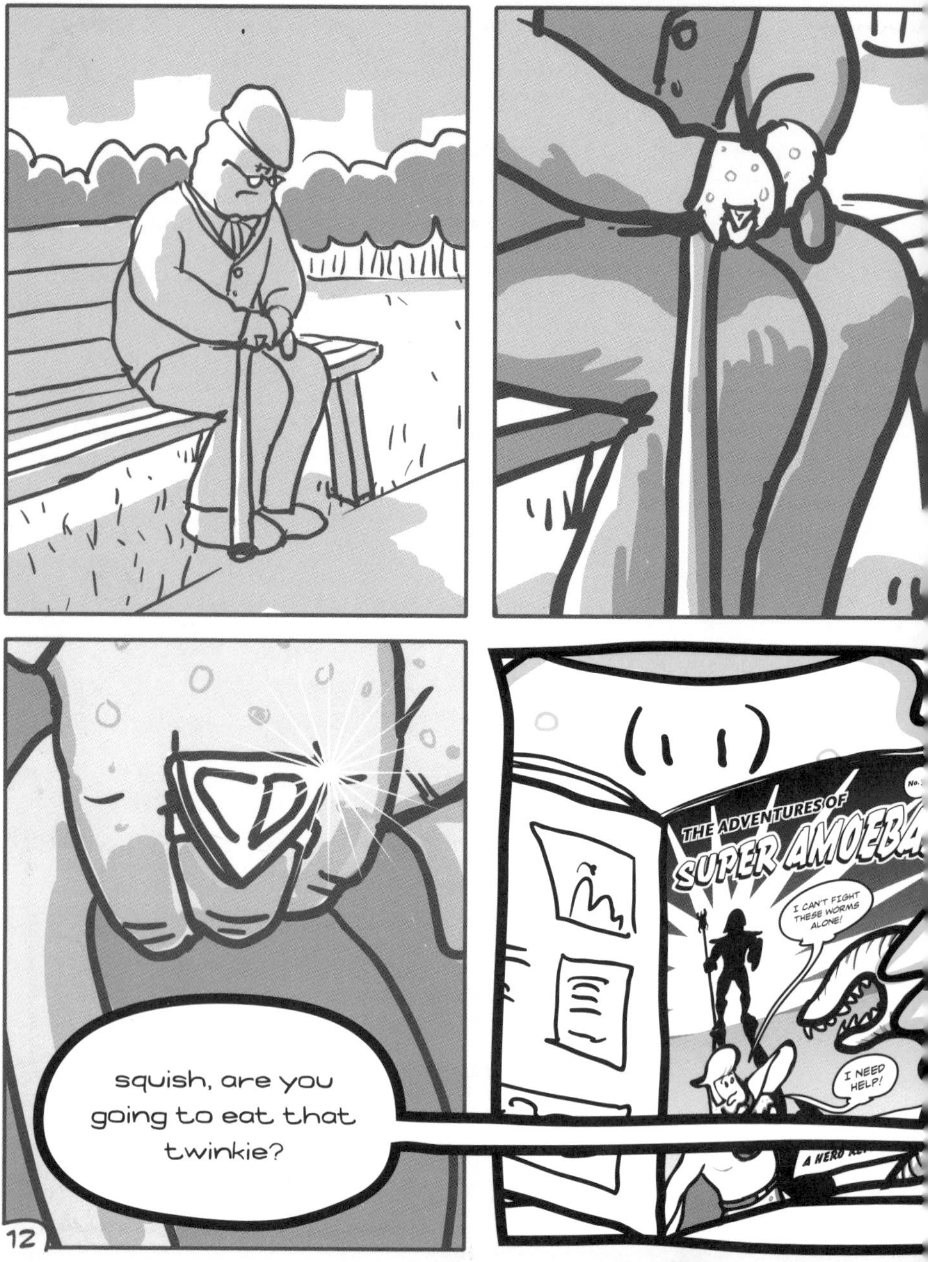
squish, are you going to eat that twinkie?
THE ADVENTURES OF
SUPER AMOEB
I CAN'T FIGHT THESE WORMS ALONE!
I NEED HELP!

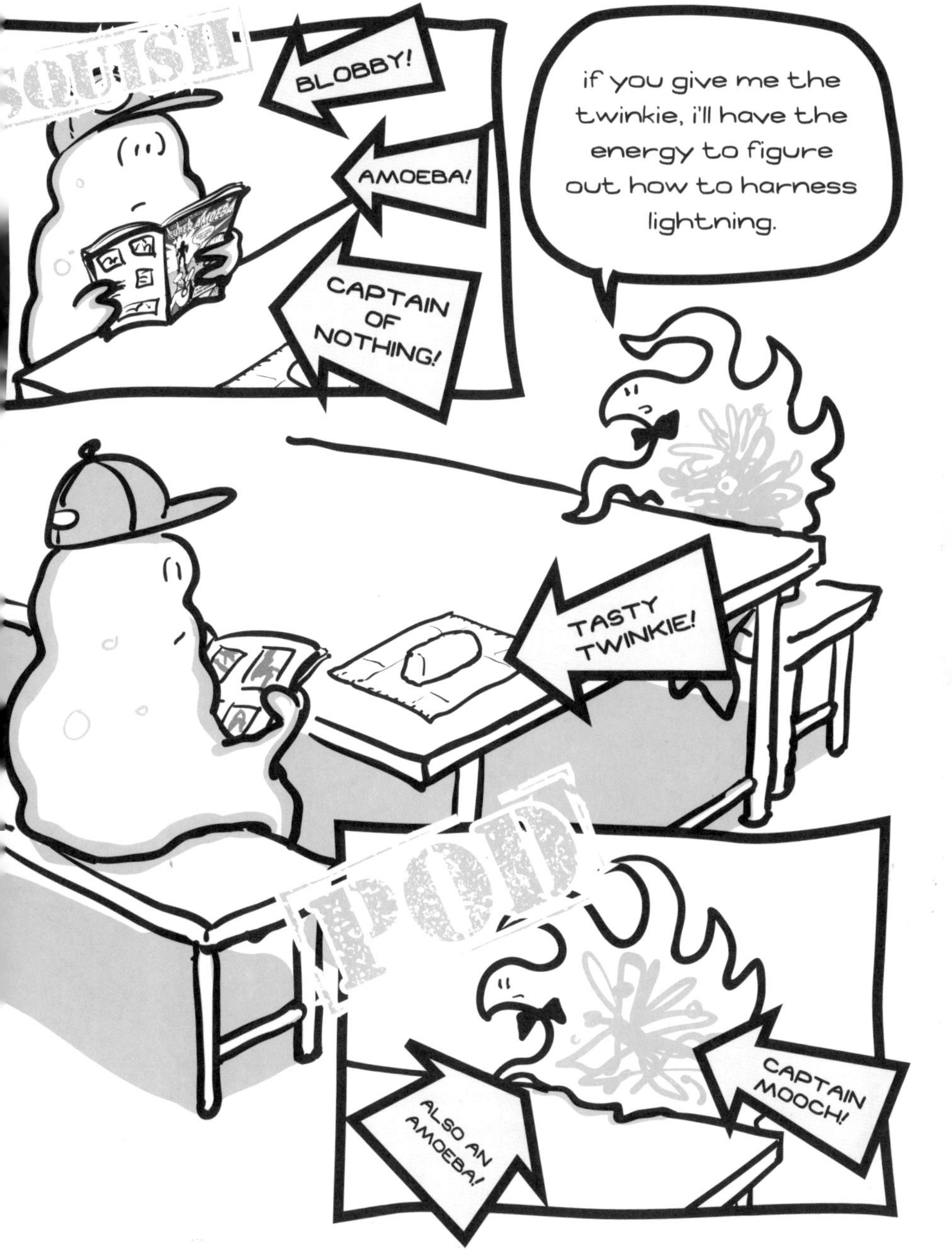
SQUISH
BLOBBY!
AMOEBA!
CAPTAIN OF NOTHING!
if you give me the twinkie, i'll have the energy to figure out how to harness lightning.
TASTY TWINKIE!
POP
CAPTAIN MOOCH!
ALSO AN AMOEBA!

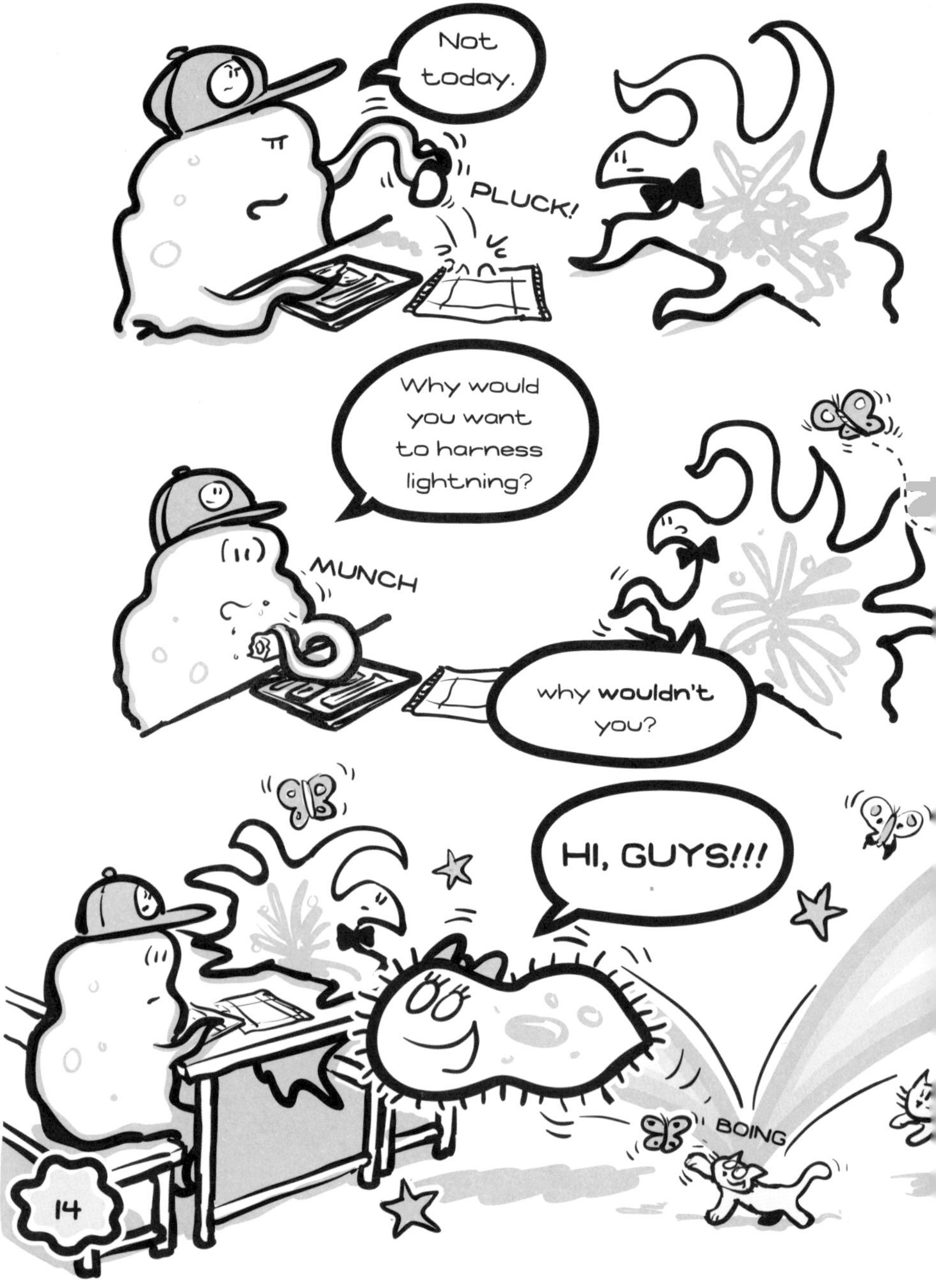
Not today.
PLUCK!
Why would you want to harness lightning?
MUNCH
why wouldn't you?
HI, GUYS!!!
BOING

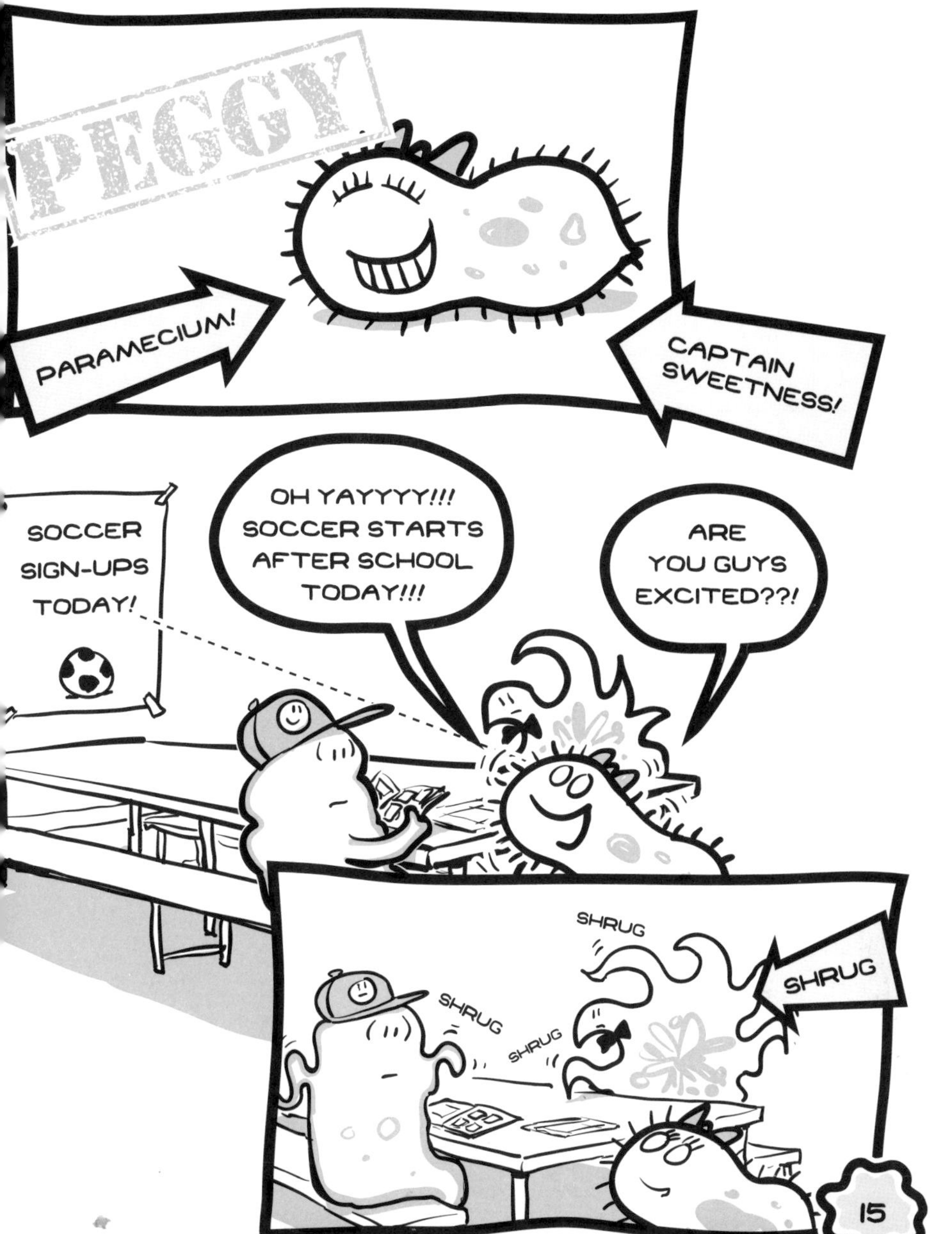
PEGGY
PARAMECIUM!
CAPTAIN SWEETNESS!
SOCCER SIGN-UPS TODAY!
OH YAYYYY!!! SOCCER STARTS AFTER SCHOOL TODAY!!!
ARE YOU GUYS EXCITED??!
SHRUG
SHRUG
SHRUG
SHRUG

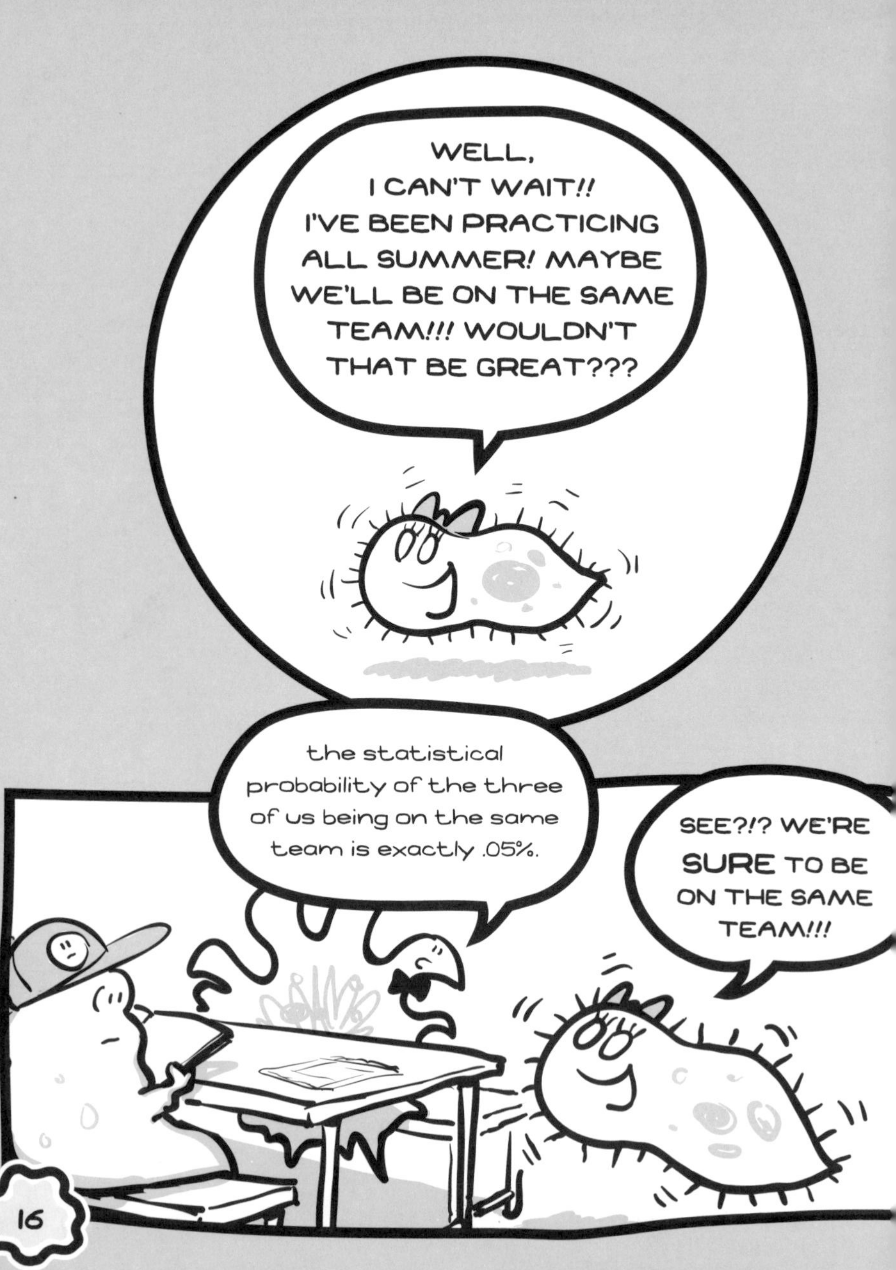
WELL, I CAN'T WAIT!! I'VE BEEN PRACTICING ALL SUMMER! MAYBE WE'LL BE ON THE SAME TEAM!!! WOULDN'T THAT BE GREAT???
the statistical probability of the three of us being on the same team is exactly .05%.
SEE?!? WE'RE **SURE** TO BE ON THE SAME TEAM!!!

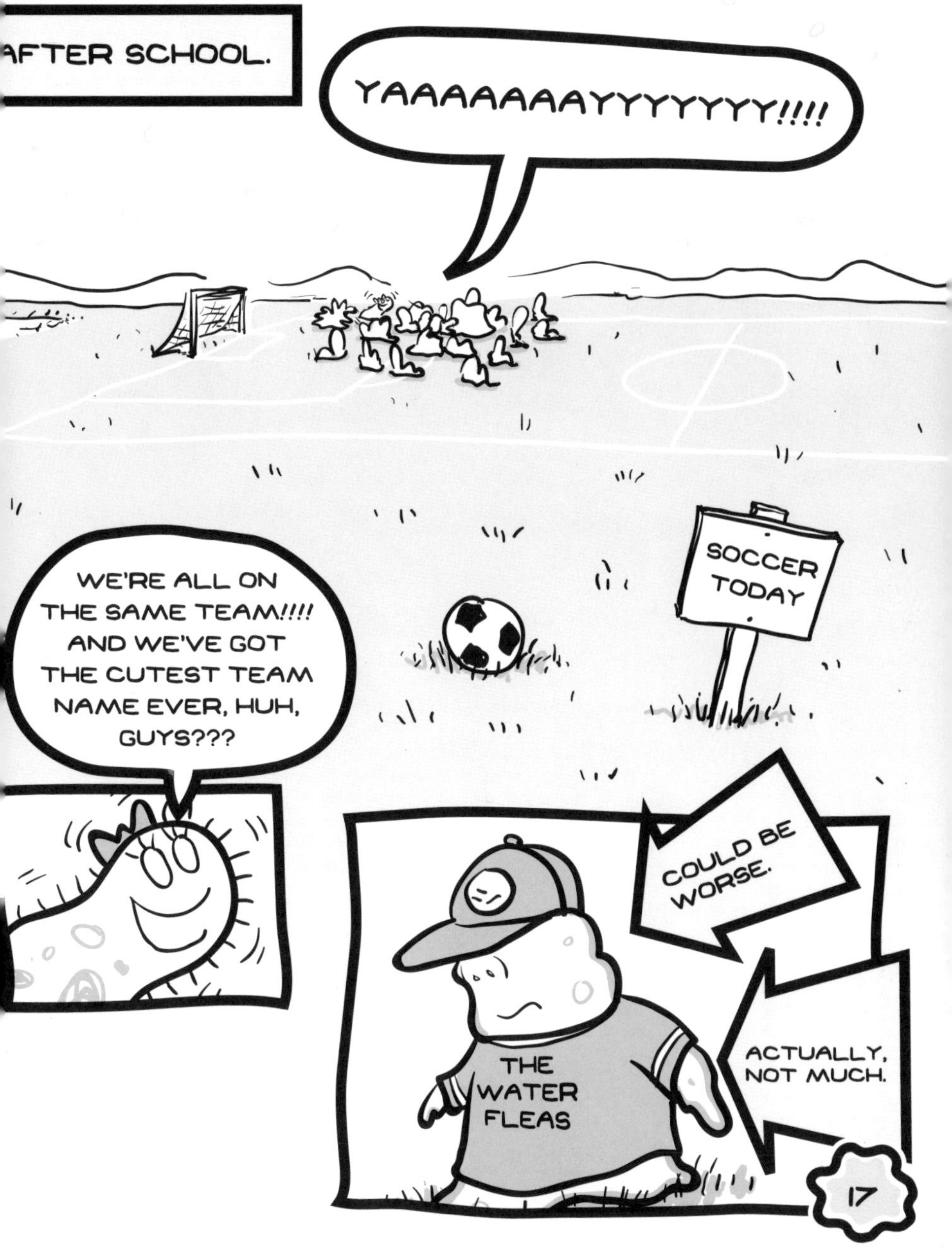
AFTER SCHOOL.
YAAAAAAAAYYYYYYYY!!!!
SOCCER TODAY
WE'RE ALL ON THE SAME TEAM!!!! AND WE'VE GOT THE CUTEST TEAM NAME EVER, HUH, GUYS???
COULD BE WORSE.
THE WATER FLEAS
ACTUALLY, NOT MUCH.

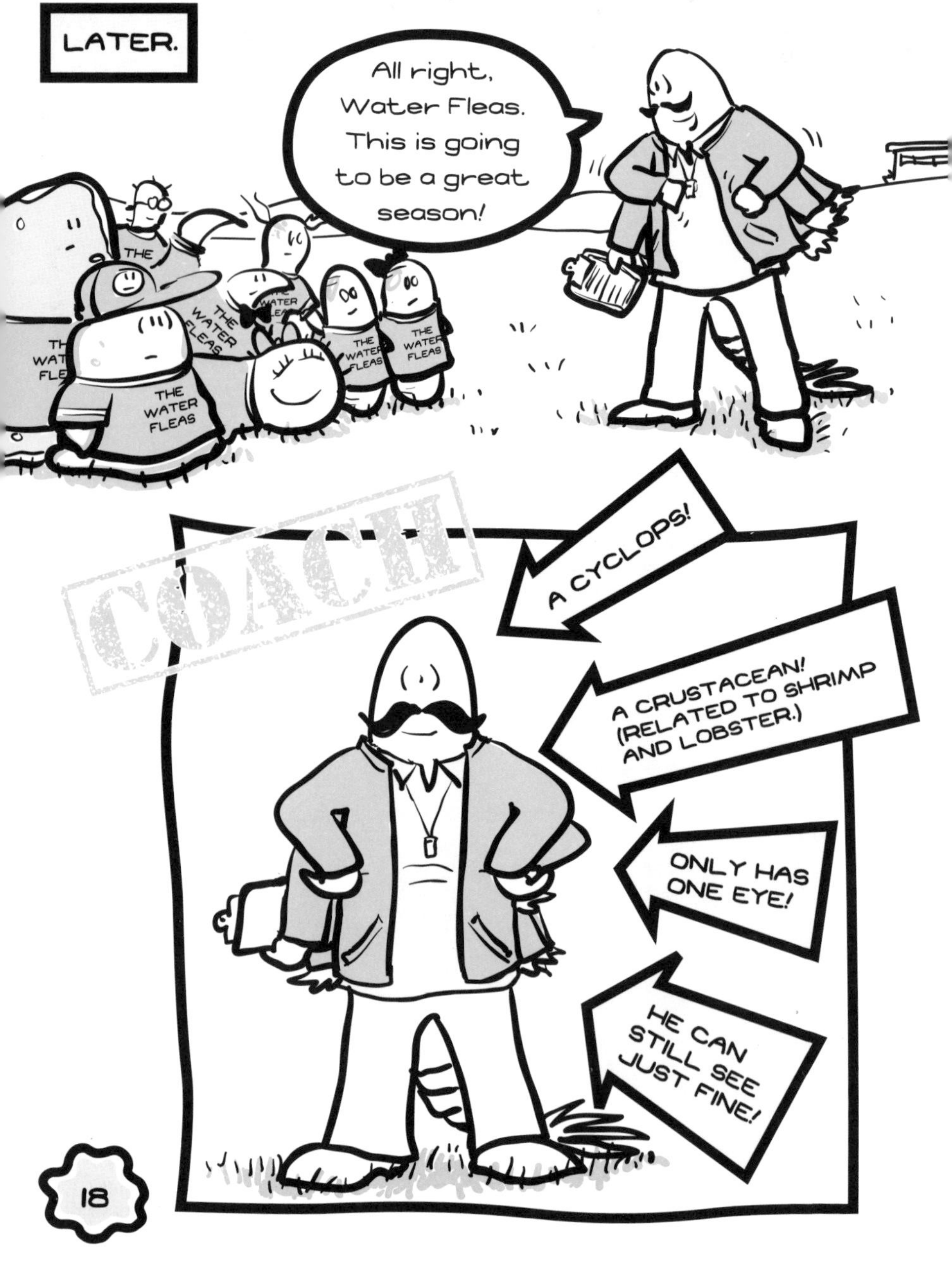
LATER.
All right, Water Fleas. This is going to be a great season!
THE WATER FLEAS
COACH
A CYCLOPS!
A CRUSTACEAN! (RELATED TO SHRIMP AND LOBSTER.)
ONLY HAS ONE EYE!
HE CAN STILL SEE JUST FINE!

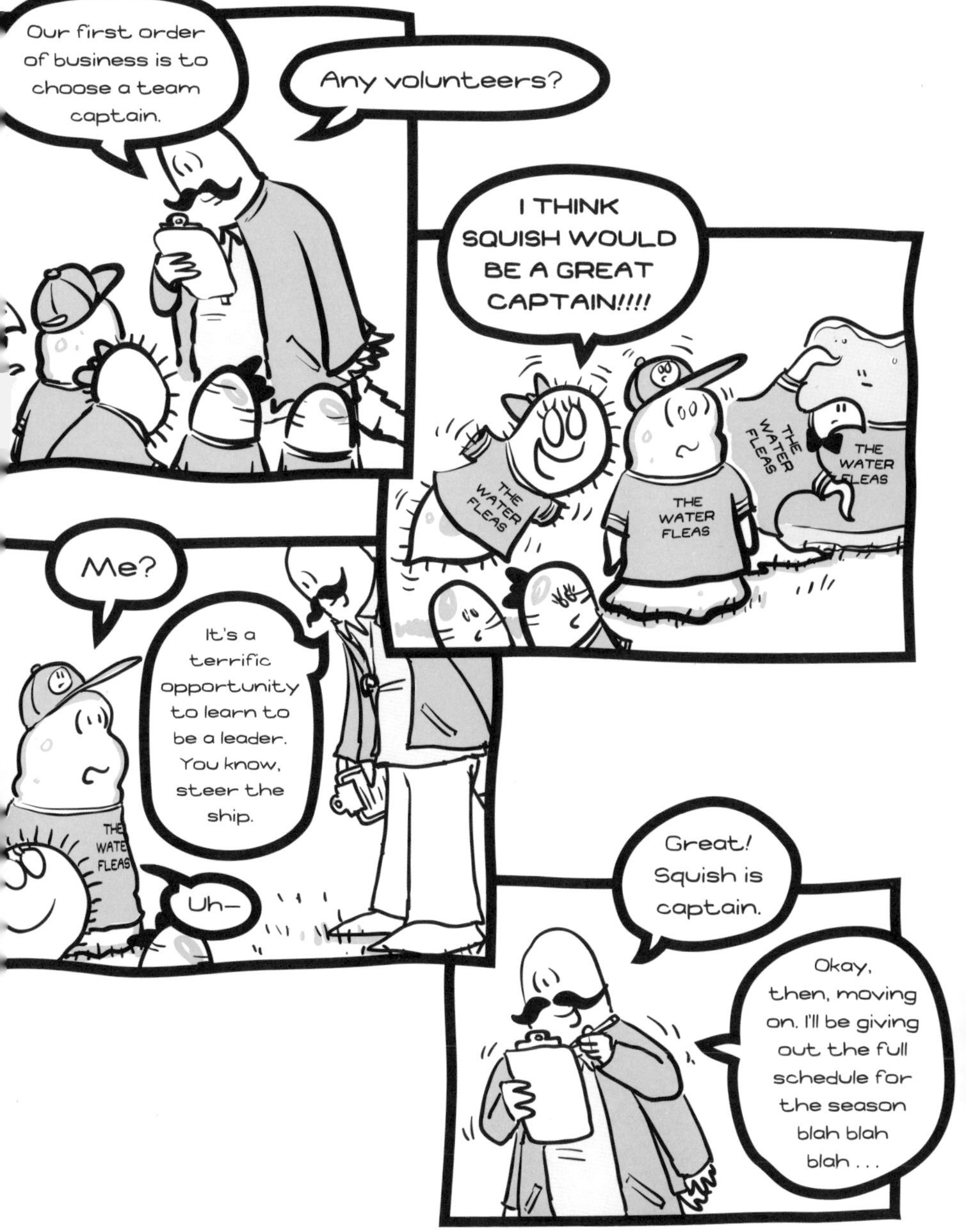
Our first order of business is to choose a team captain.
Any volunteers?
I THINK SQUISH WOULD BE A GREAT CAPTAIN!!!!
THE WATER FLEAS
THE WATER FLEAS
THE WATER FLEAS
THE WATER FLEAS
Me?
It's a terrific opportunity to learn to be a leader. You know, steer the ship.
Uh—
Great! Squish is captain.
Okay, then, moving on. I'll be giving out the full schedule for the season blah blah blah . . .

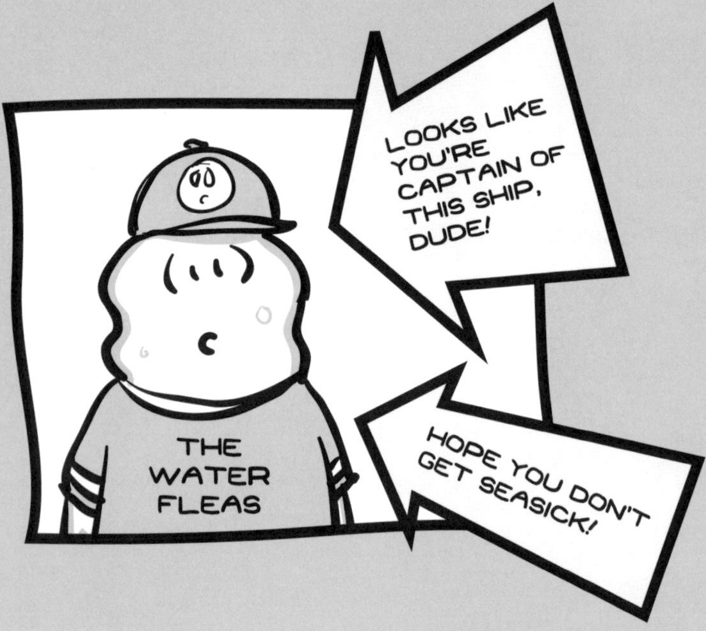
THE WATER FLEAS
LOOKS LIKE YOU'RE CAPTAIN OF THIS SHIP, DUDE!
HOPE YOU DON'T GET SEASICK!

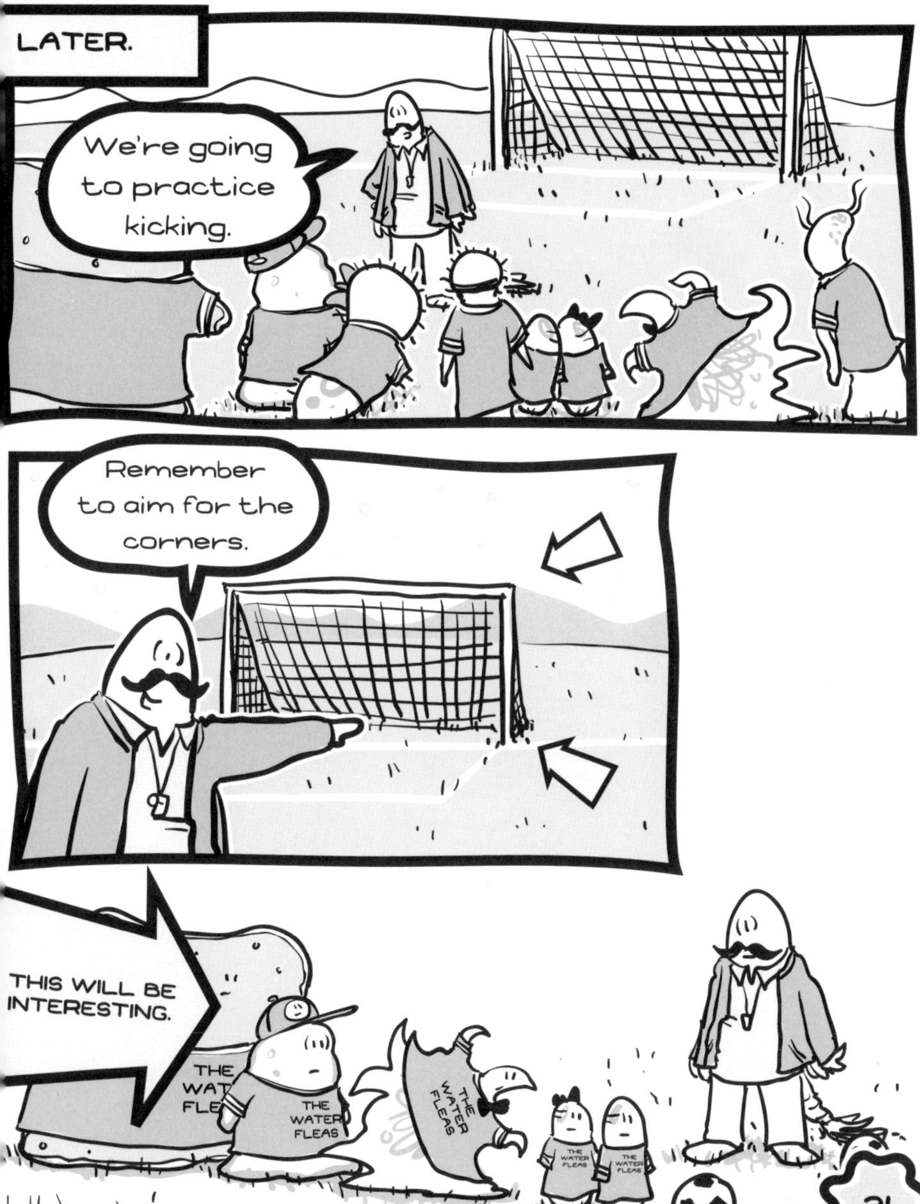
LATER.
We're going to practice kicking.
Remember to aim for the corners.
THIS WILL BE INTERESTING.
THE WAT FLE
THE WATER FLEAS
THE WATER FLEAS
THE WATER FLEAS
THE WATER FLEAS

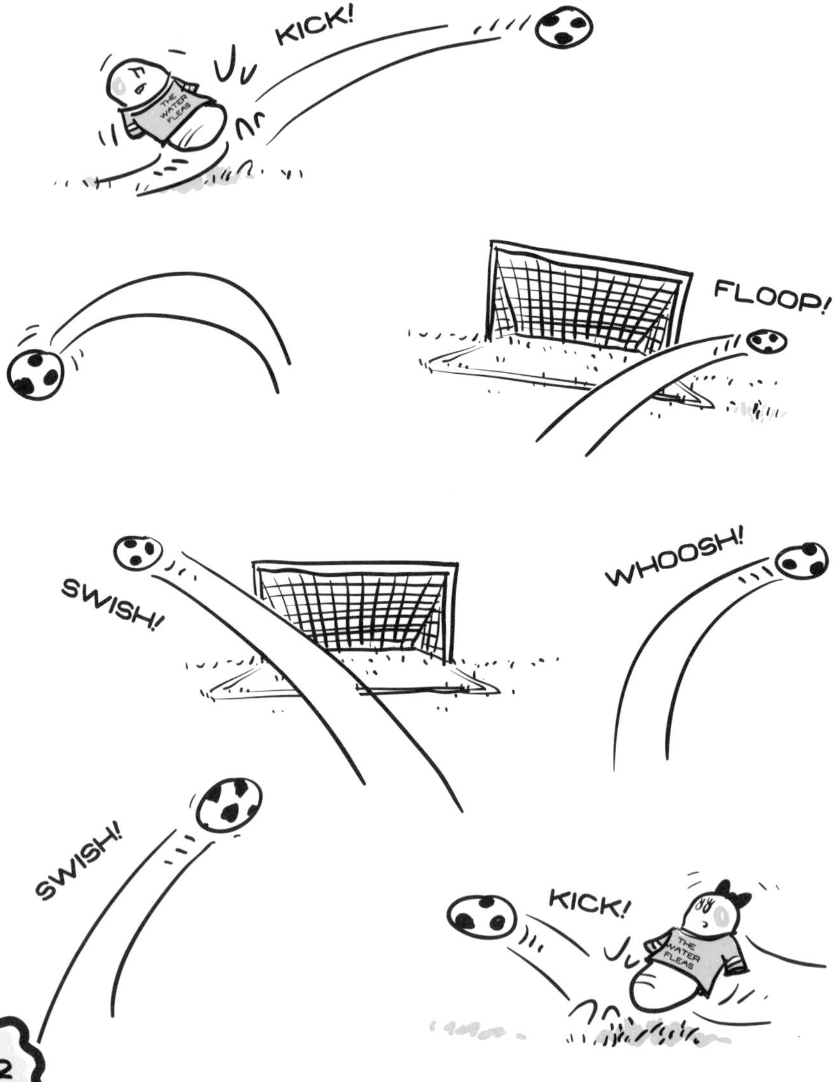
KICK!
THE WATER FLEAS
FLOOP!
SWISH!
WHOOSH!
SWISH!
KICK!
THE WATER FLEAS

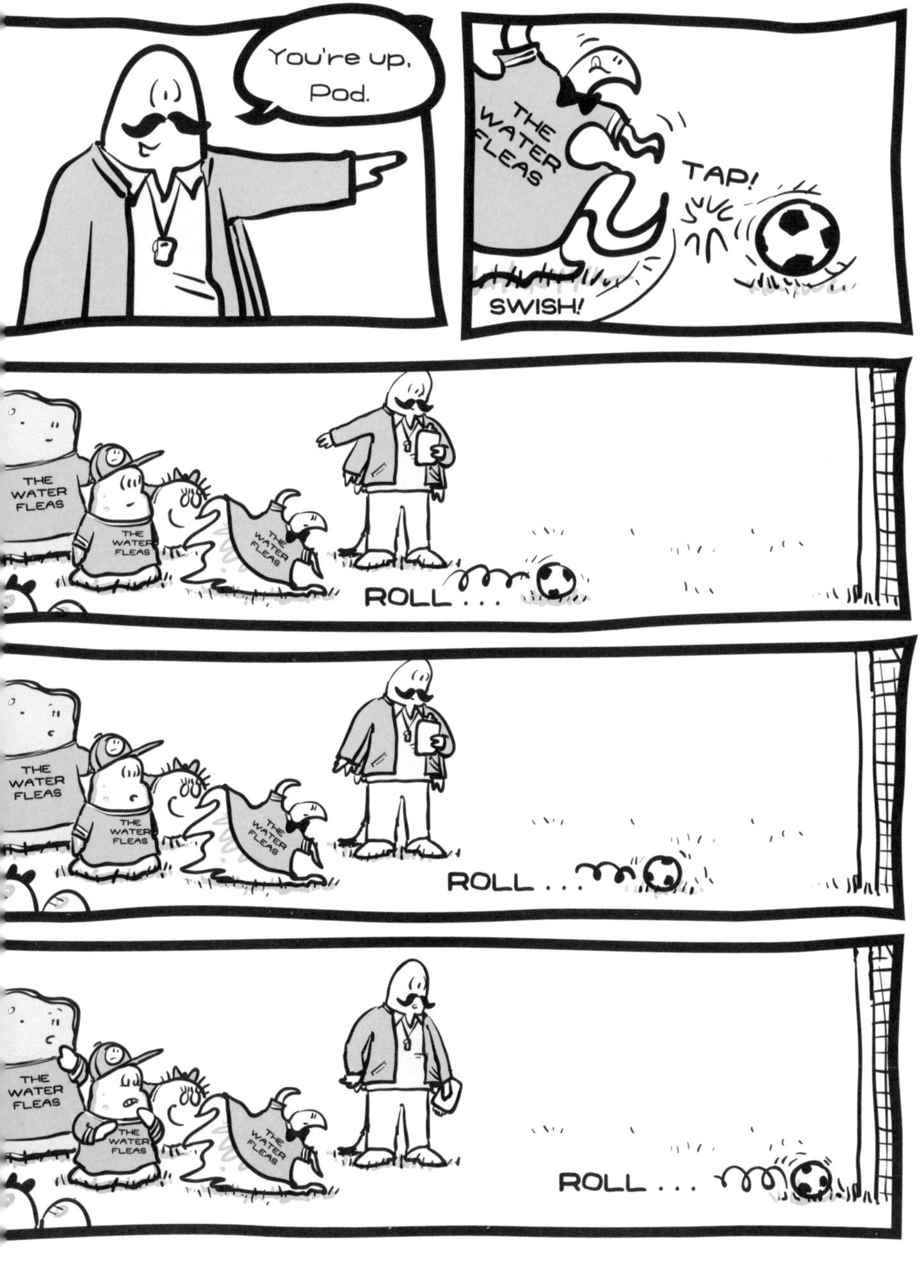
You're up, Pod.
THE WATER FLEAS
TAP!
SWISH!
THE WATER FLEAS
THE WATER FLEAS
THE WATER FLEAS
ROLL...
THE WATER FLEAS
THE WATER FLEAS
THE WATER FLEAS
ROLL...
THE WATER FLEAS
THE WATER FLEAS
THE WATER FLEAS
ROLL...

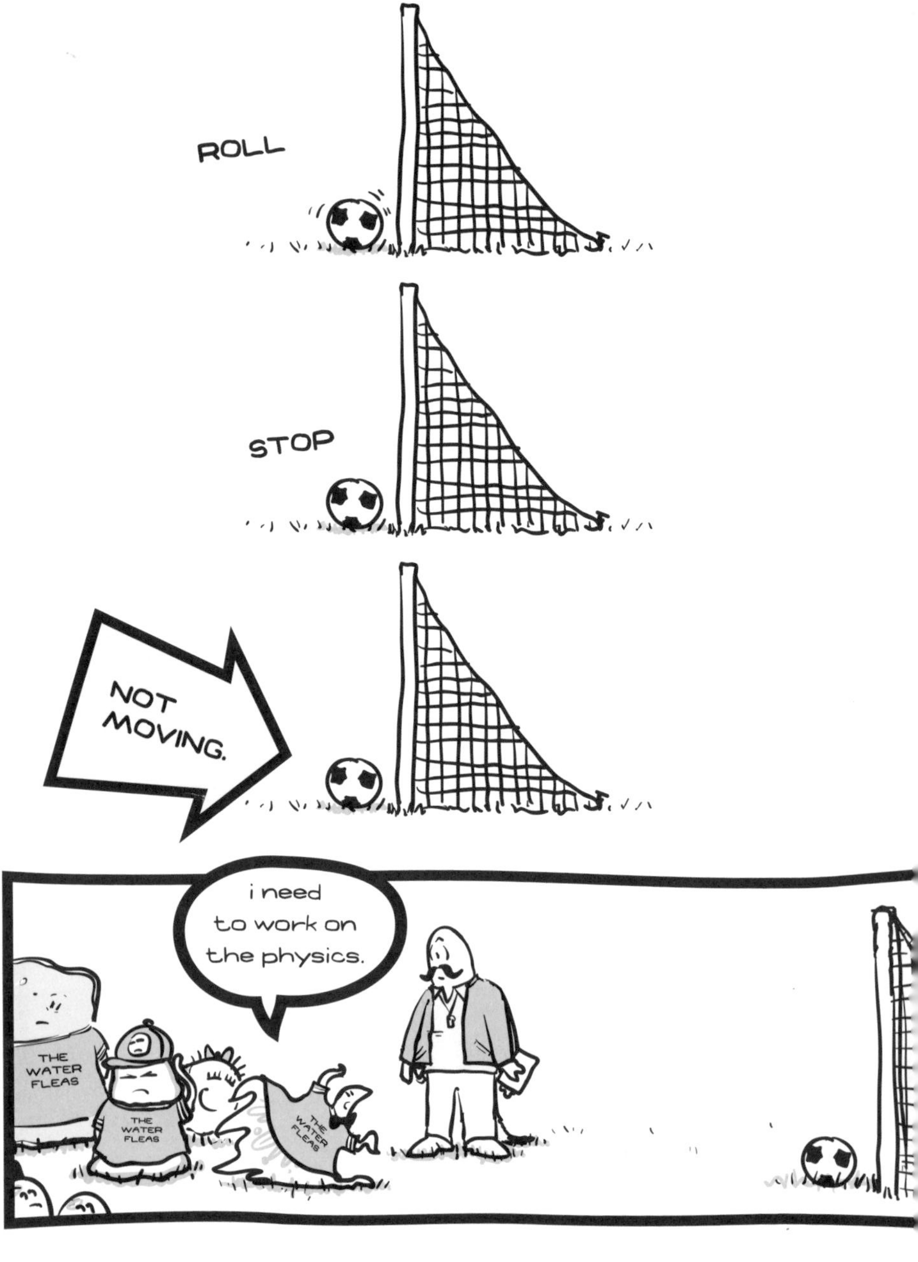
ROLL
STOP
NOT MOVING.
i need to work on the physics.
THE WATER FLEAS
THE WATER FLEAS
THE WATER FLEAS

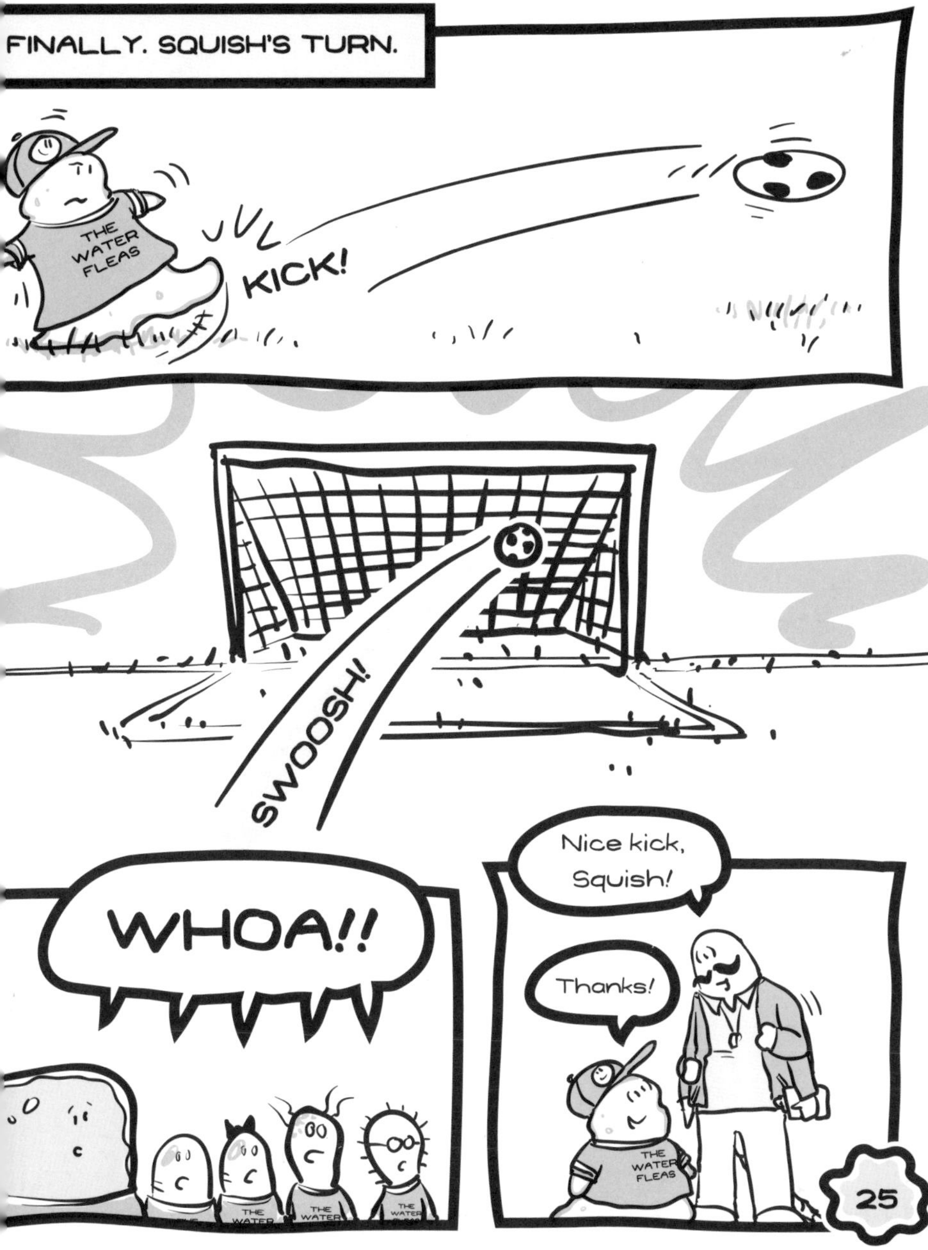
FINALLY. SQUISH'S TURN.
THE WATER FLEAS
KICK!
SWOOSH!
WHOA!!
Nice kick, Squish!
Thanks!
THE WATER FLEAS

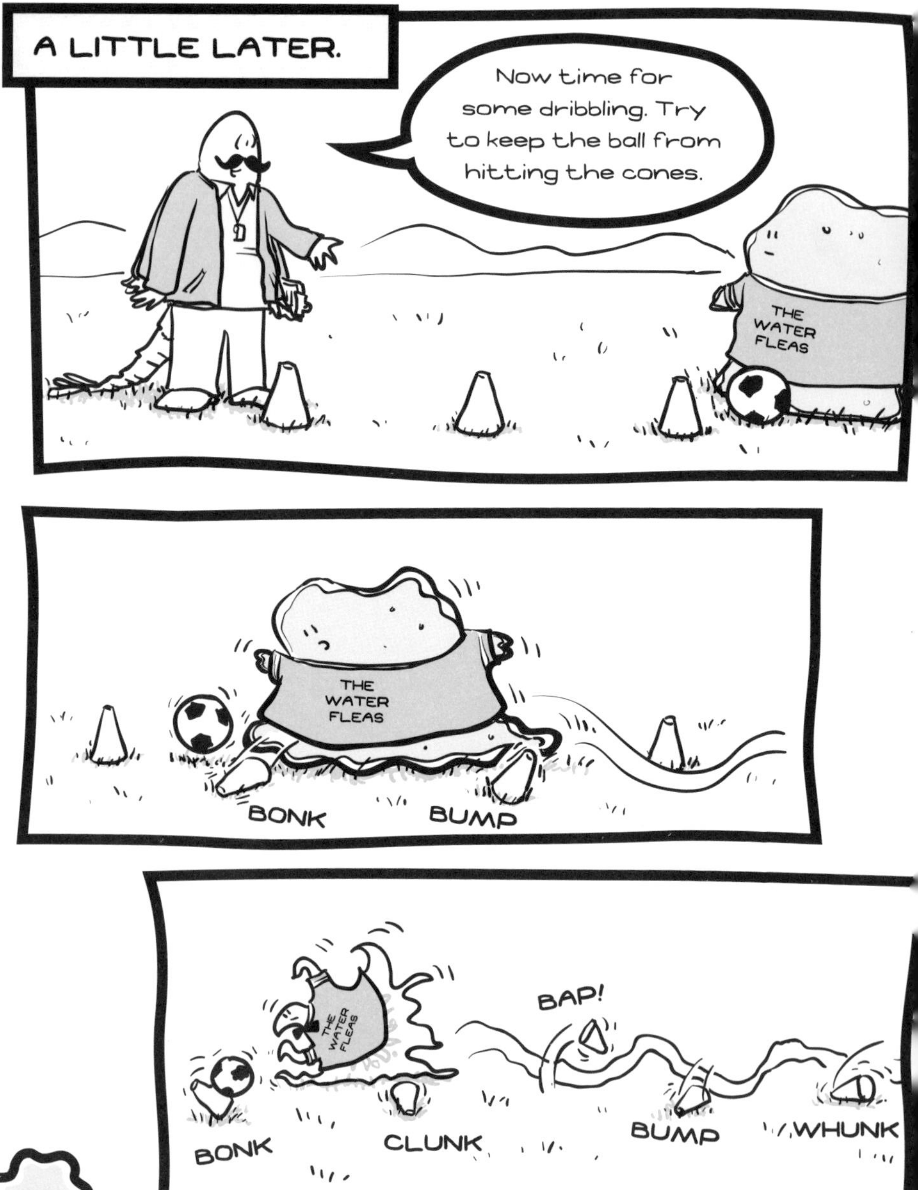
A LITTLE LATER.
Now time for some dribbling. Try to keep the ball from hitting the cones.
THE WATER FLEAS
THE WATER FLEAS
BONK
BUMP
THE WATER FLEAS
BAP!
BONK
CLUNK
BUMP
WHUNK

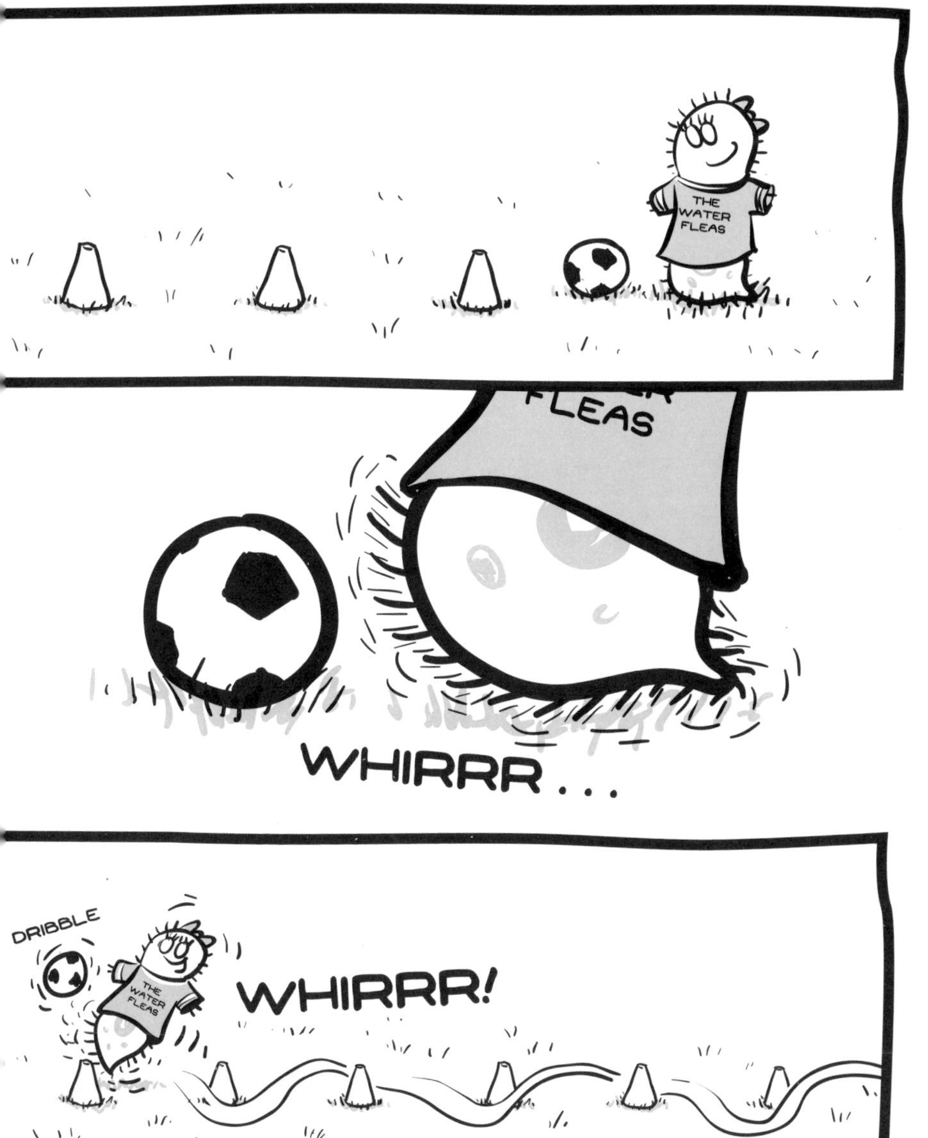
THE WATER FLEAS
FLEAS
WHIRRR...
DRIBBLE
THE WATER FLEAS
WHIRRR!

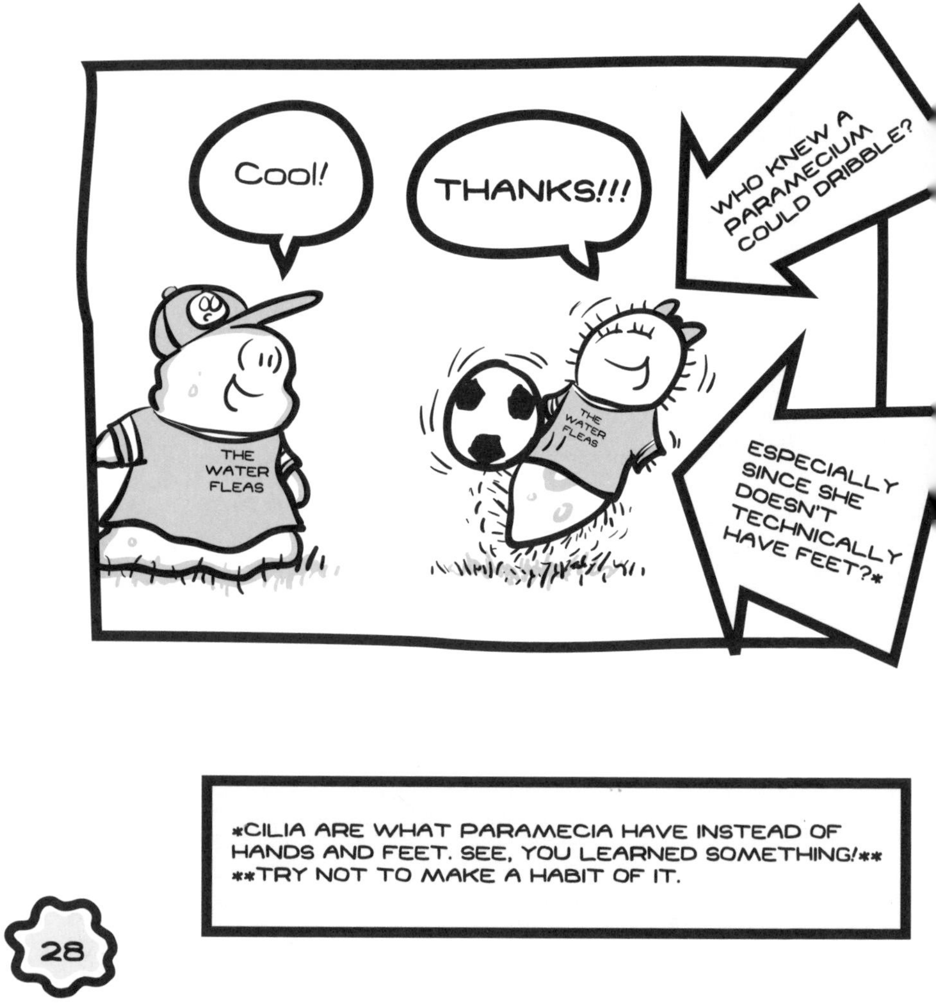
Cool!
THANKS!!!
WHO KNEW A PARAMECIUM COULD DRIBBLE?
ESPECIALLY SINCE SHE DOESN'T TECHNICALLY HAVE FEET?*
THE WATER FLEAS
THE WATER FLEAS

*CILIA ARE WHAT PARAMECIA HAVE INSTEAD OF HANDS AND FEET. SEE, YOU LEARNED SOMETHING!**
**TRY NOT TO MAKE A HABIT OF IT.

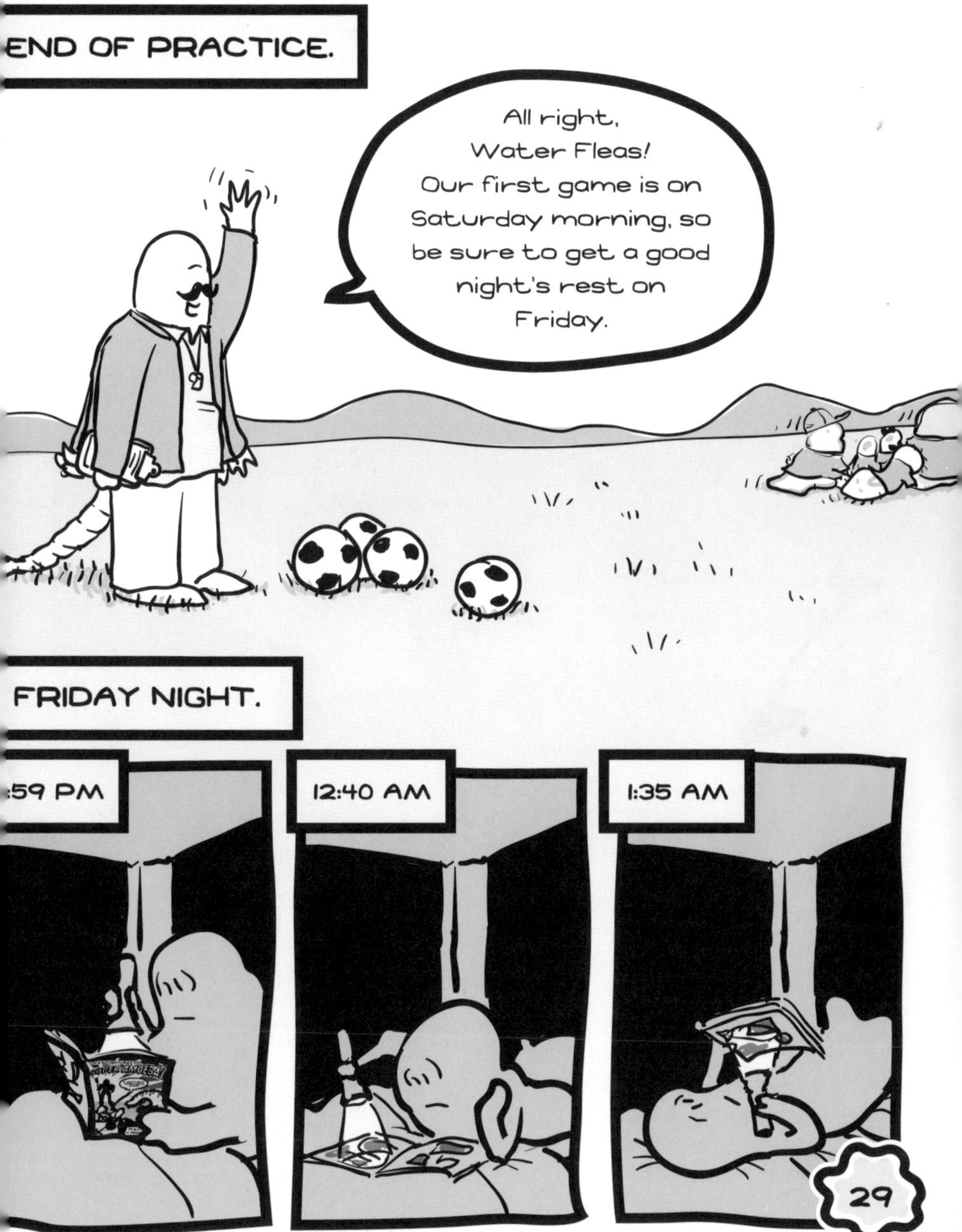
END OF PRACTICE.
All right, Water Fleas! Our first game is on Saturday morning, so be sure to get a good night's rest on Friday.
FRIDAY NIGHT.
:59 PM
12:40 AM
1:35 AM

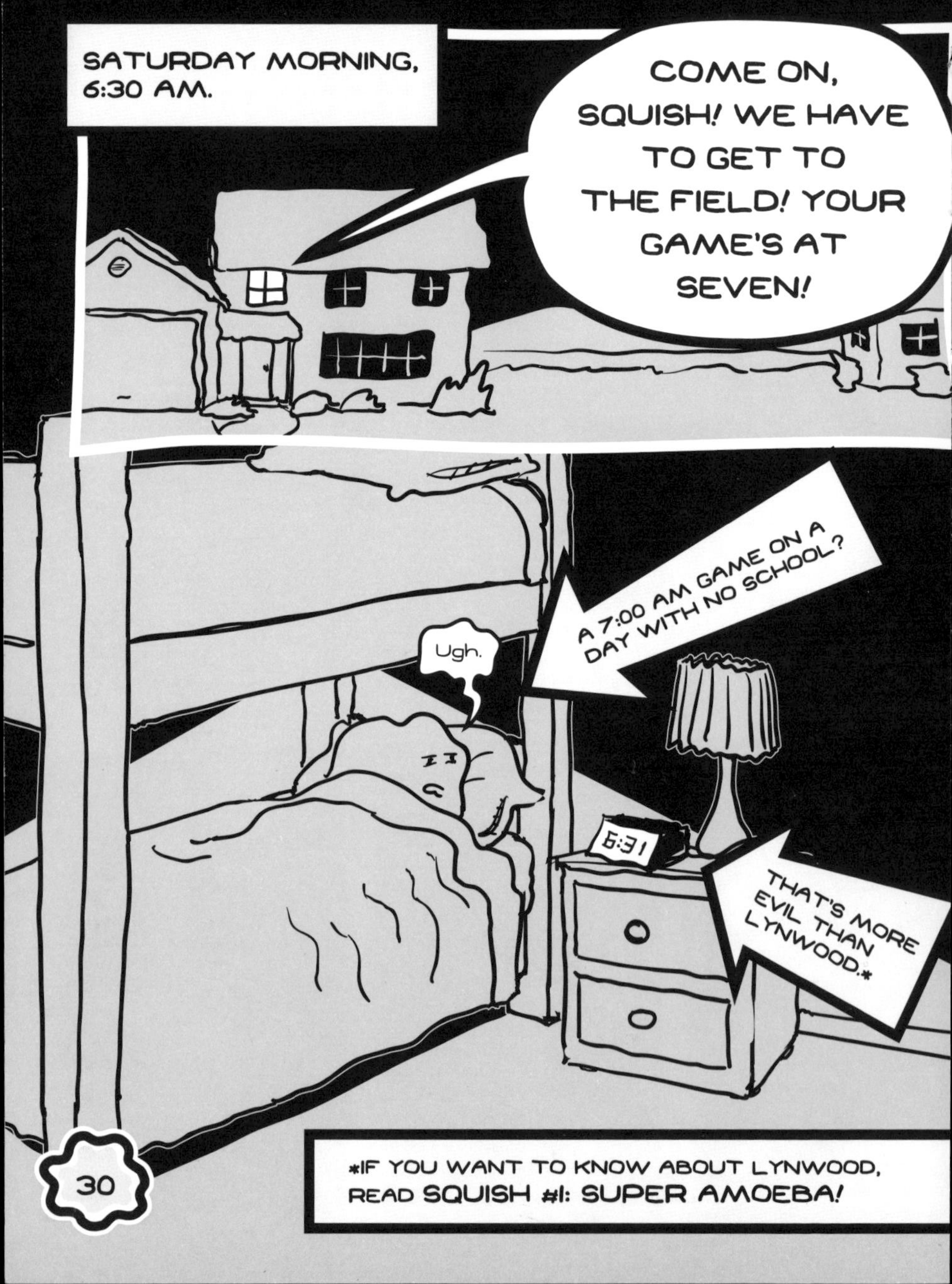
SATURDAY MORNING, 6:30 AM.
COME ON, SQUISH! WE HAVE TO GET TO THE FIELD! YOUR GAME'S AT SEVEN!
Ugh.
A 7:00 AM GAME ON A DAY WITH NO SCHOOL?
6:31
THAT'S MORE EVIL THAN LYNWOOD.*

*IF YOU WANT TO KNOW ABOUT LYNWOOD, READ SQUISH #1: SUPER AMOEBA!

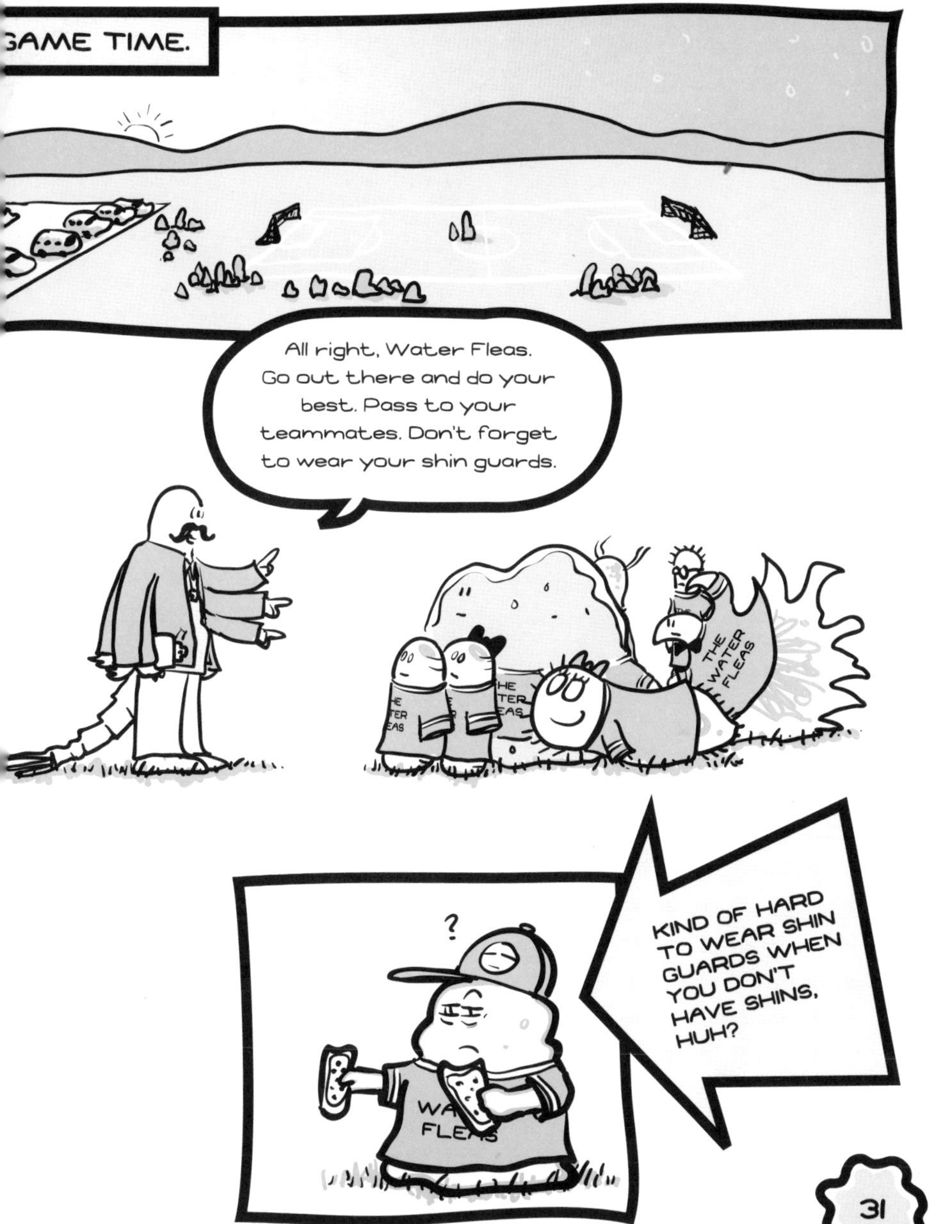
GAME TIME.
All right, Water Fleas. Go out there and do your best. Pass to your teammates. Don't forget to wear your shin guards.
THE WATER FLEAS
KIND OF HARD TO WEAR SHIN GUARDS WHEN YOU DON'T HAVE SHINS, HUH?
?

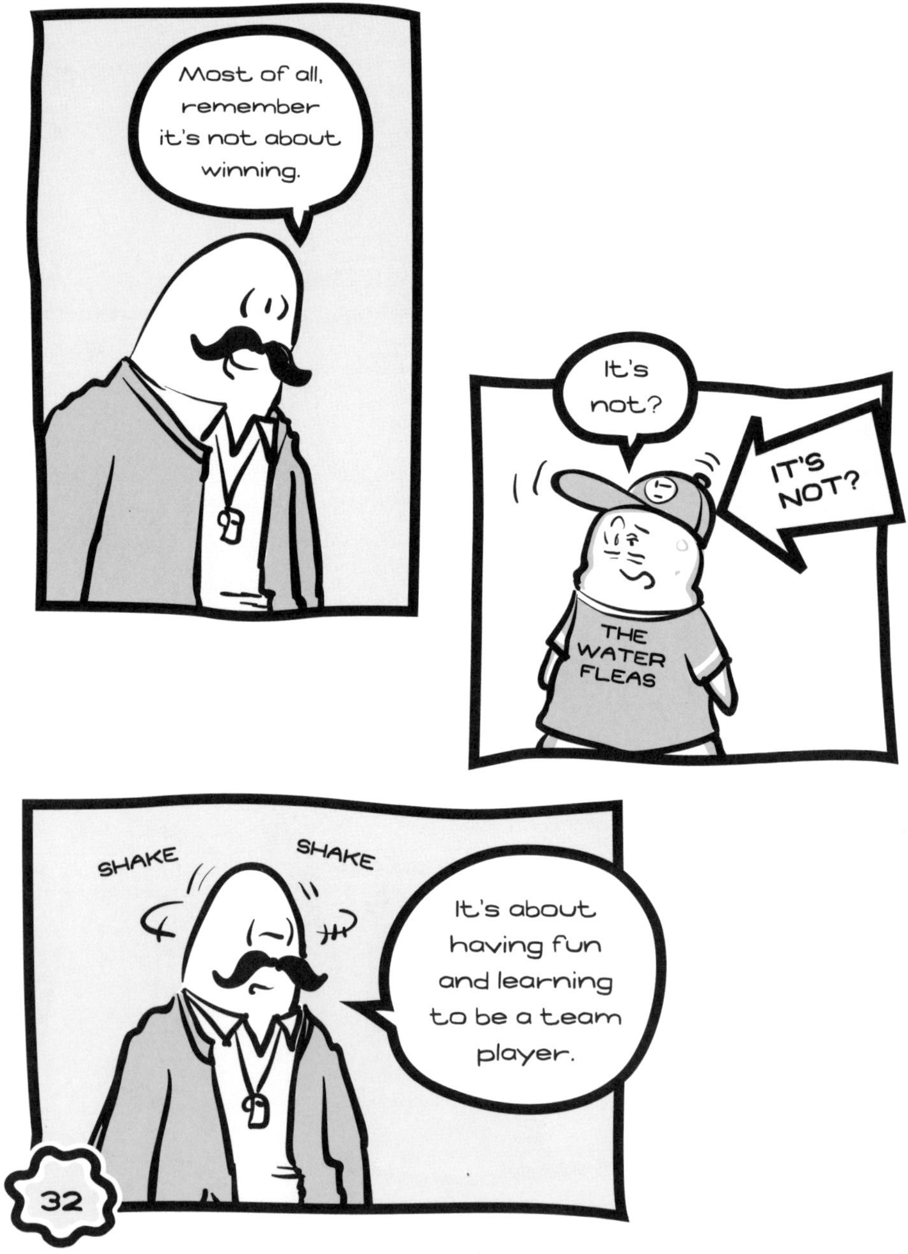
Most of all, remember it's not about winning.
It's not?
IT'S NOT?
THE WATER FLEAS
SHAKE
SHAKE
It's about having fun and learning to be a team player.

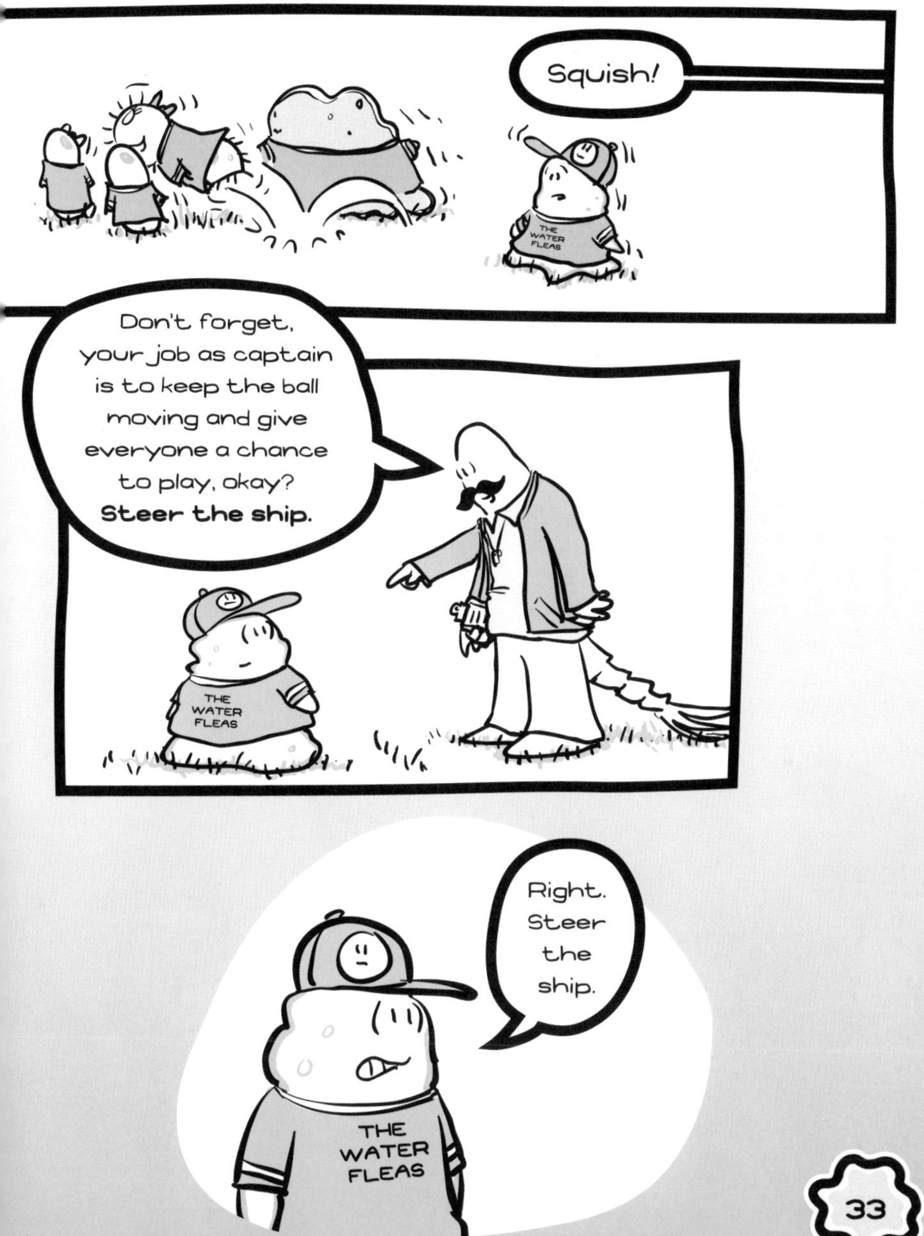
Squish!
THE WATER FLEAS
Don't forget, your job as captain is to keep the ball moving and give everyone a chance to play, okay? **Steer the ship.**
THE WATER FLEAS
Right. Steer the ship.
THE WATER FLEAS

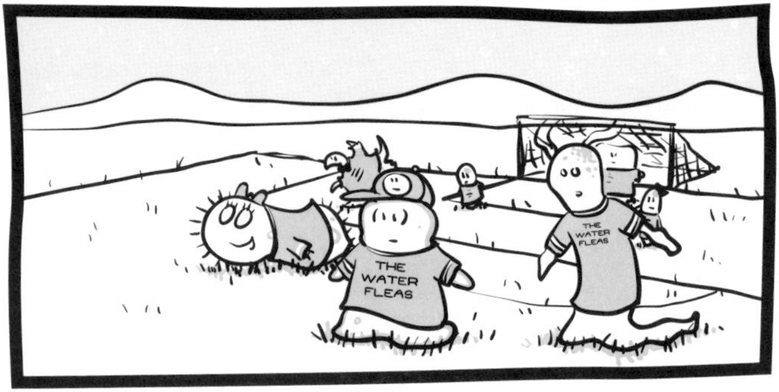
THE WATER FLEAS
THE WATER FLEAS

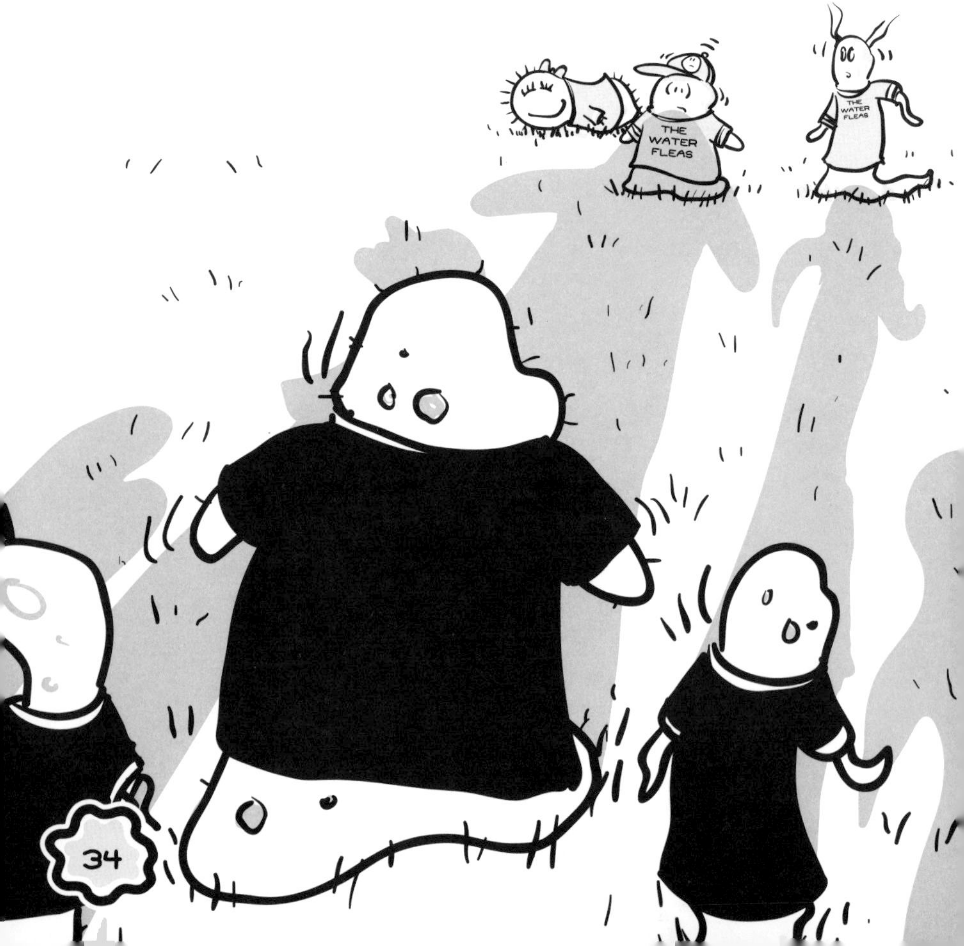
THE WATER FLEAS
THE WATER FLEAS

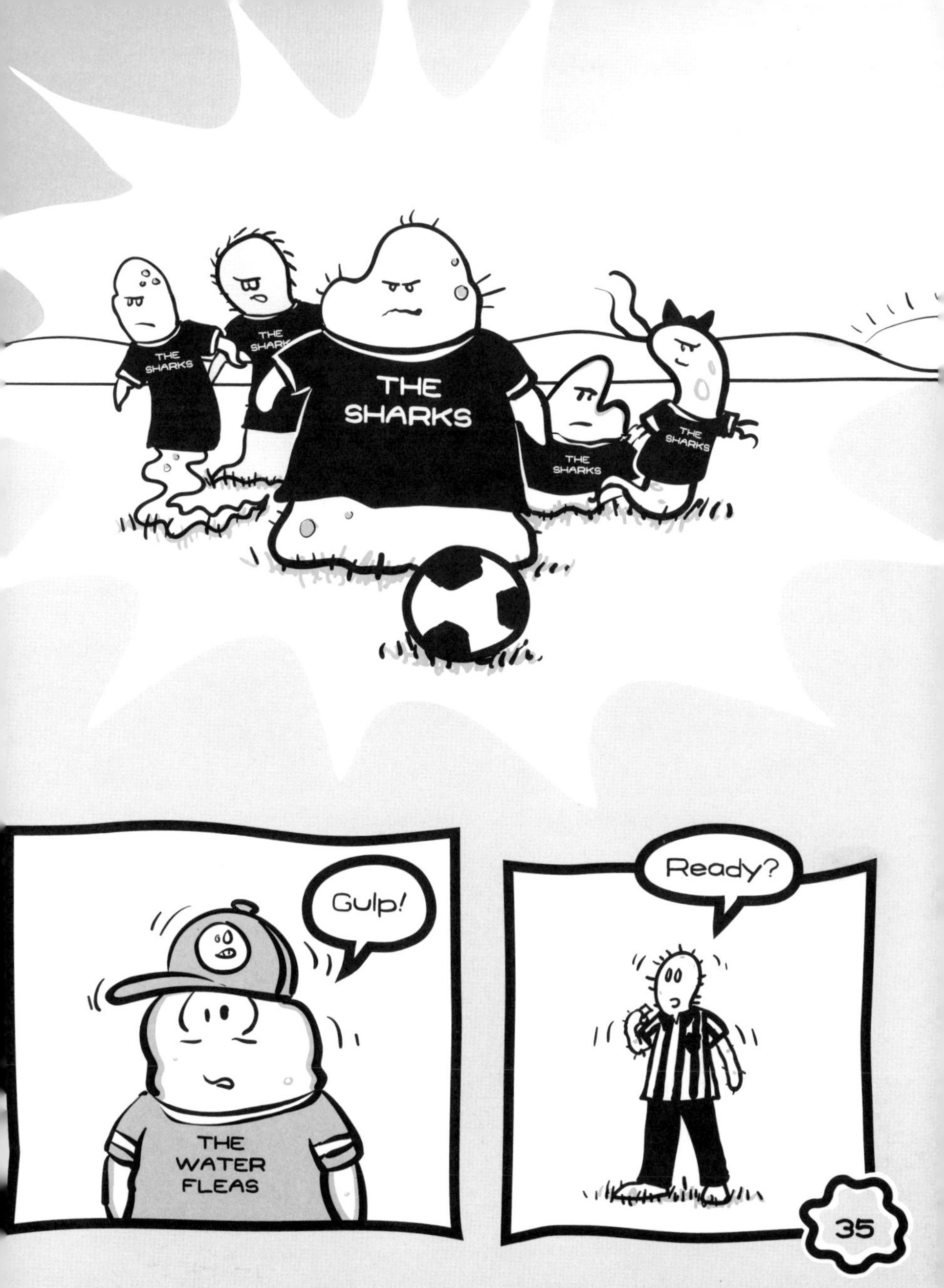
THE SHARKS
THE SHARKS
THE SHARKS
THE SHARKS
THE SHARKS
Gulp!
THE WATER FLEAS
Ready?

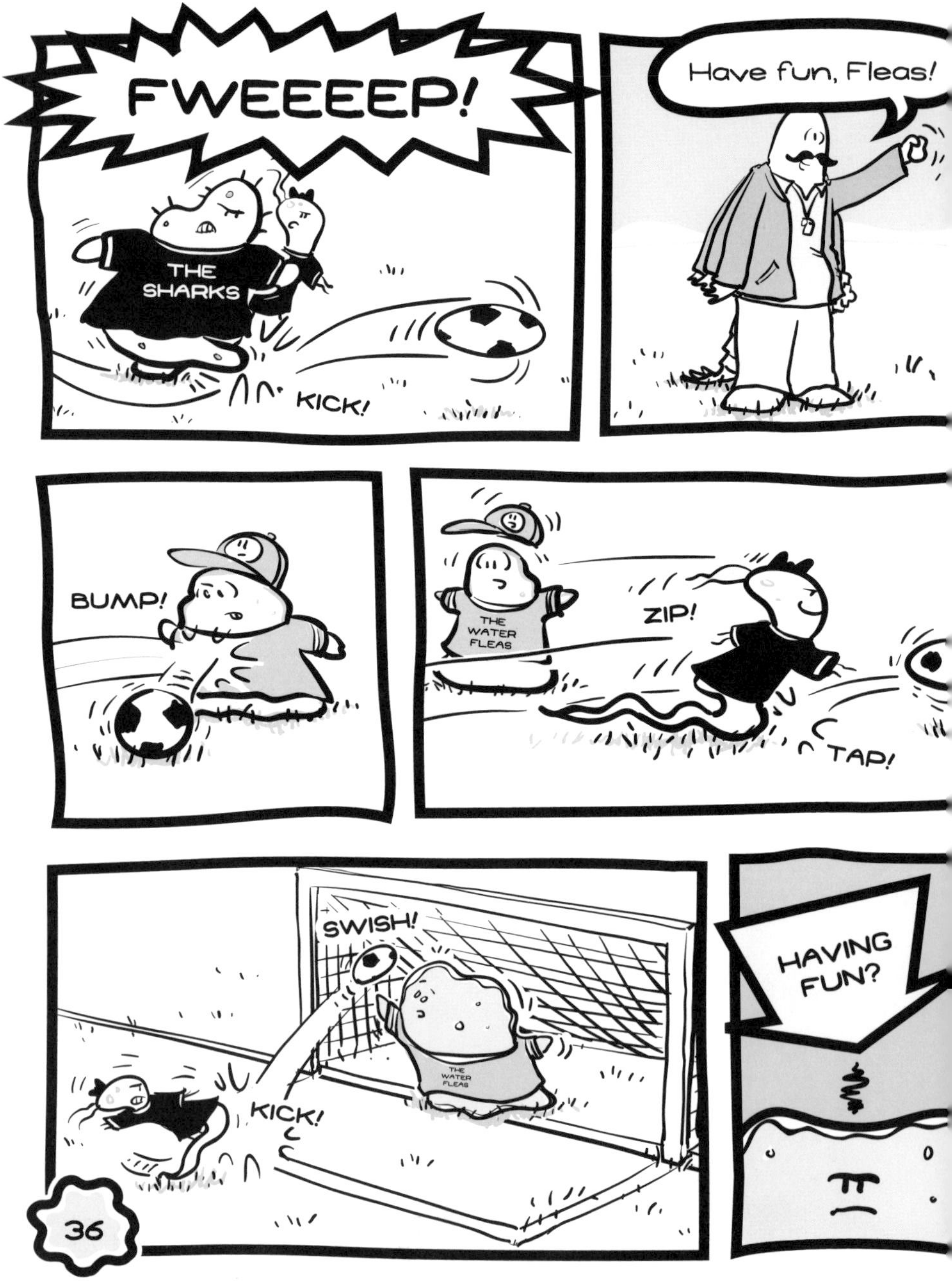
FWEEEEEP!
THE SHARKS
KICK!
Have fun, Fleas!
BUMP!
THE WATER FLEAS
ZIP!
TAP!
SWISH!
THE WATER FLEAS
KICK!
HAVING FUN?

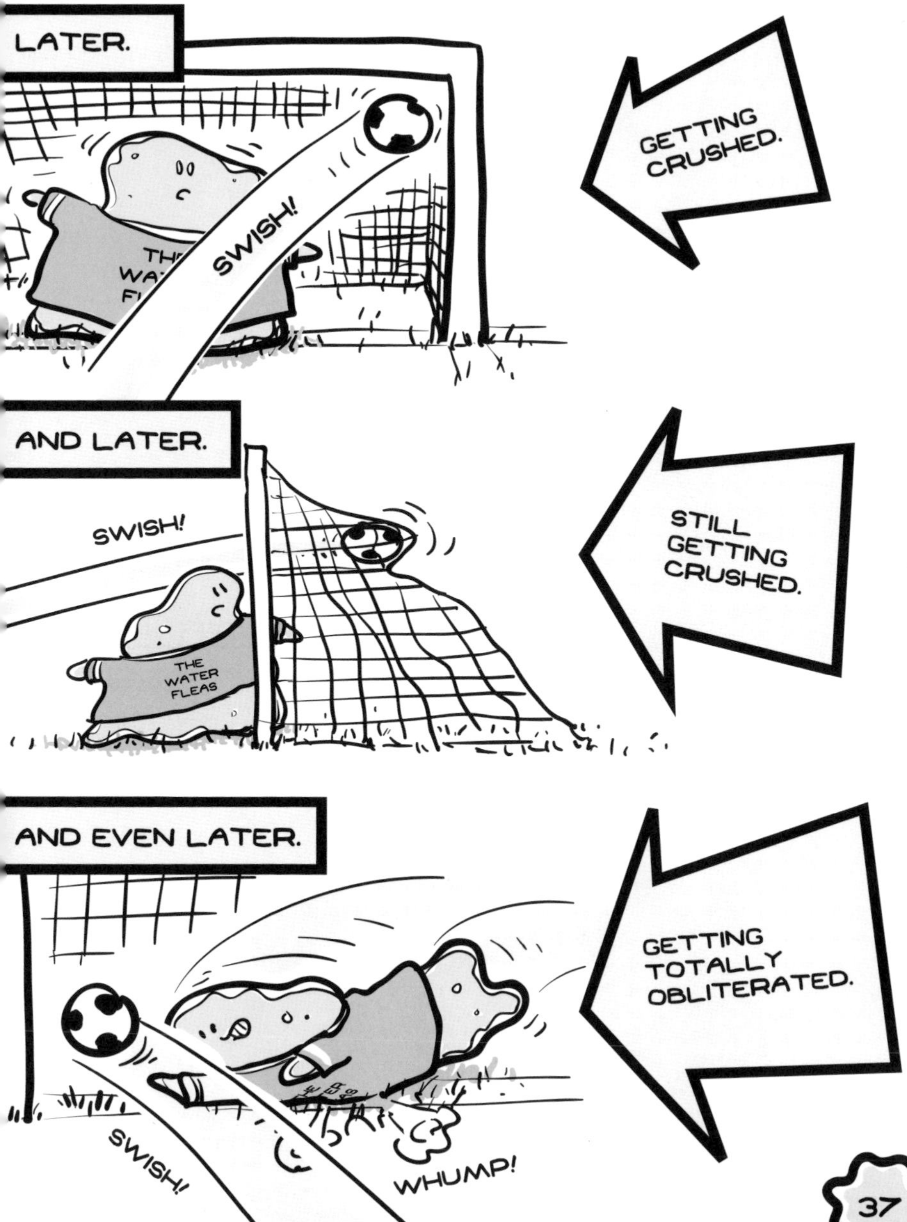
LATER.
GETTING CRUSHED.
SWISH!
AND LATER.
STILL GETTING CRUSHED.
SWISH!
THE WATER FLEAS
AND EVEN LATER.
GETTING TOTALLY OBLITERATED.
SWISH!
WHUMP!

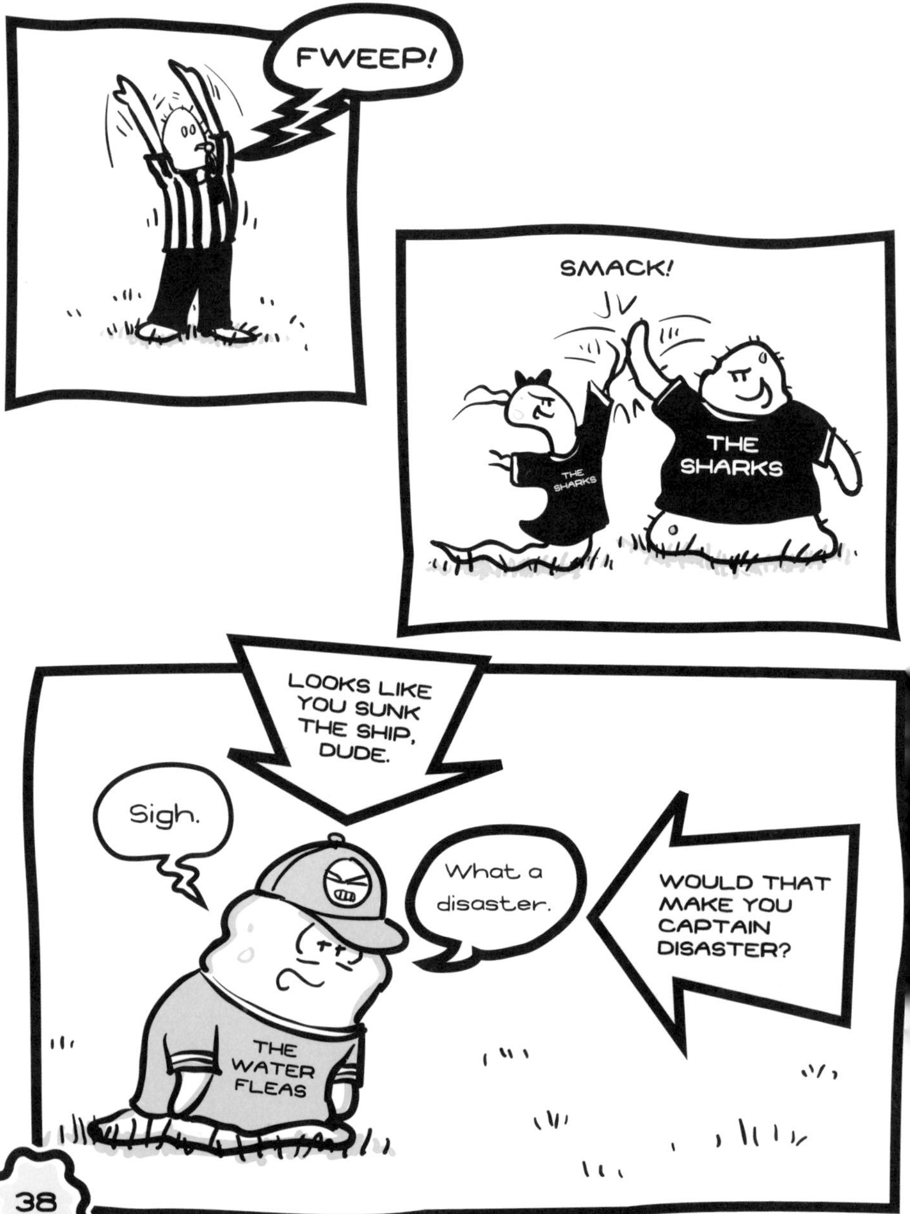
FWEEP!
SMACK!
THE SHARKS
THE SHARKS
LOOKS LIKE YOU SUNK THE SHIP, DUDE.
Sigh.
What a disaster.
WOULD THAT MAKE YOU CAPTAIN DISASTER?
THE WATER FLEAS

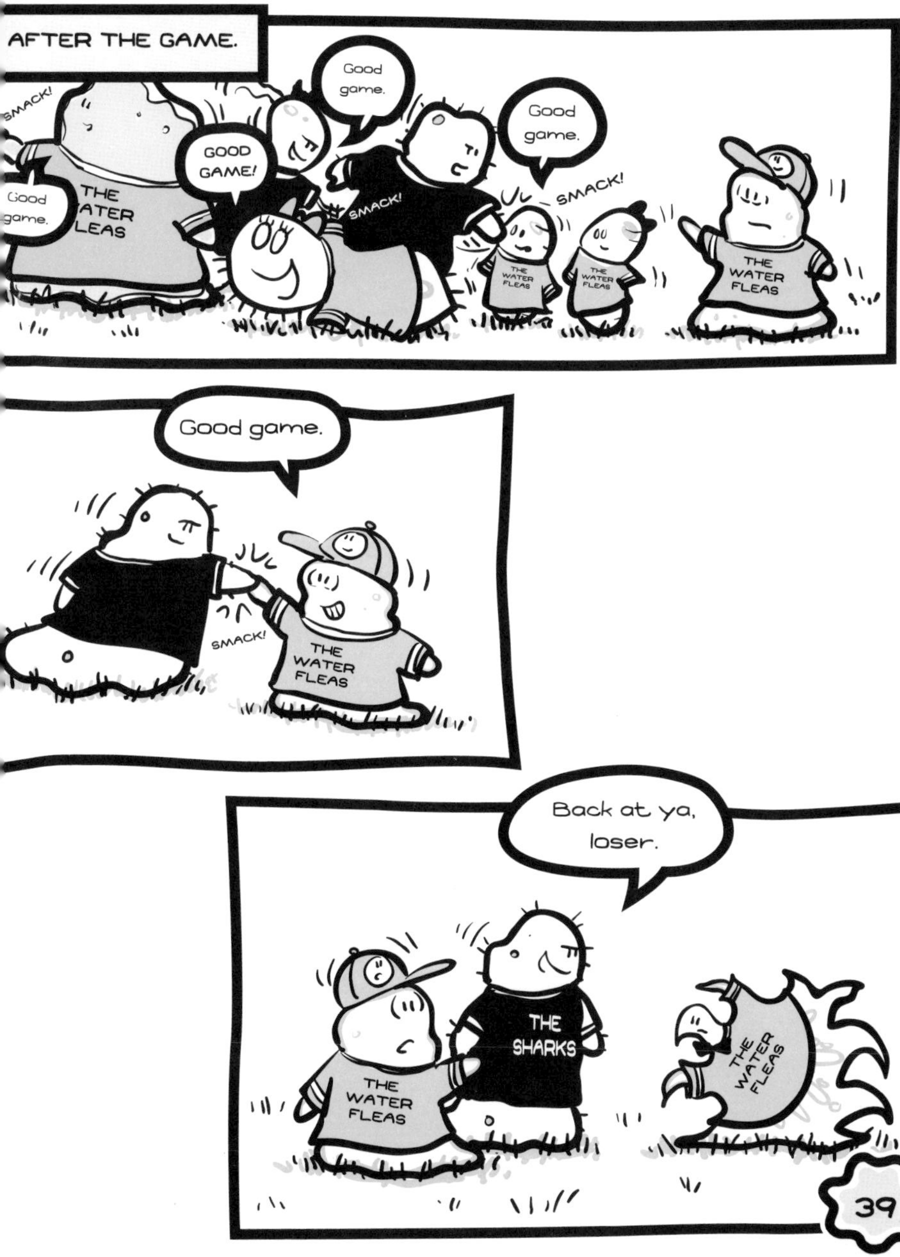
AFTER THE GAME.
SMACK!
Good game.
THE WATER FLEAS
GOOD GAME!
Good game.
SMACK!
Good game.
SMACK!
THE WATER FLEAS
THE WATER FLEAS
THE WATER FLEAS
Good game.
SMACK!
THE WATER FLEAS
Back at ya, loser.
THE WATER FLEAS
THE SHARKS
THE WATER FLEAS

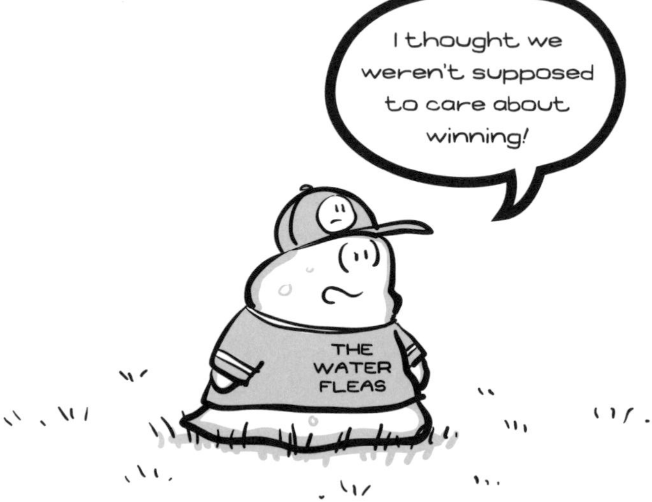
I thought we weren't supposed to care about winning!
THE WATER FLEAS

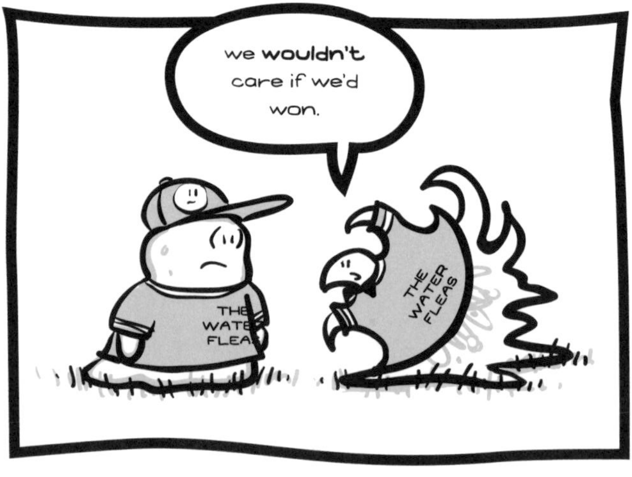
we **wouldn't** care if we'd won.
THE WATER FLEAS

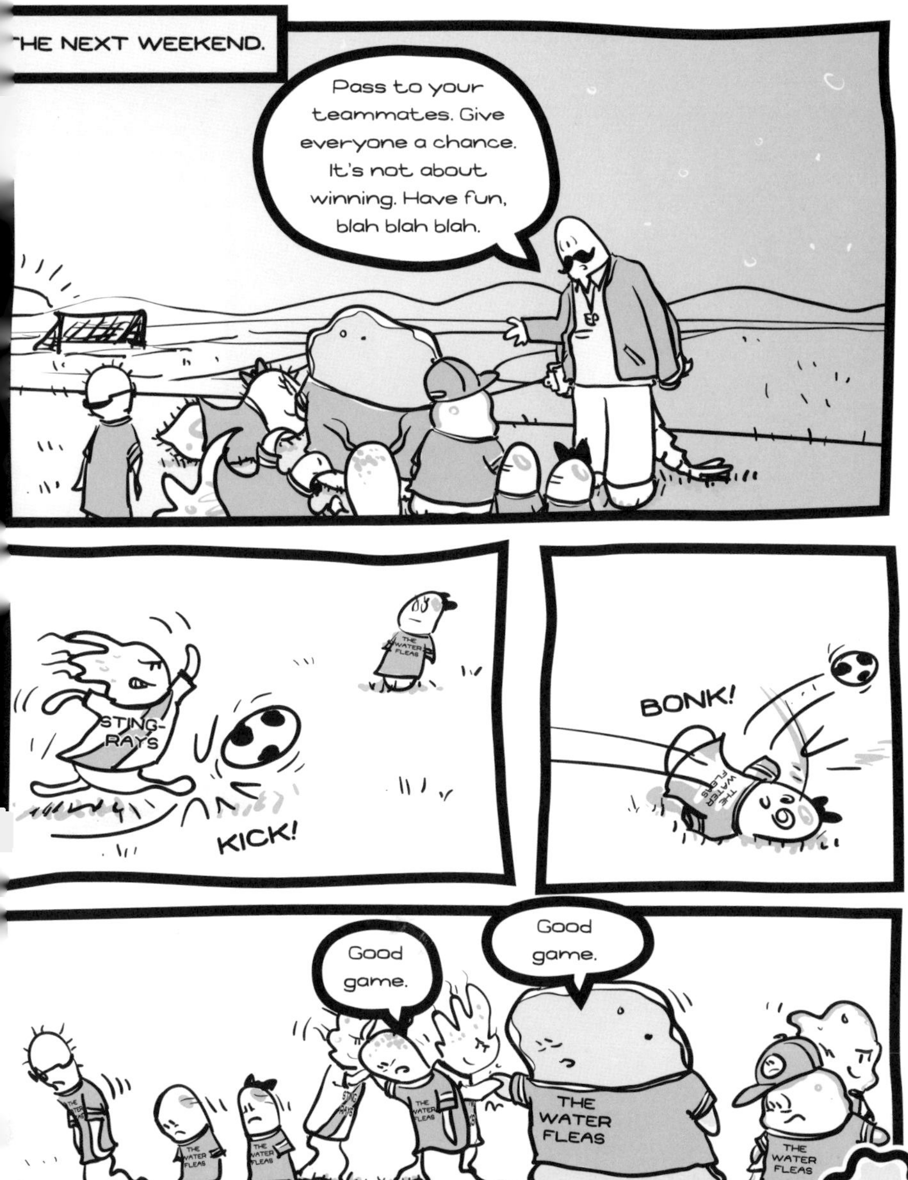

THE NEXT WEEKEND.
Pass to your teammates. Give everyone a chance. It's not about winning. Have fun, blah blah blah.
STING-RAYS
THE WATER FLEAS
KICK!
BONK!
THE WATER FLEAS
Good game.
Good game.
THE WATER FLEAS

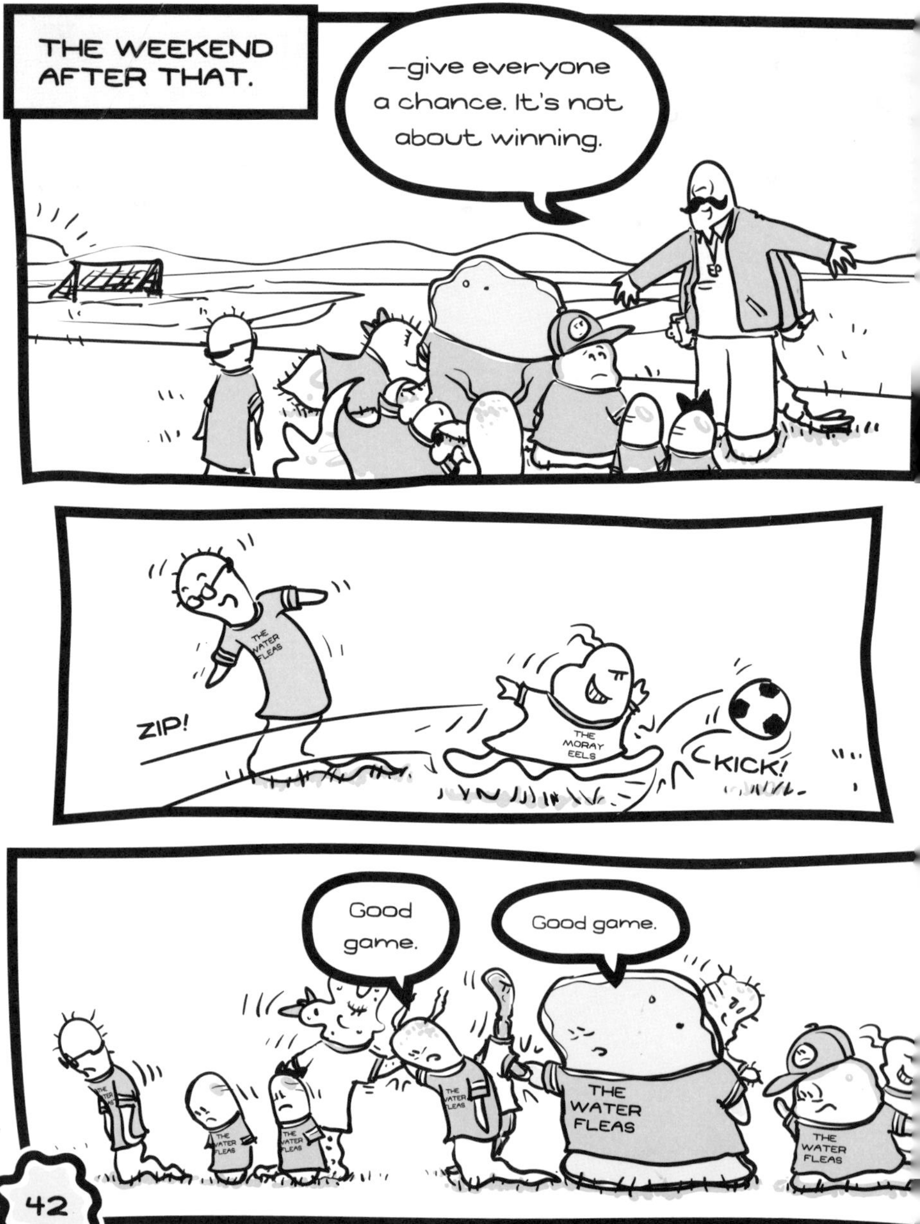
THE WEEKEND AFTER THAT.
—give everyone a chance. It's not about winning.
EP
THE WATER FLEAS
ZIP!
THE MORAY EELS
KICK!
Good game.
Good game.
THE WATER FLEAS
THE WATER FLEAS
THE WATER FLEAS

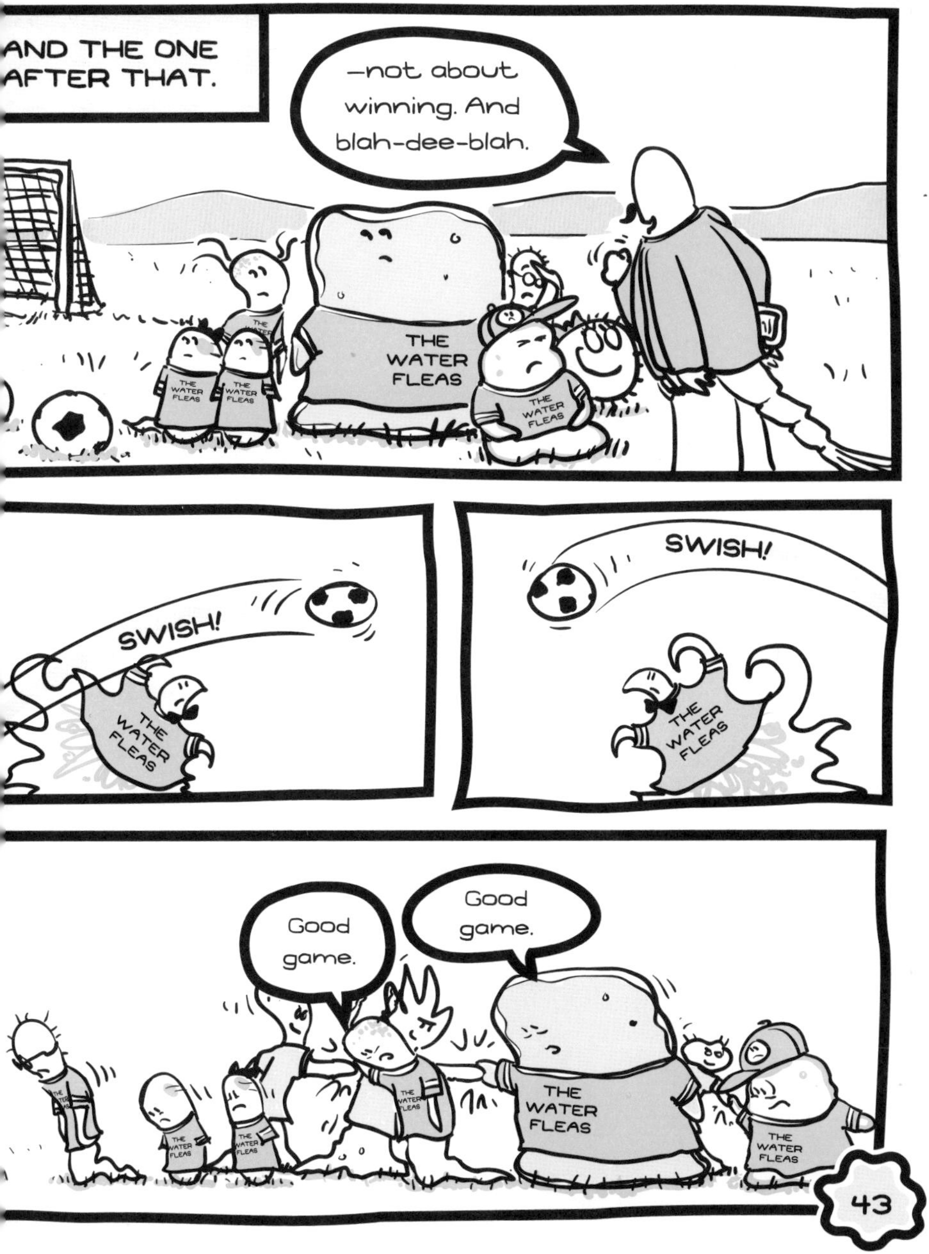
AND THE ONE AFTER THAT.
—not about winning. And blah-dee-blah.
THE WATER FLEAS
SWISH!
THE WATER FLEAS
SWISH!
THE WATER FLEAS
Good game.
Good game.
THE WATER FLEAS

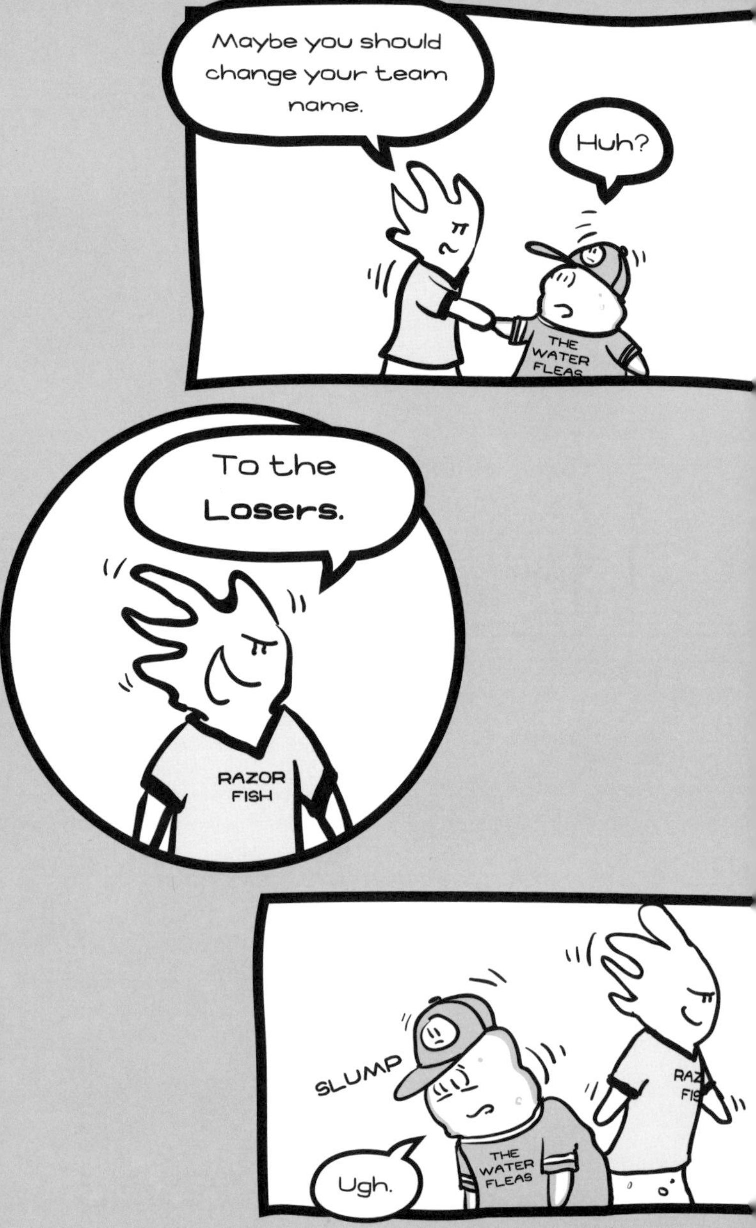
Maybe you should change your team name.
Huh?
THE WATER FLEAS
To the Losers.
RAZOR FISH
SLUMP
Ugh.
THE WATER FLEAS

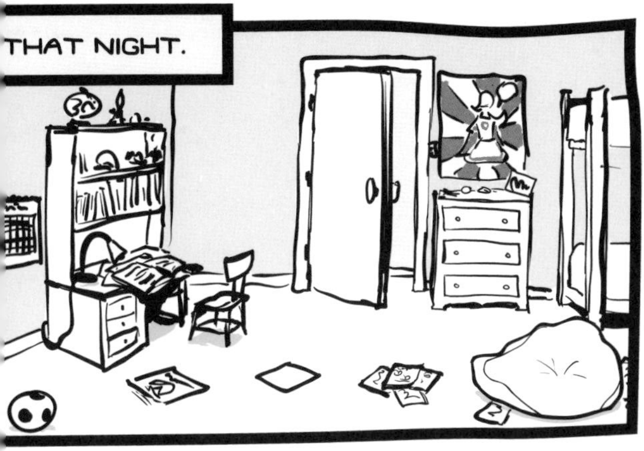
THAT NIGHT.

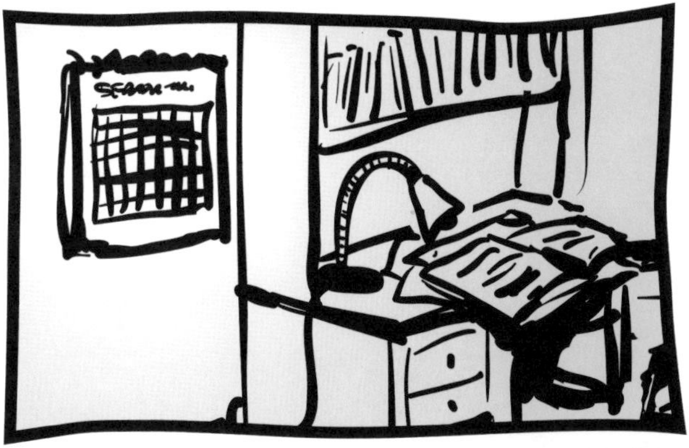

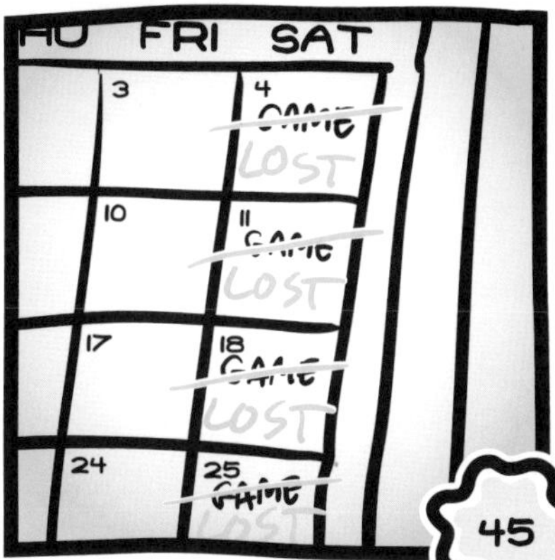
FRI SAT
3
4
GAME
LOST
10
11
GAME
LOST
17
18
GAME
LOST
24
25
GAME

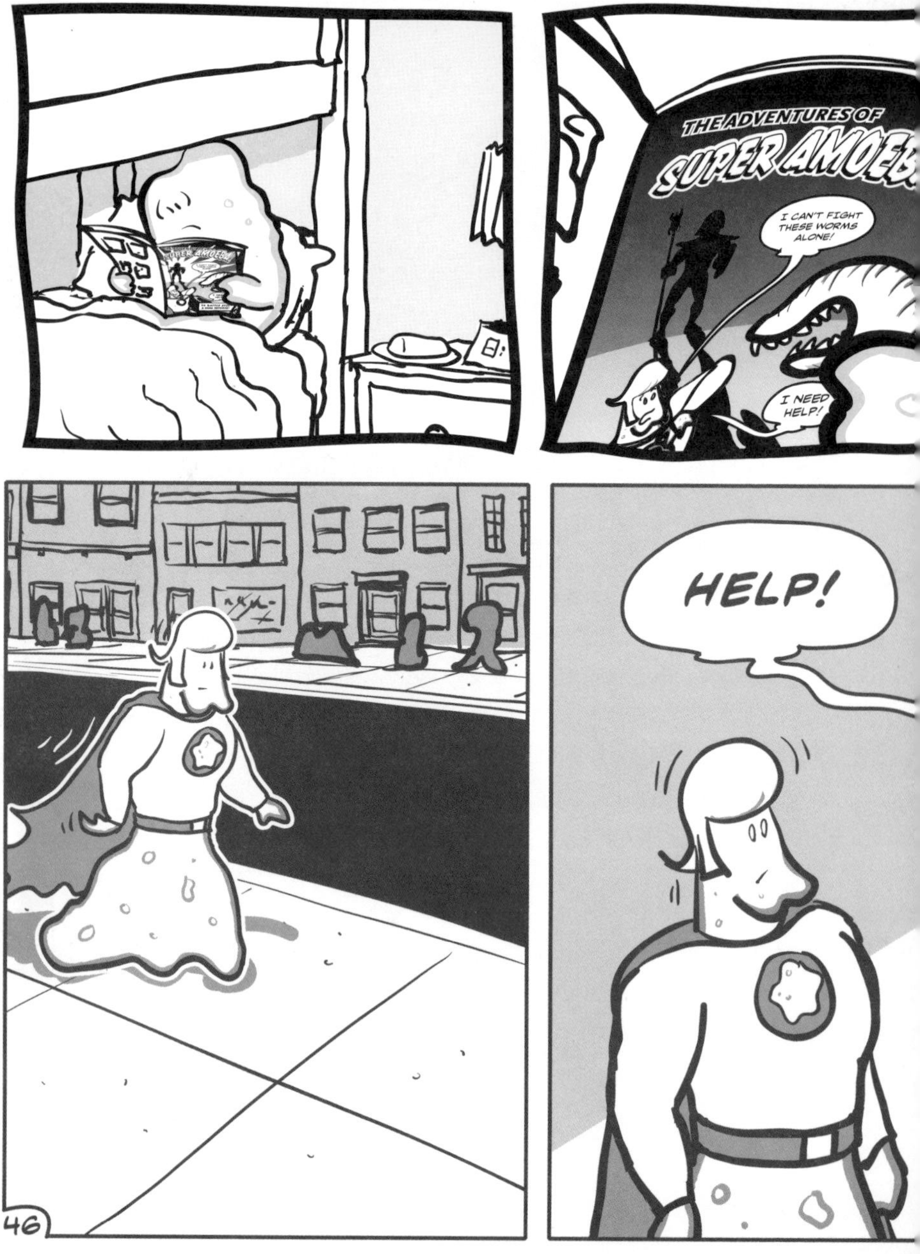
THE ADVENTURES OF
SUPER AMOEB
I CAN'T FIGHT THESE WORMS ALONE!
I NEED HELP!
HELP!

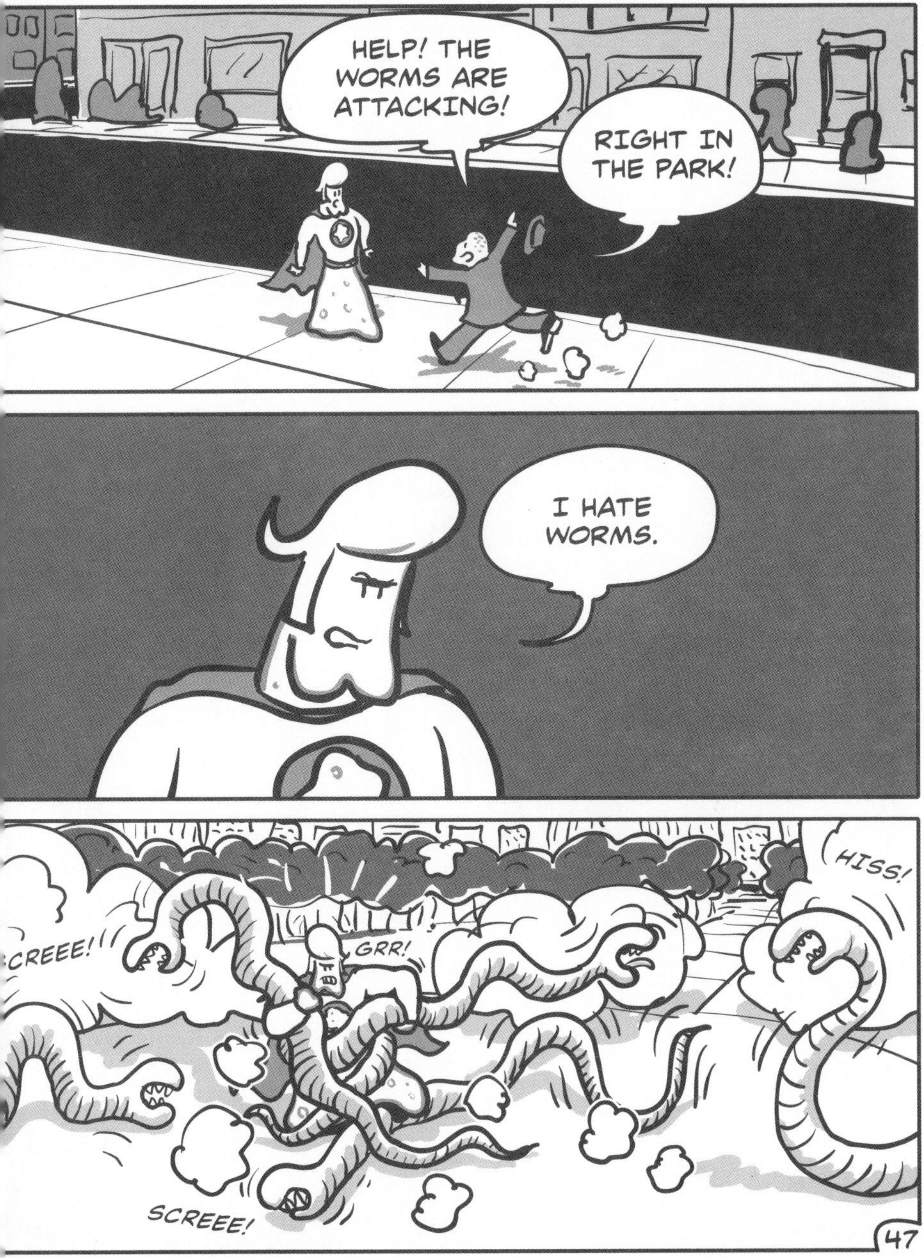
HELP! THE WORMS ARE ATTACKING!
RIGHT IN THE PARK!
I HATE WORMS.
HISS!
SCREEE!
GRR!
SCREEE!

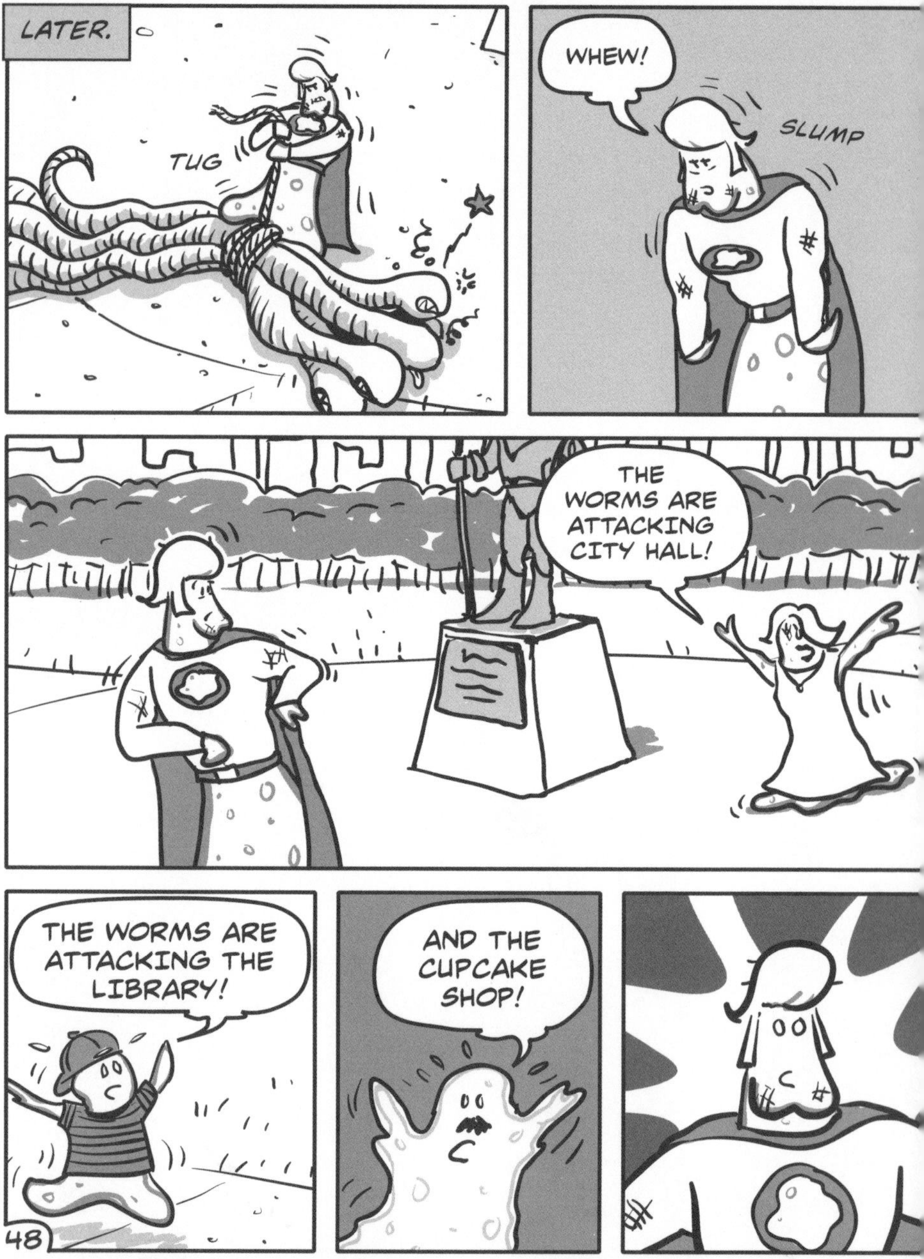
LATER.
TUG
WHEW!
SLUMP
THE WORMS ARE ATTACKING CITY HALL!
THE WORMS ARE ATTACKING THE LIBRARY!
AND THE CUPCAKE SHOP!

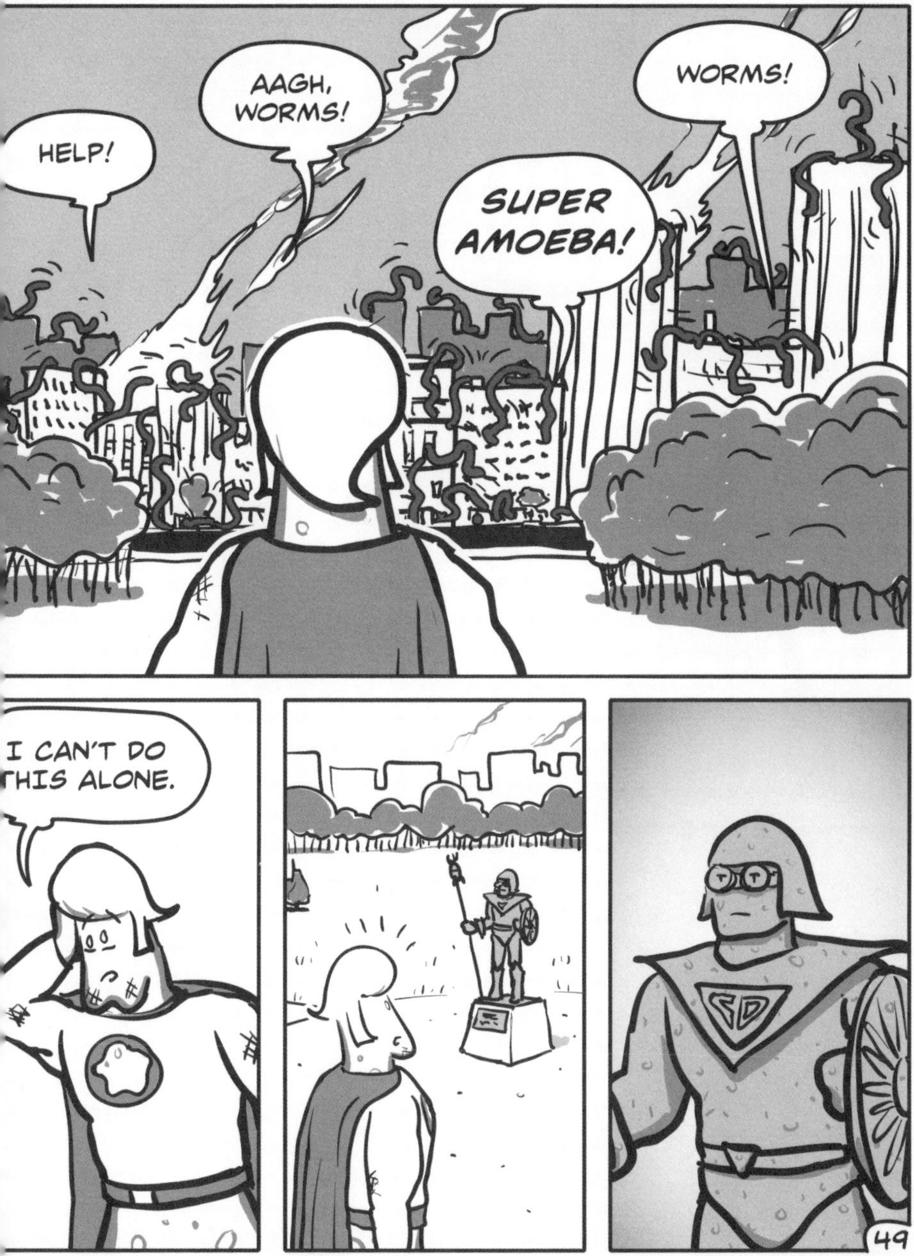
HELP!
AAGH, WORMS!
SUPER AMOEBA!
WORMS!
I CAN'T DO THIS ALONE.

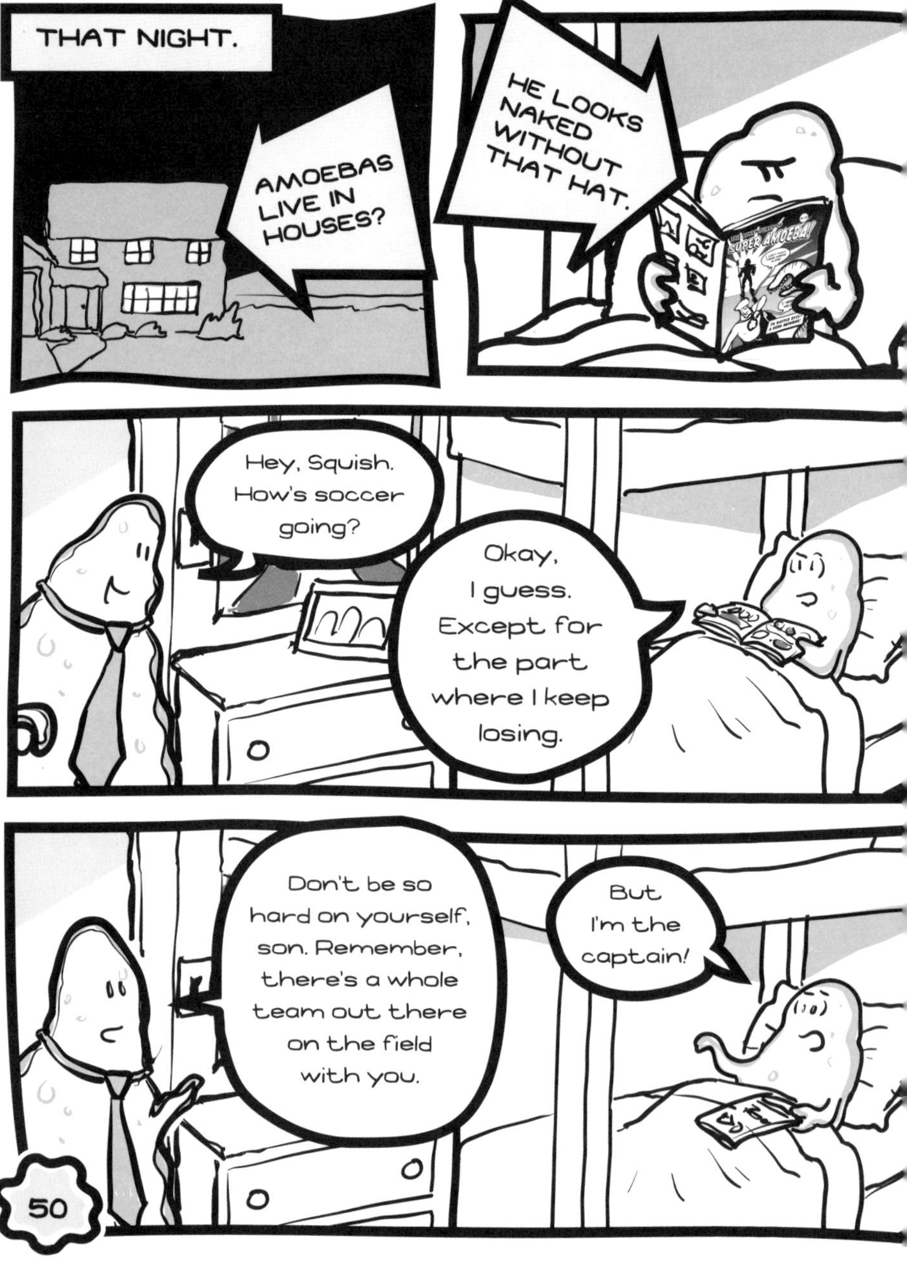
THAT NIGHT.
AMOEBAS LIVE IN HOUSES?
HE LOOKS NAKED WITHOUT THAT HAT.
SUPER AMOEBA!
Hey, Squish. How's soccer going?
Okay, I guess. Except for the part where I keep losing.
Don't be so hard on yourself, son. Remember, there's a whole team out there on the field with you.
But I'm the captain!

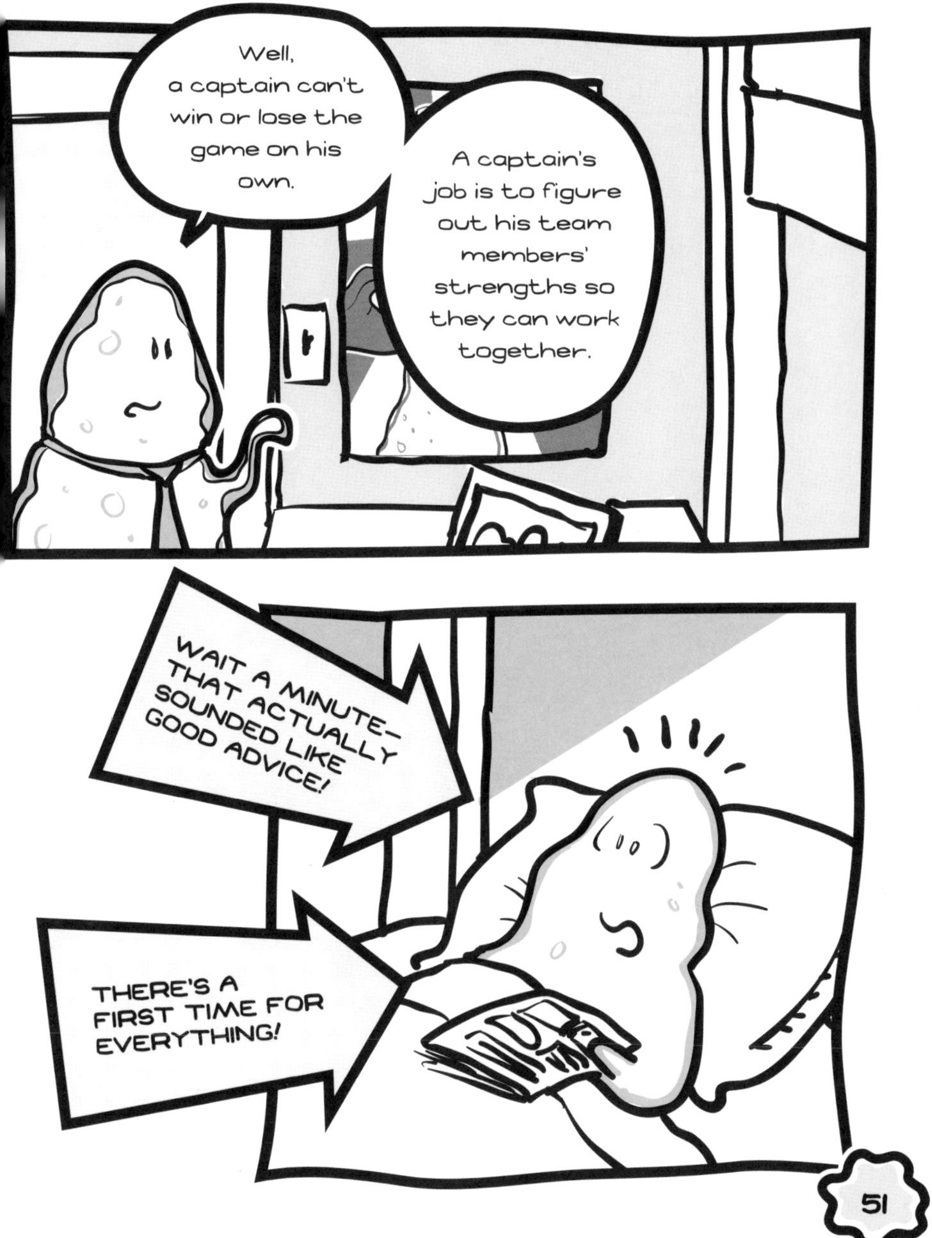
Well, a captain can't win or lose the game on his own.
A captain's job is to figure out his team members' strengths so they can work together.
WAIT A MINUTE– THAT ACTUALLY SOUNDED LIKE GOOD ADVICE!
THERE'S A FIRST TIME FOR EVERYTHING!

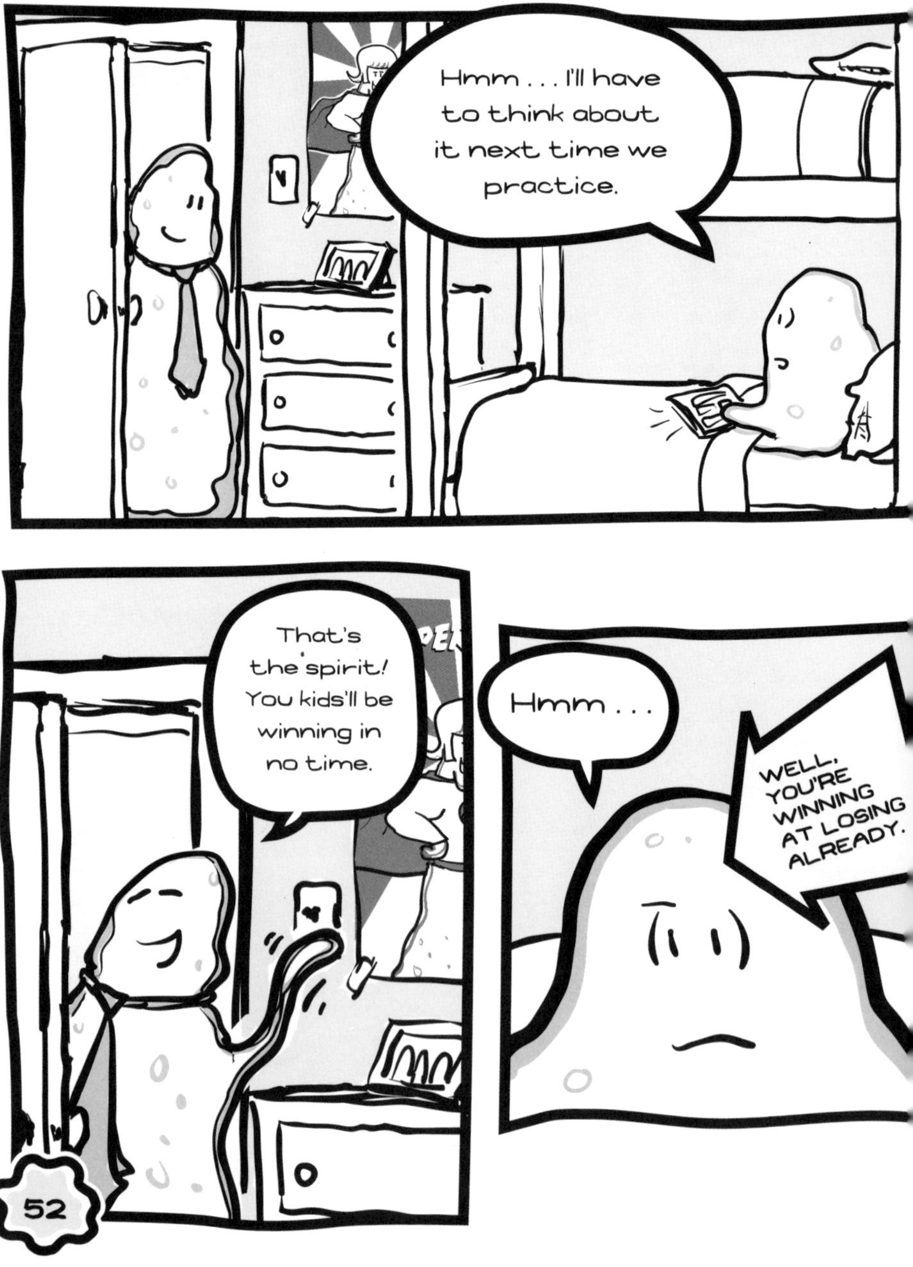
Hmm . . . I'll have to think about it next time we practice.
That's the spirit! You kids'll be winning in no time.
Hmm . . .
WELL, YOU'RE WINNING AT LOSING ALREADY.

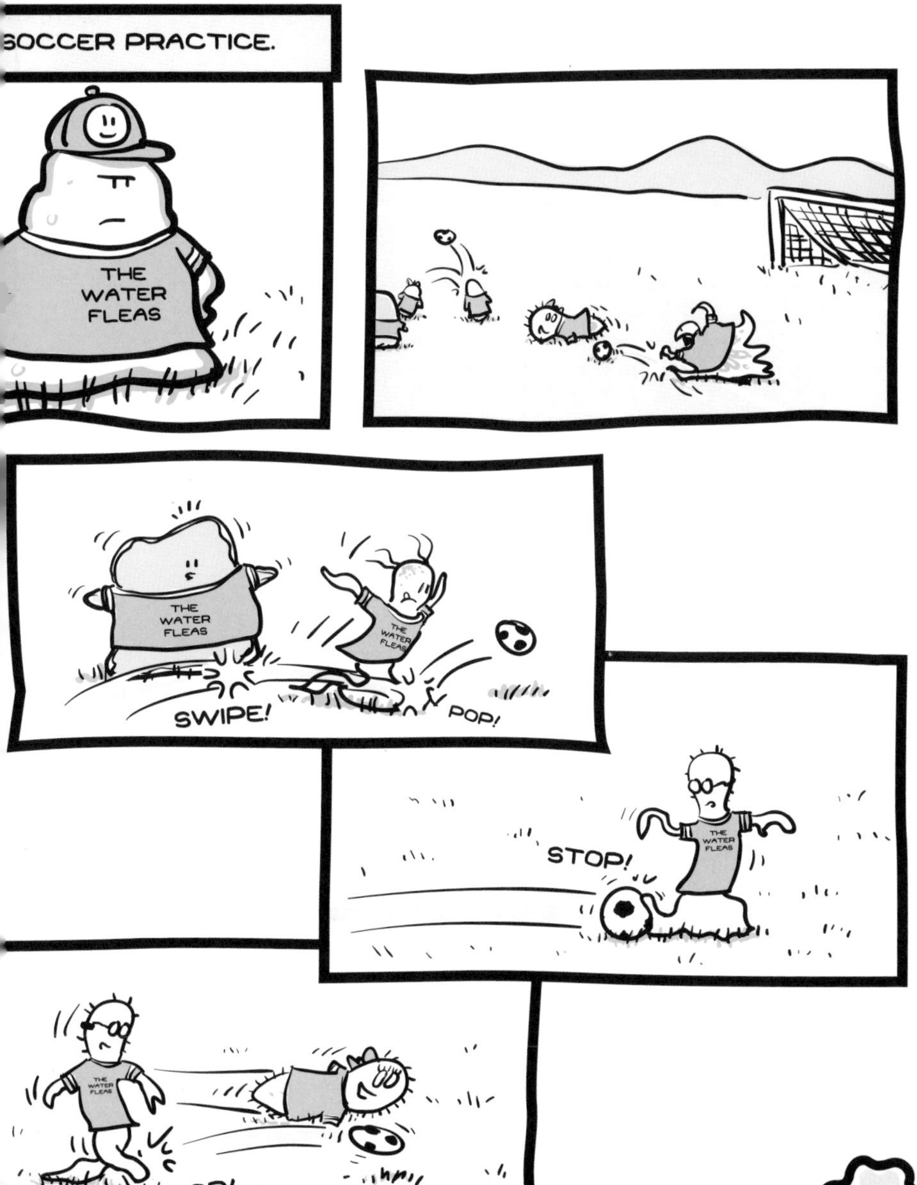
SOCCER PRACTICE.
THE WATER FLEAS
THE WATER FLEAS
THE WATER FLEAS
SWIPE!
POP!
STOP!
THE WATER FLEAS
THE WATER FLEAS
POP!

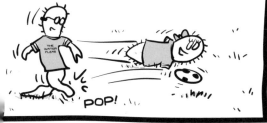

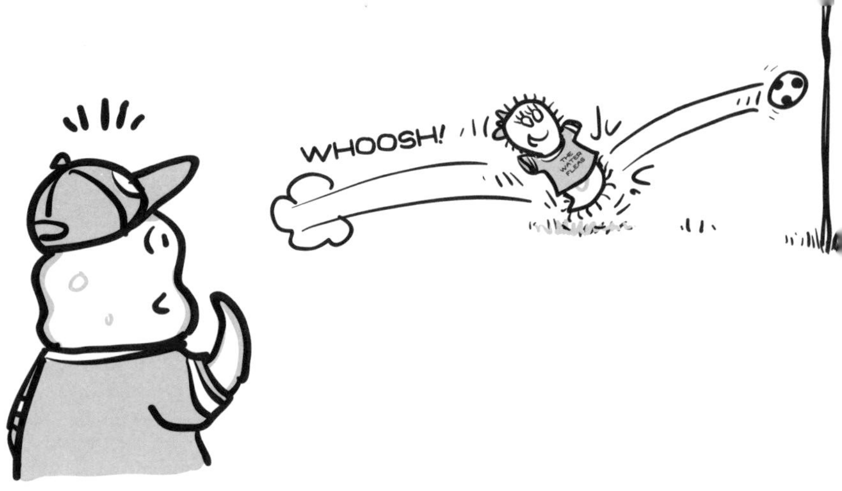
WHOOSH!
THE WATER FLEAS

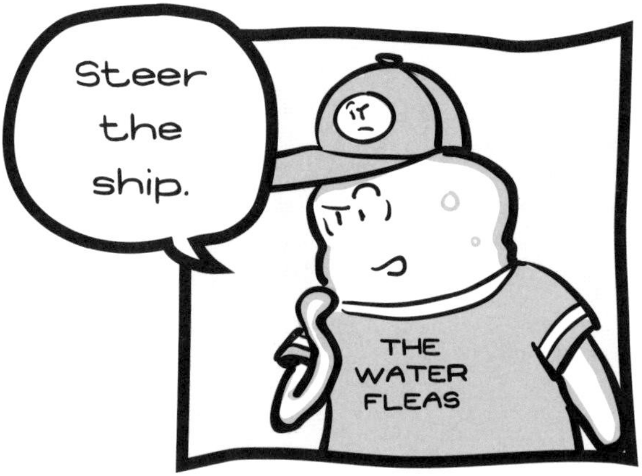
Steer the ship.
THE WATER FLEAS

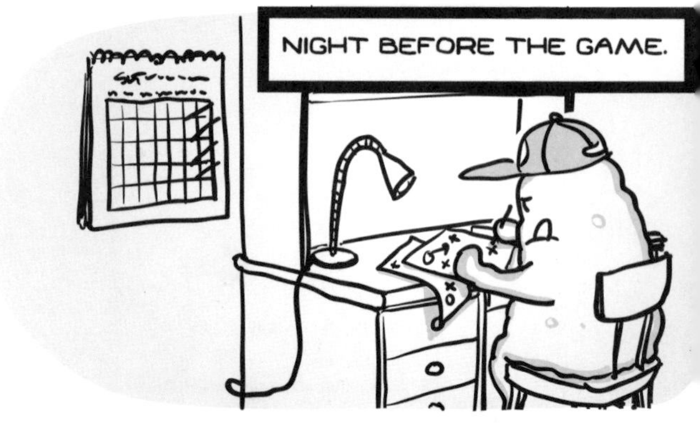
NIGHT BEFORE THE GAME.

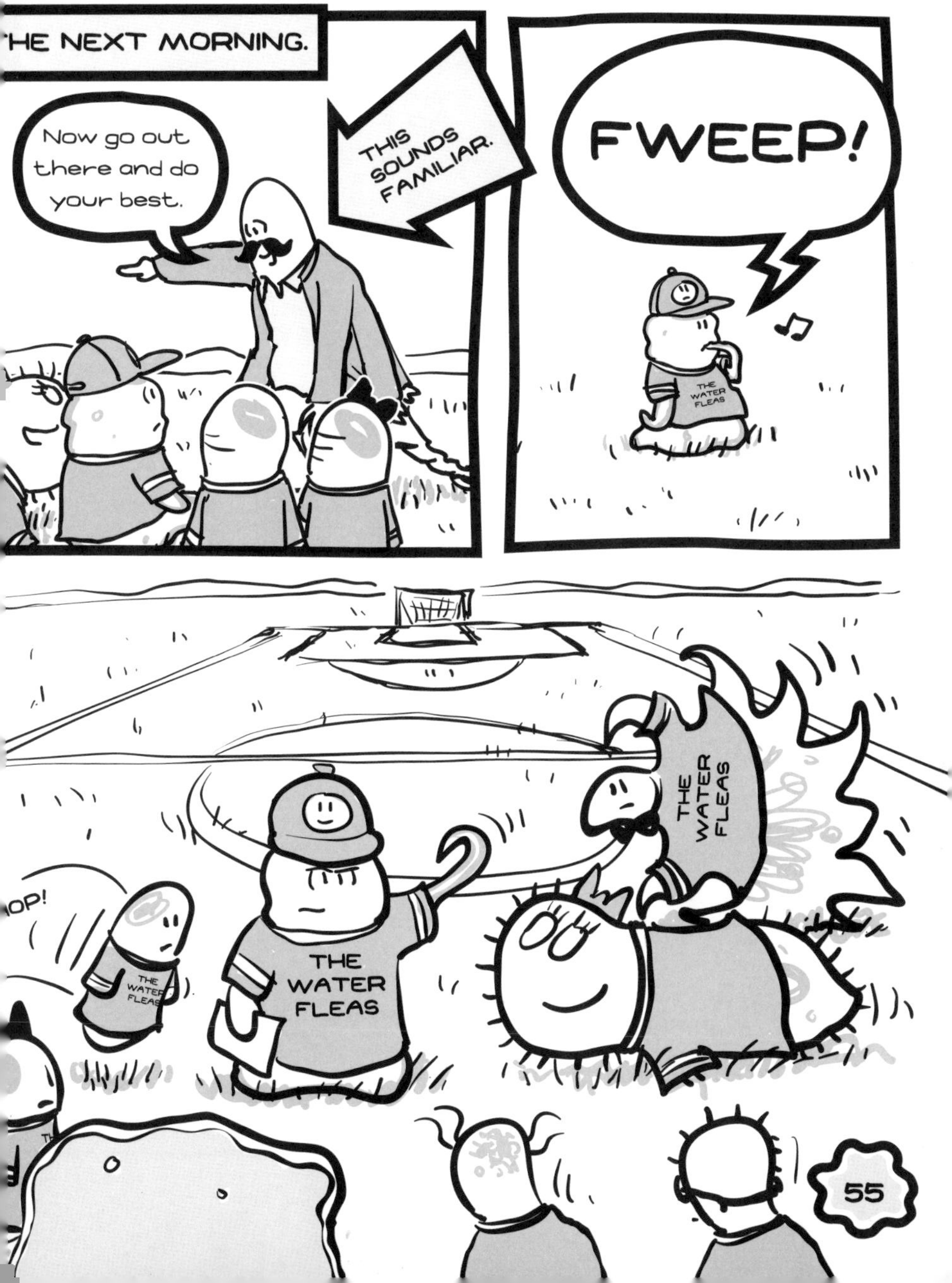

THE NEXT MORNING.
Now go out there and do your best.
THIS SOUNDS FAMILIAR.
FWEEP!
THE WATER FLEAS
THE WATER FLEAS
THE WATER FLEAS
THE WATER FLEAS
THE WATER FLEAS

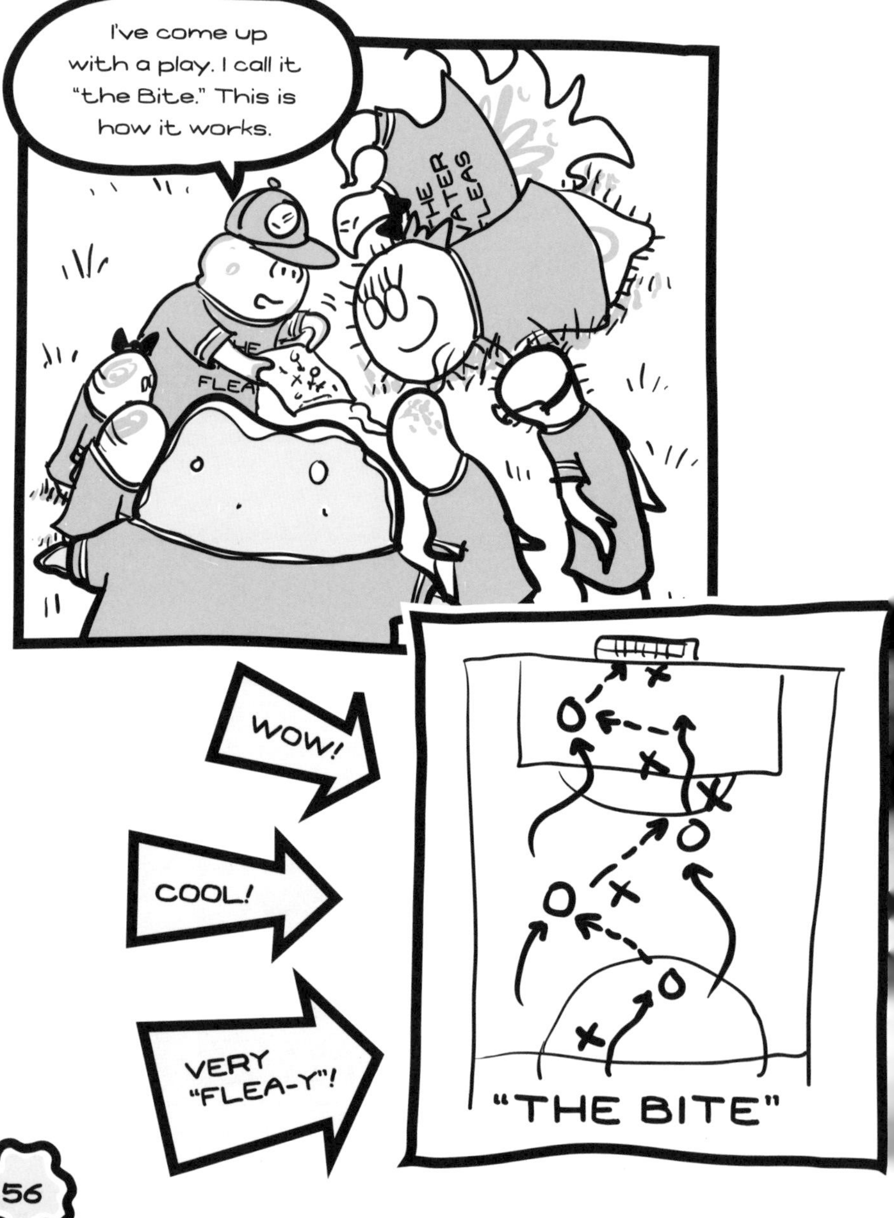
I've come up with a play. I call it "the Bite." This is how it works.
THE FLEA
THE ATER LEAS
WOW!
COOL!
VERY "FLEA-Y"!
"THE BITE"

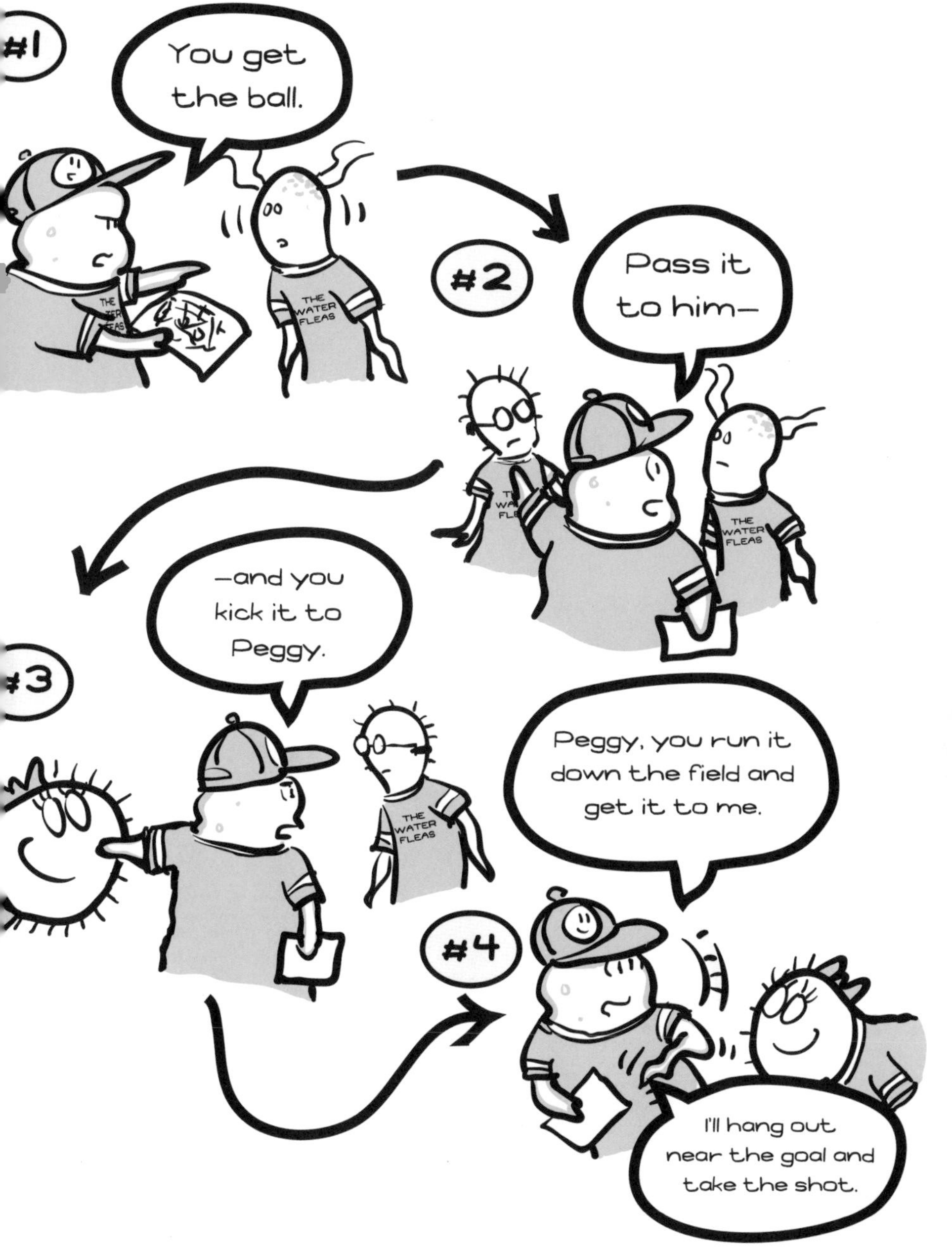
#1
You get the ball.
THE WATER FLEAS
#2
Pass it to him—
THE WATER FLEAS
—and you kick it to Peggy.
#3
THE WATER FLEAS
Peggy, you run it down the field and get it to me.
#4
I'll hang out near the goal and take the shot.

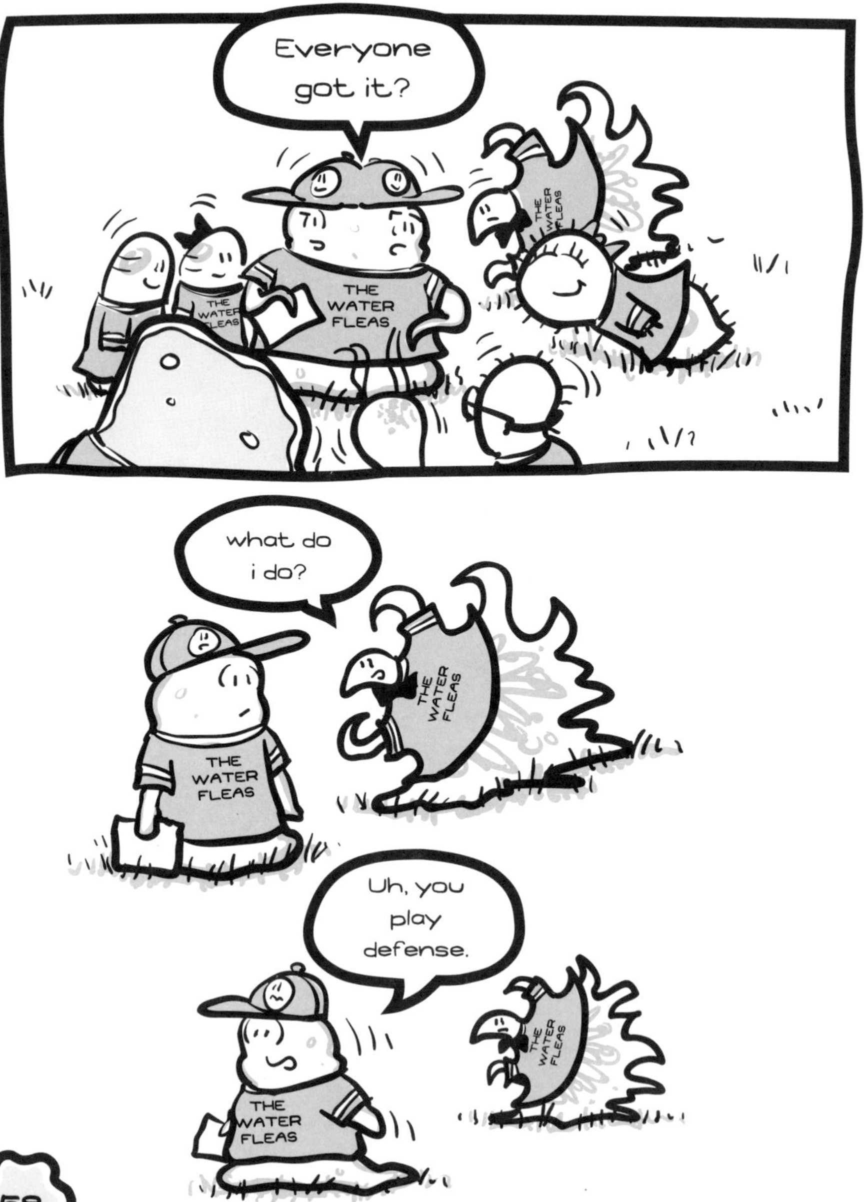
Everyone got it?
THE WATER FLEAS
what do i do?
Uh, you play defense.

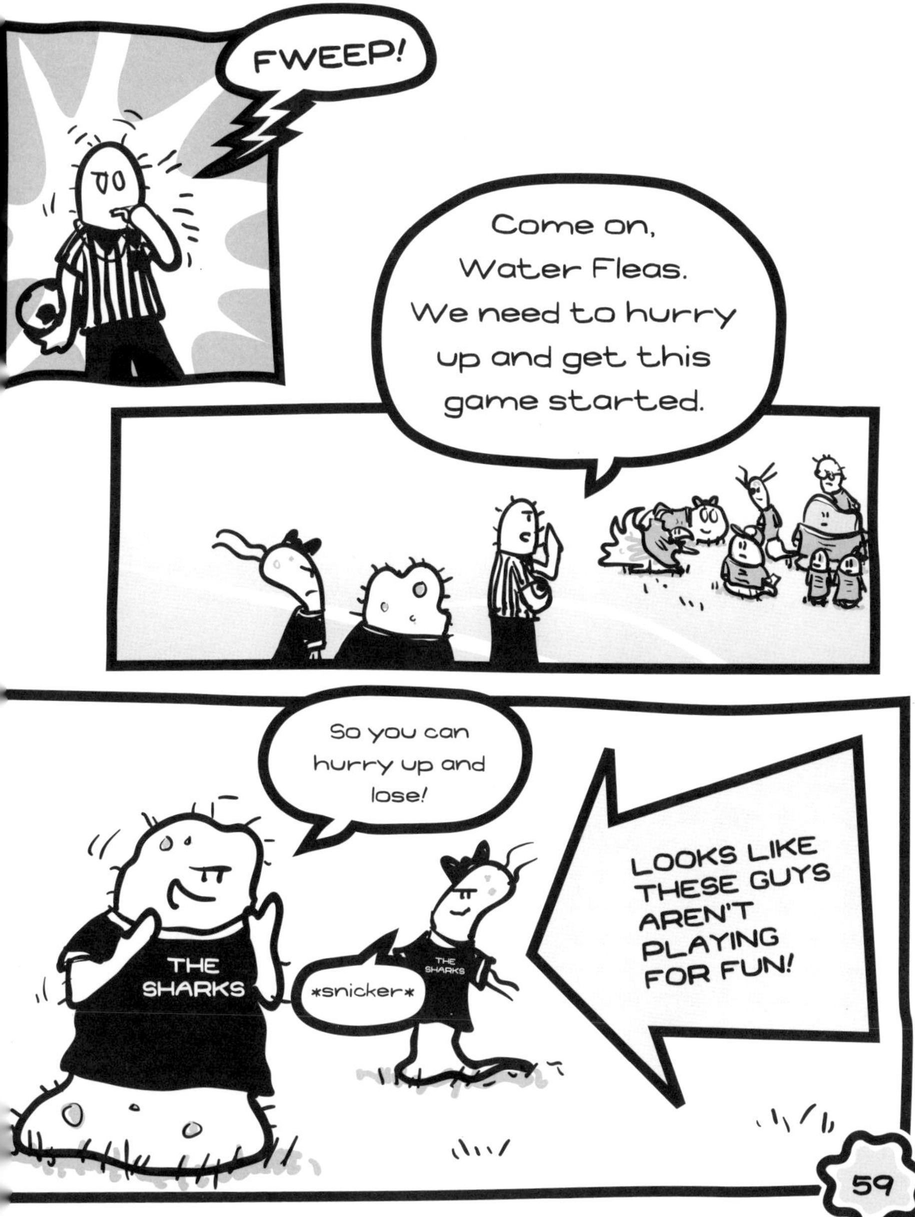
FWEEP!
Come on, Water Fleas. We need to hurry up and get this game started.
So you can hurry up and lose!
THE SHARKS
snicker
THE SHARKS
LOOKS LIKE THESE GUYS AREN'T PLAYING FOR FUN!

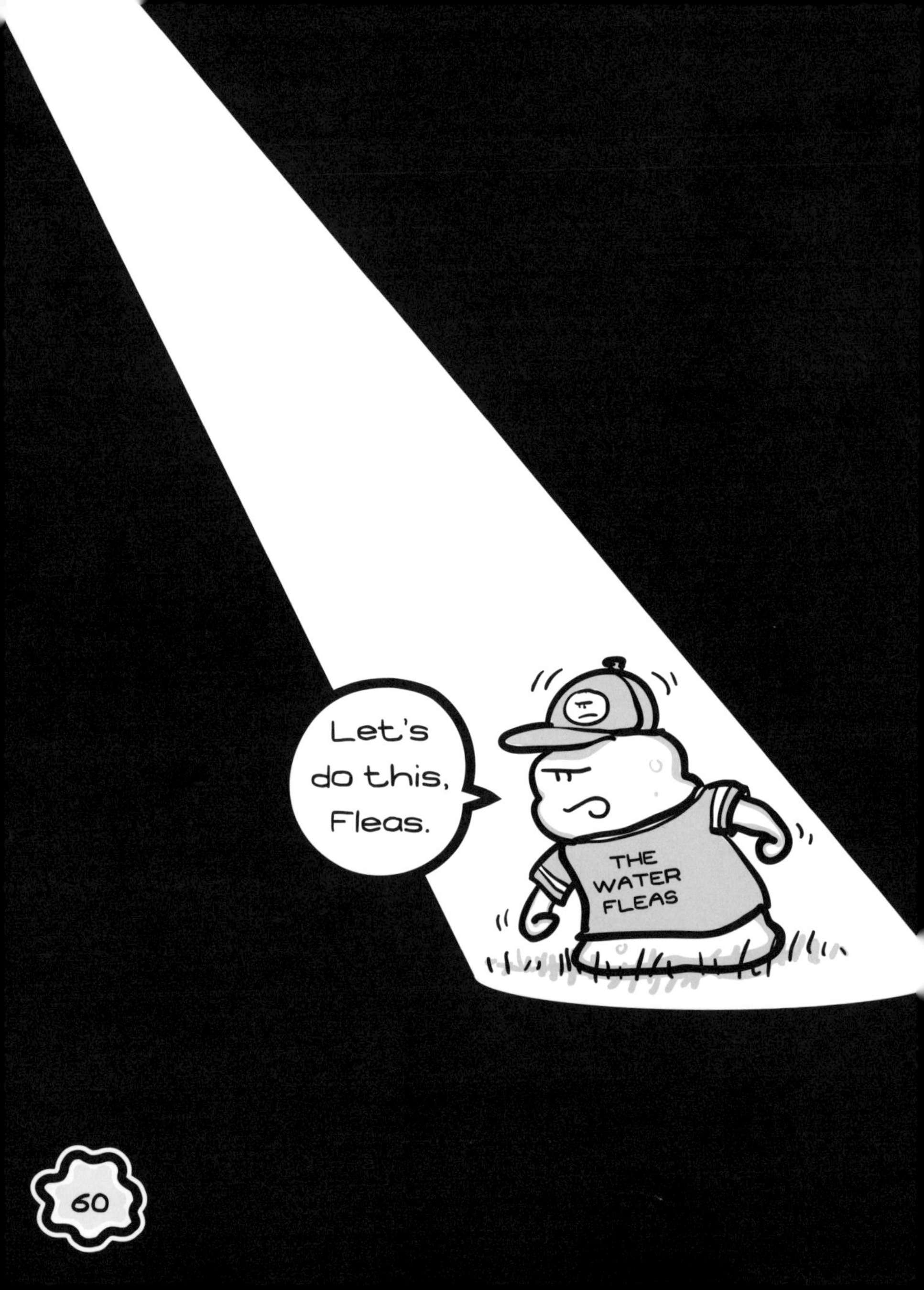
Let's do this, Fleas.
THE WATER FLEAS

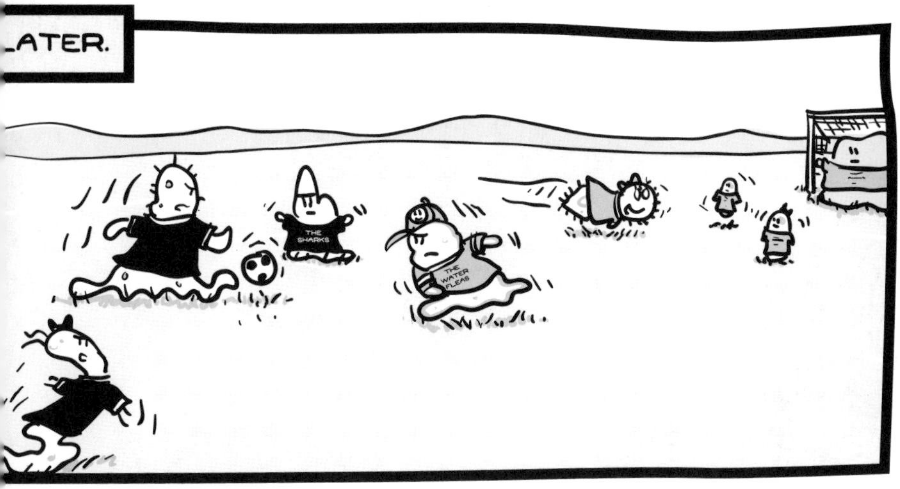
LATER.
THE SHARKS
THE WATER FLEAS

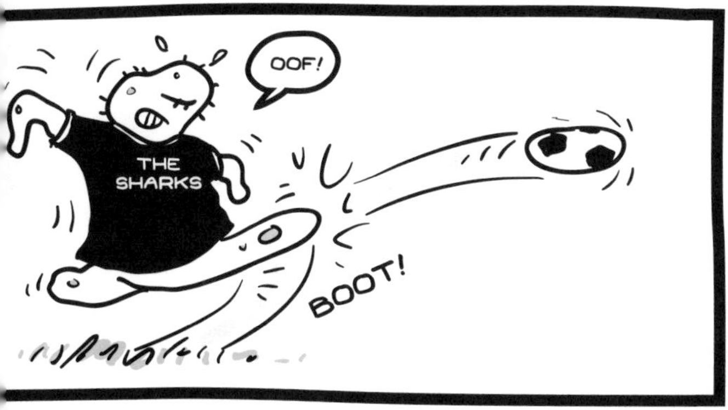
OOF!
THE SHARKS
BOOT!

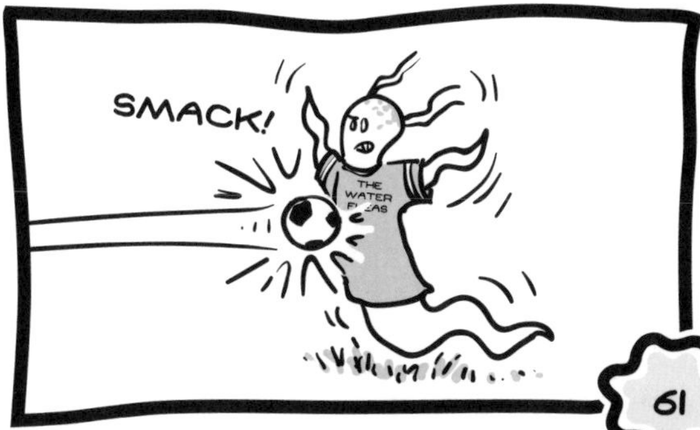
SMACK!
THE WATER FLEAS

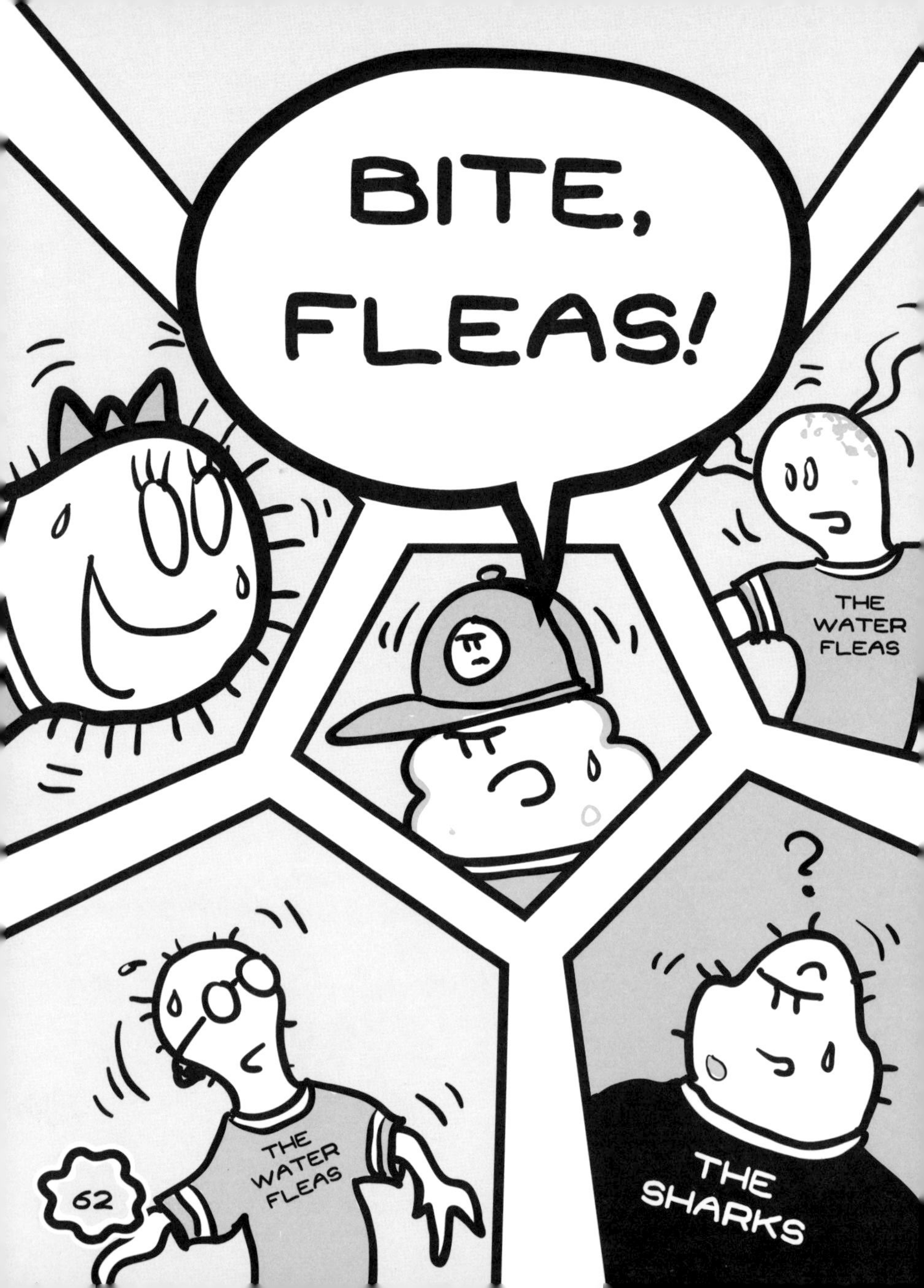
BITE, FLEAS!
THE WATER FLEAS
?
THE WATER FLEAS
THE SHARKS
62

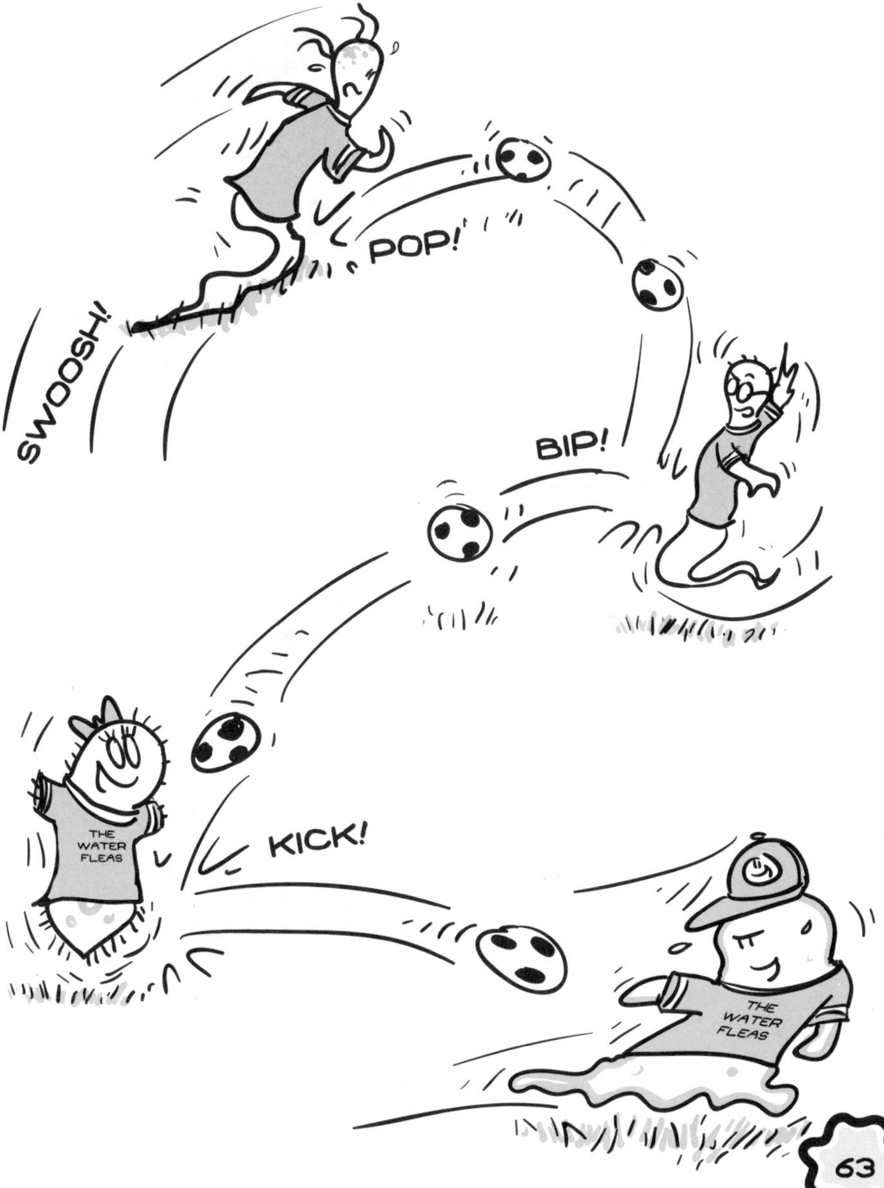
SWOOSH!
POP!
BIP!
THE WATER FLEAS
KICK!
THE WATER FLEAS

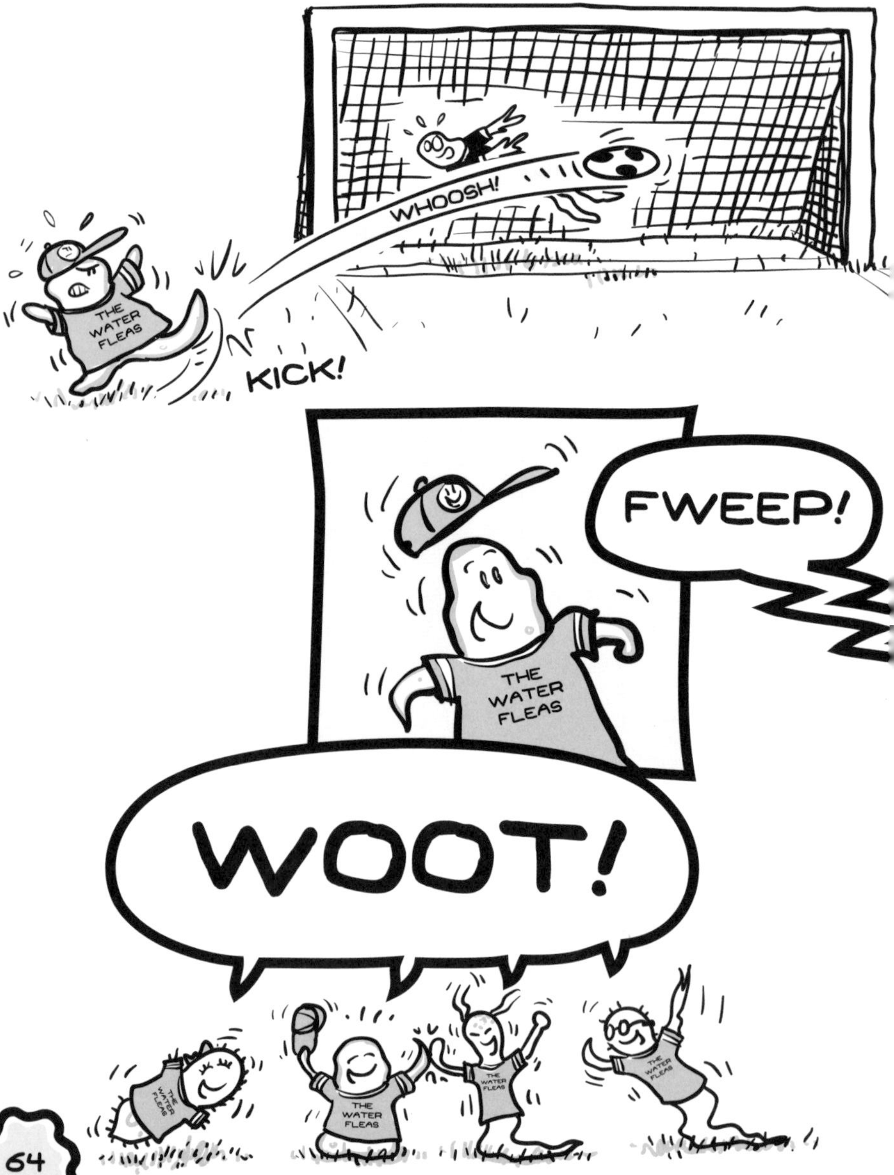
WHOOSH!
THE WATER FLEAS
KICK!
THE WATER FLEAS
FWEEP!
WOOT!
THE WATER FLEAS
THE WATER FLEAS
THE WATER FLEAS
THE WATER FLEAS

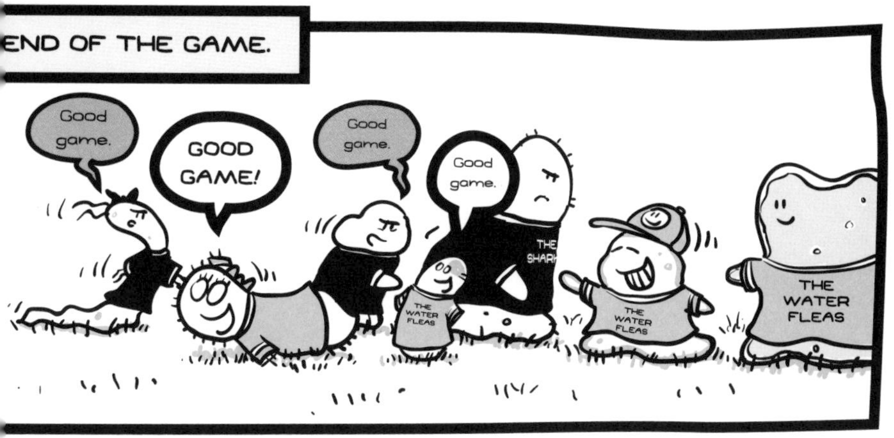
END OF THE GAME.
Good game.
GOOD GAME!
Good game.
Good game.
THE SHARK
THE WATER FLEAS
THE WATER FLEAS
THE WATER FLEAS

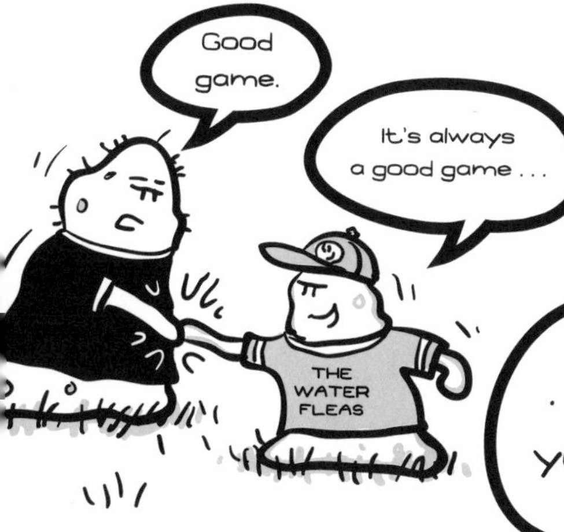
Good game.
It's always a good game . . .
THE WATER FLEAS

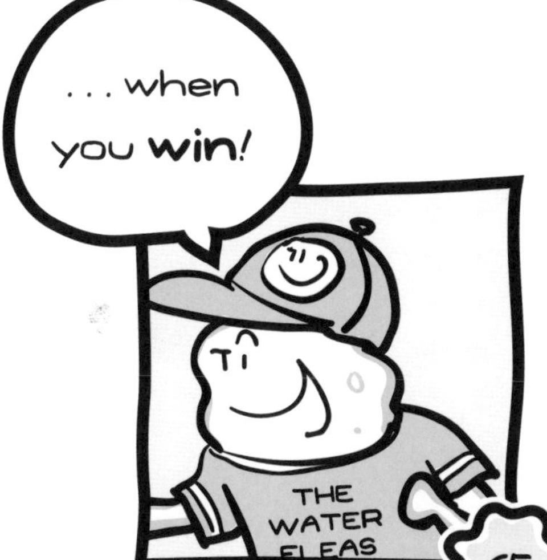
. . . when you **win**!
THE WATER FLEAS

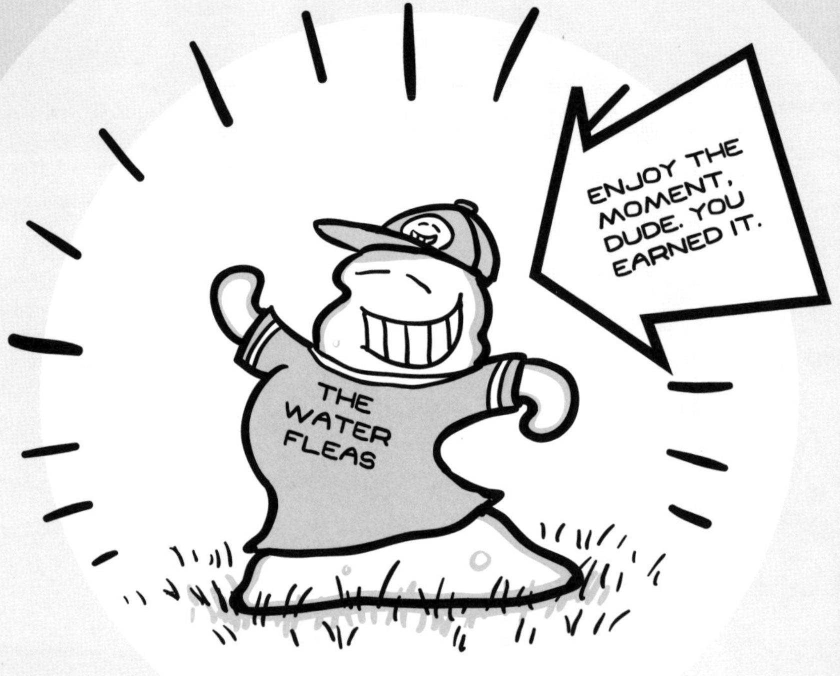
ENJOY THE MOMENT, DUDE. YOU EARNED IT.
THE WATER FLEAS

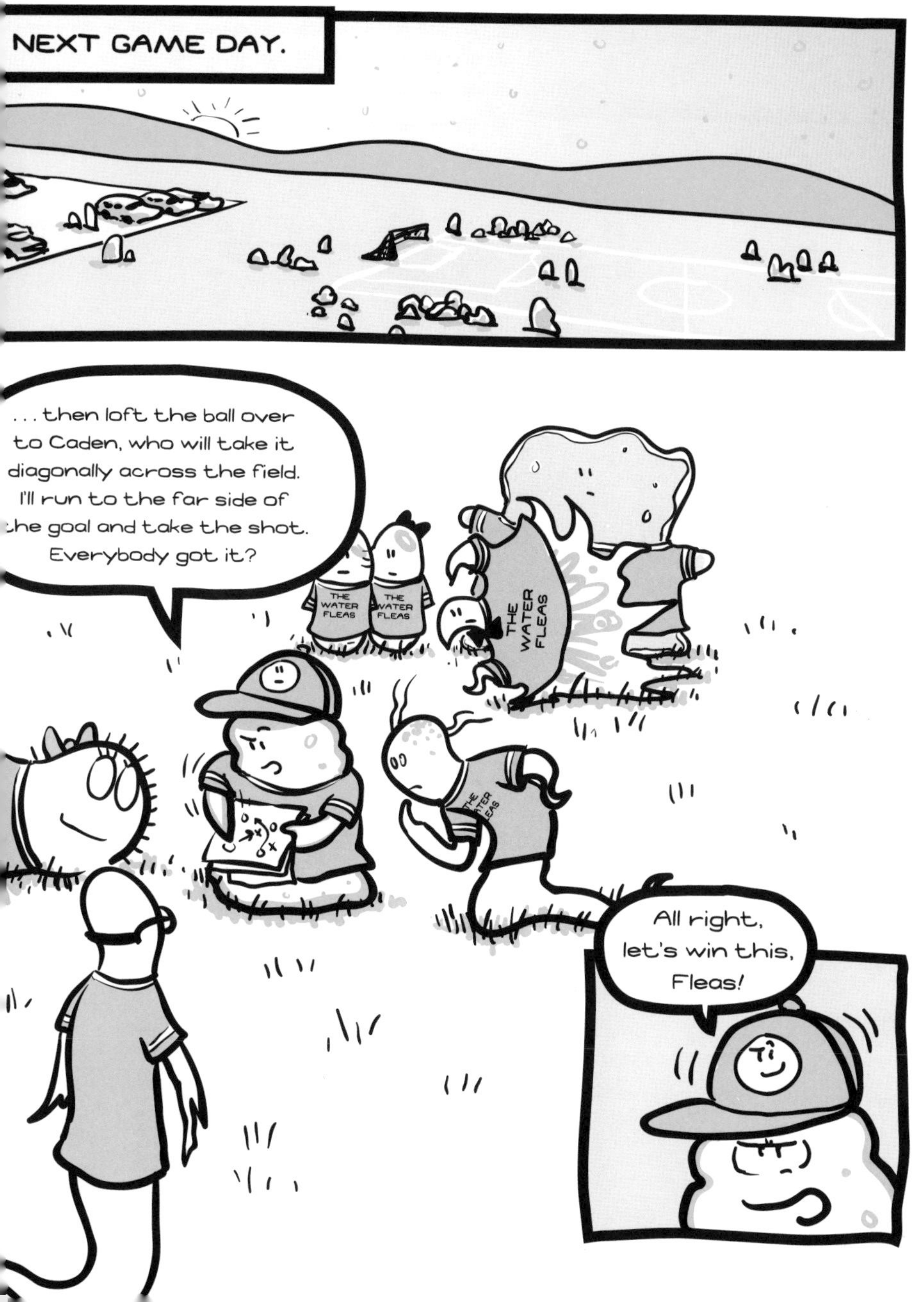
NEXT GAME DAY.
. . . then loft the ball over to Caden, who will take it diagonally across the field. I'll run to the far side of the goal and take the shot. Everybody got it?
THE WATER FLEAS
THE WATER FLEAS
THE WATER FLEAS
THE WATER FLEAS
All right, let's win this, Fleas!

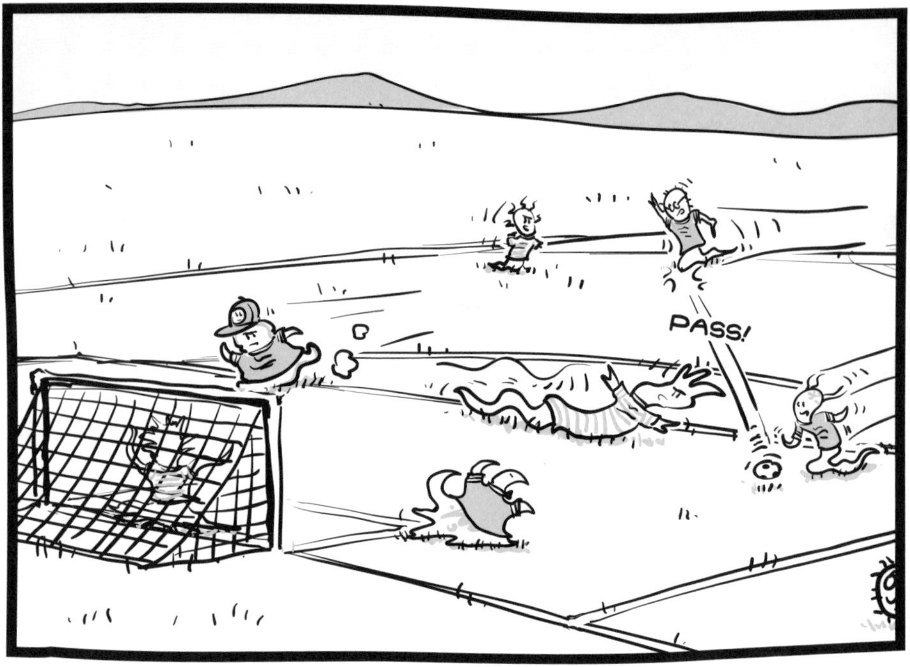
PASS!

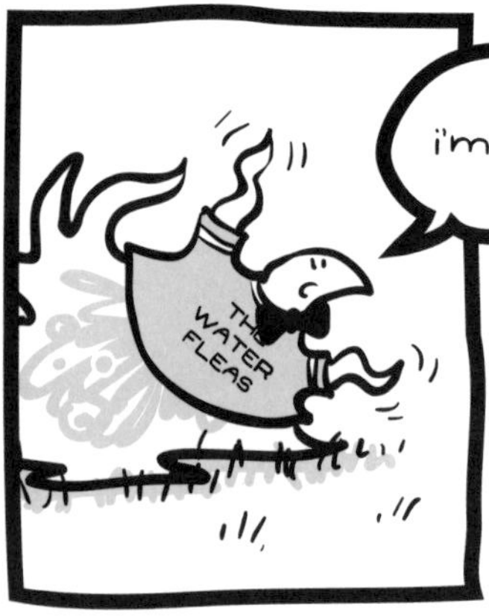
i'm open.
THE WATER FLEAS

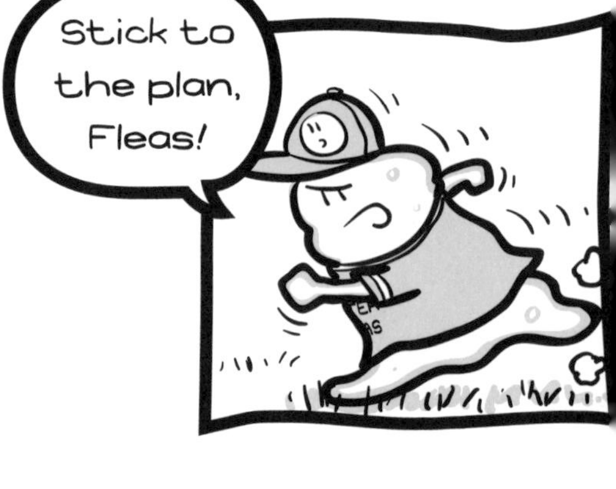
Stick to the plan, Fleas!

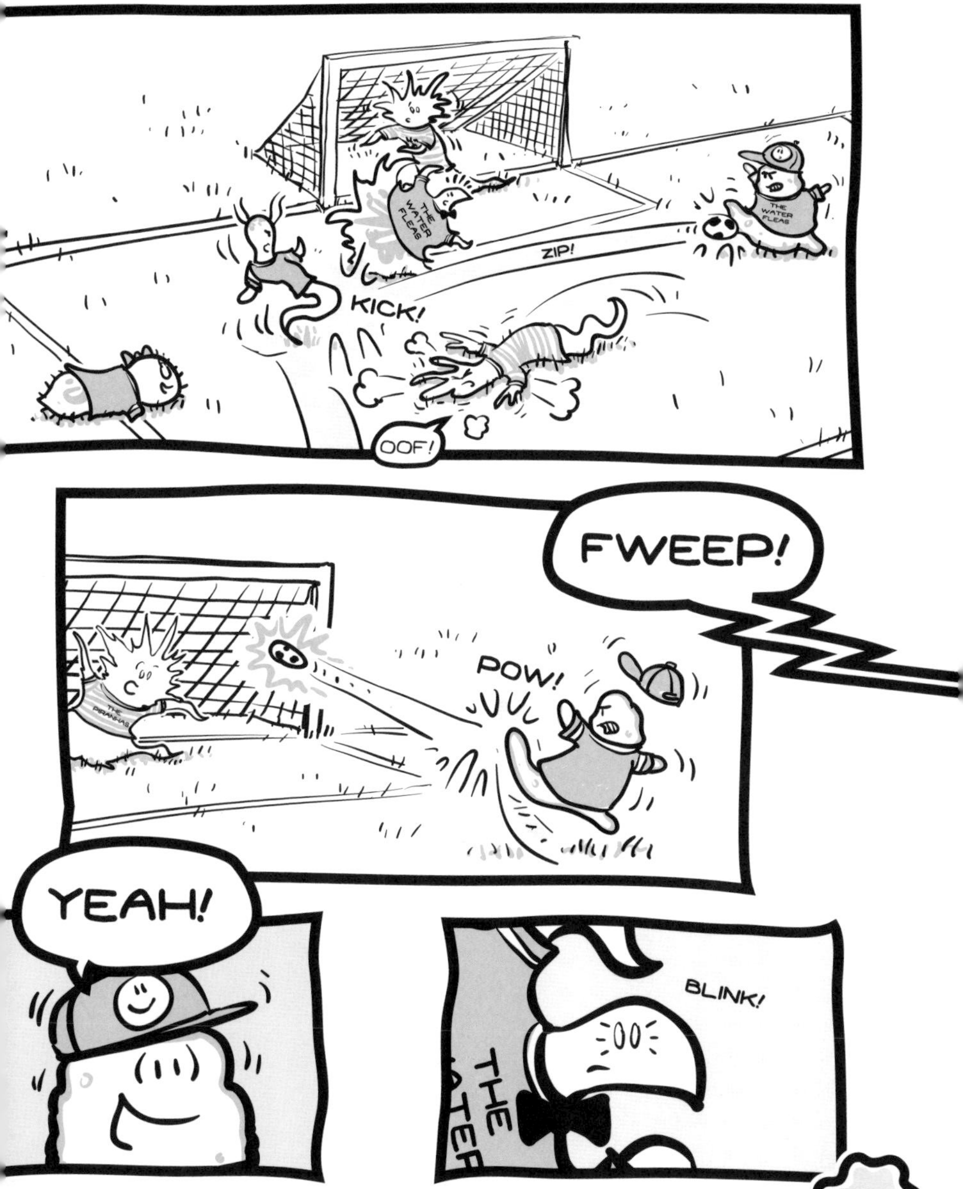
THE WATER FLEAS
THE WATER FLEAS
ZIP!
KICK!
OOF!
FWEEP!
THE PIRANHAS
POW!
YEAH!
BLINK!
THE
ATER

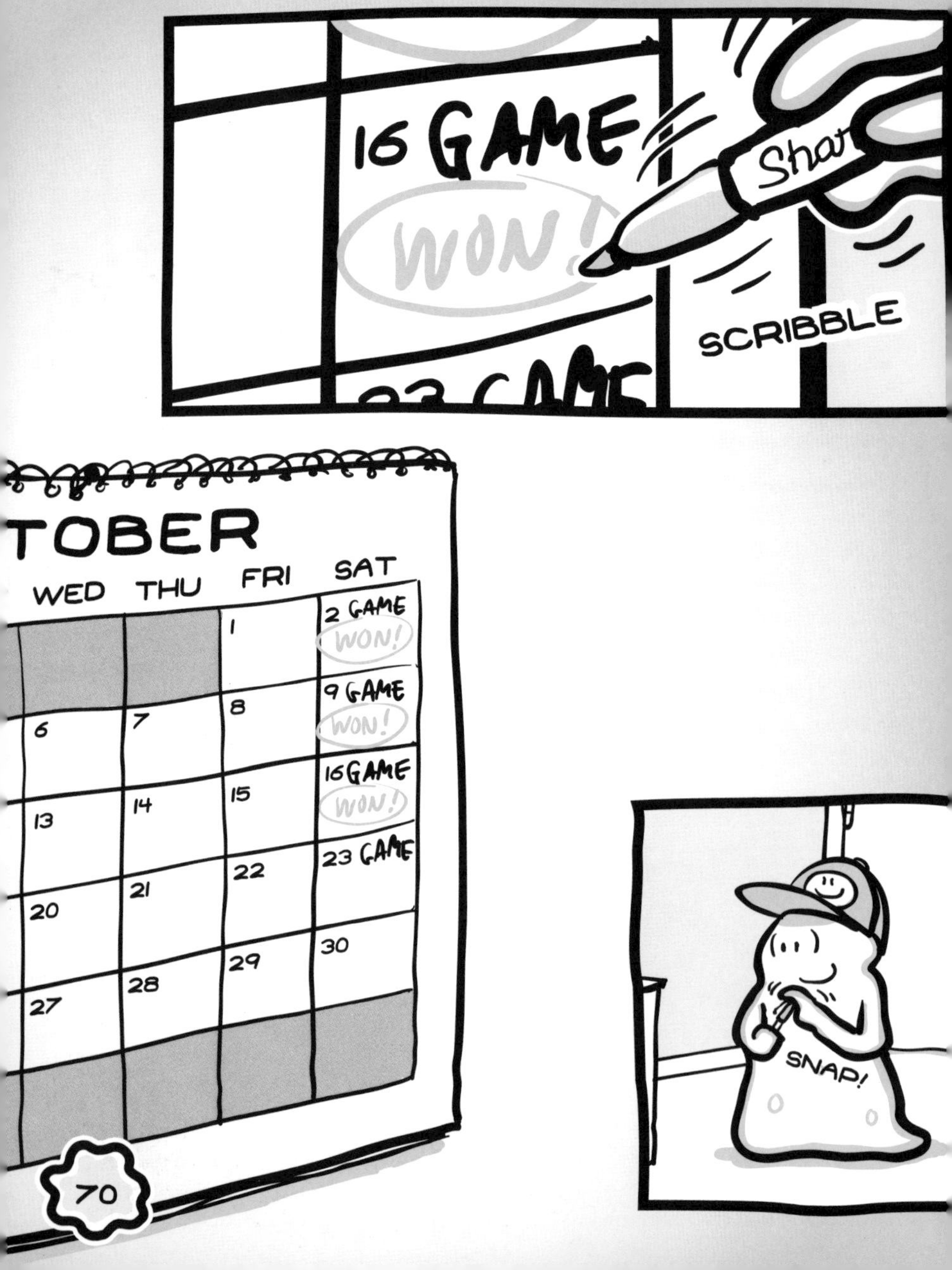
16 GAME
WON!
Shar
SCRIBBLE
23 GAME
TOBER
WED
THU
FRI
SAT
1
2 GAME
WON!
6
7
8
9 GAME
WON!
13
14
15
16 GAME
WON!
20
21
22
23 GAME
27
28
29
30
SNAP!

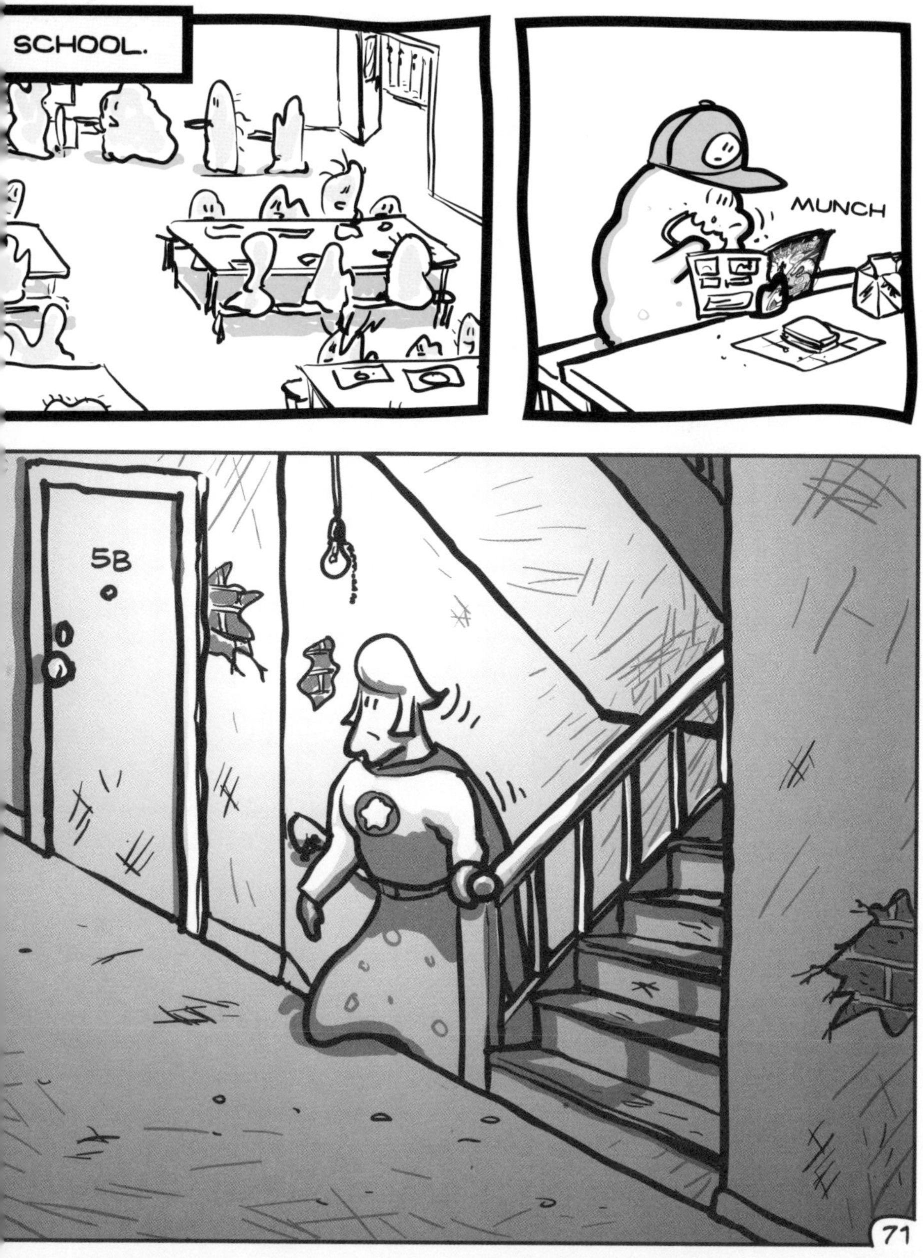
SCHOOL.
MUNCH
5B

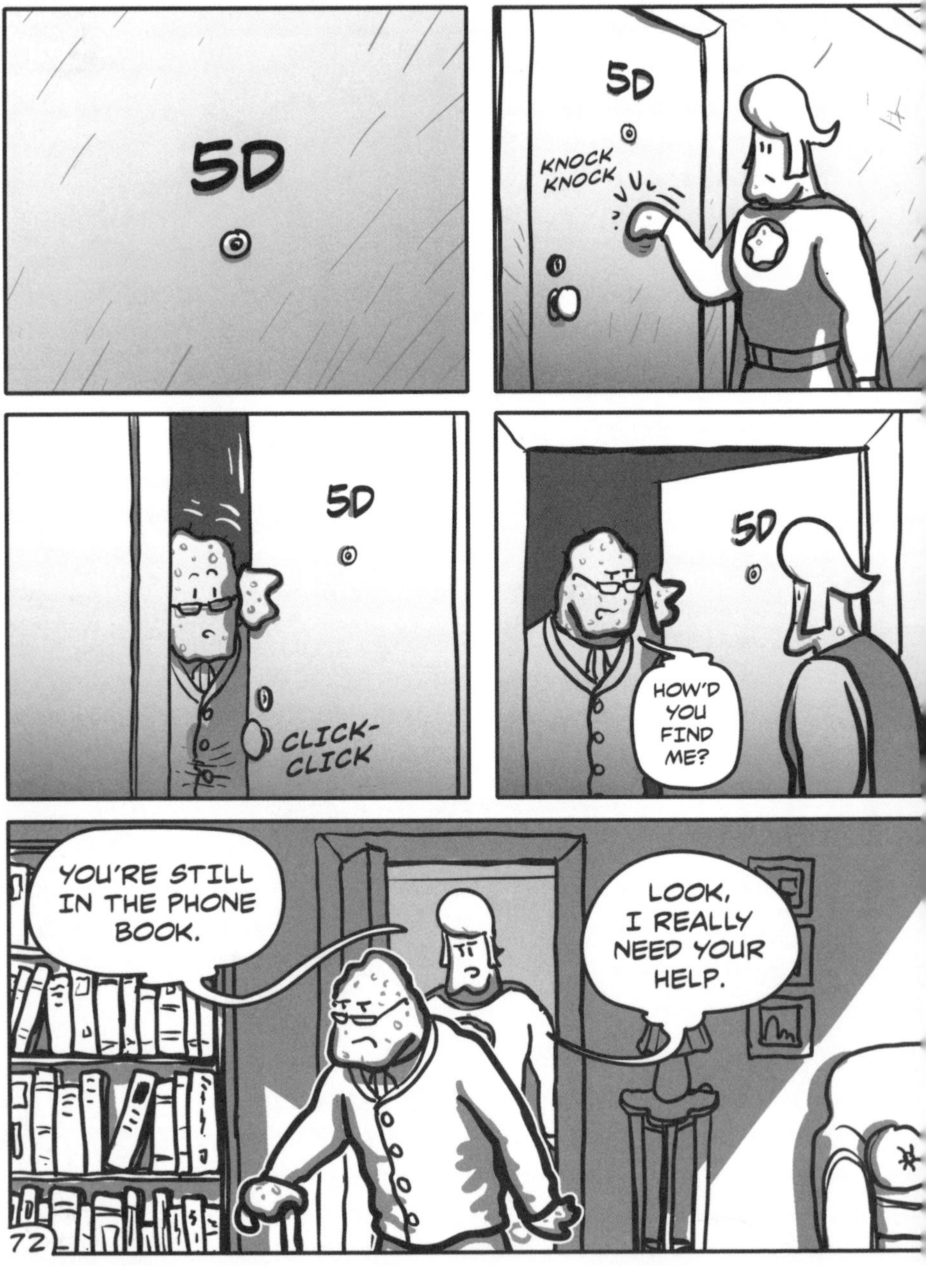
5D
5D
KNOCK KNOCK
5D
CLICK-CLICK
5D
HOW'D YOU FIND ME?
YOU'RE STILL IN THE PHONE BOOK.
LOOK, I REALLY NEED YOUR HELP.

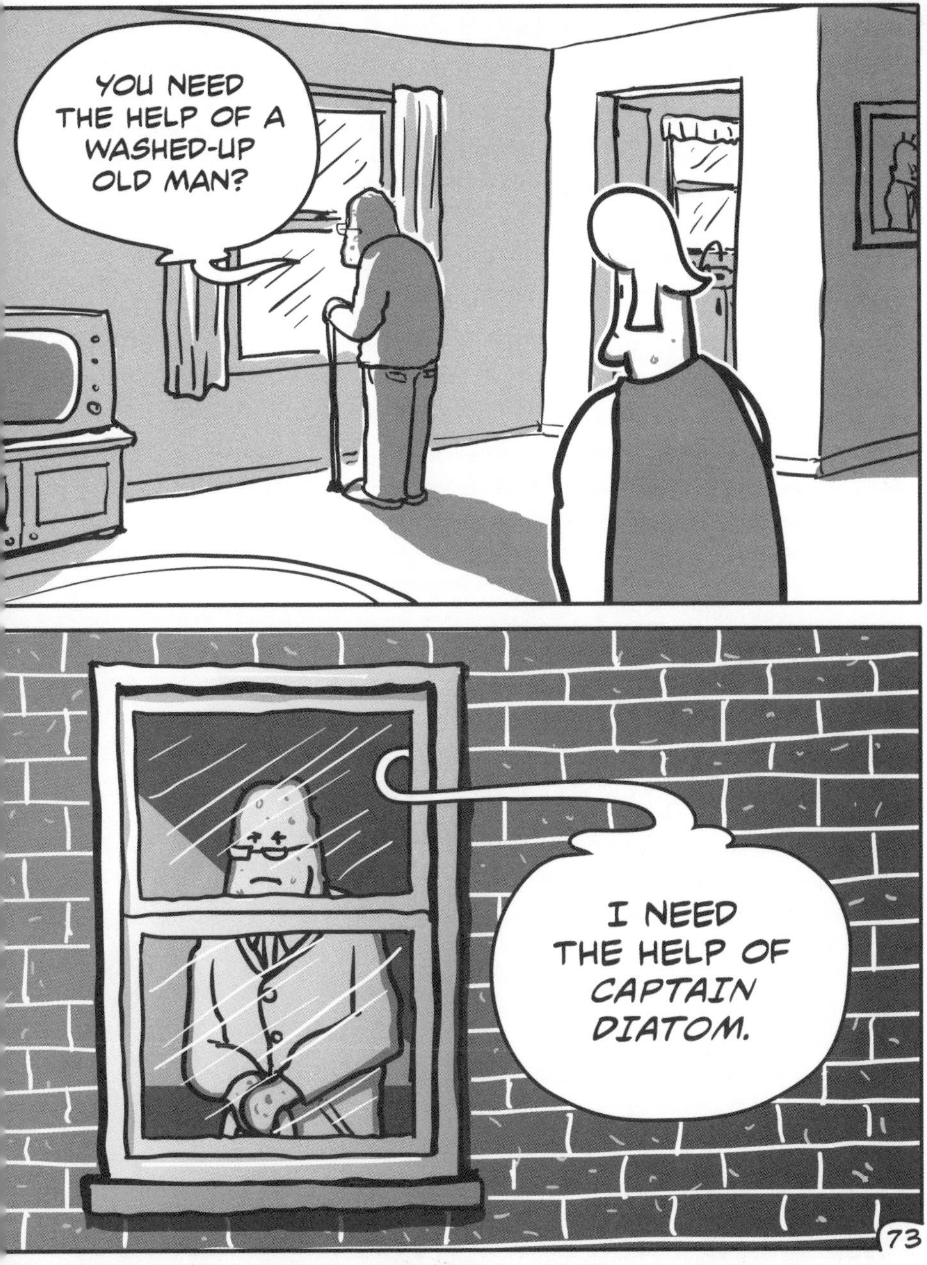
YOU NEED THE HELP OF A WASHED-UP OLD MAN?
I NEED THE HELP OF *CAPTAIN DIATOM.*

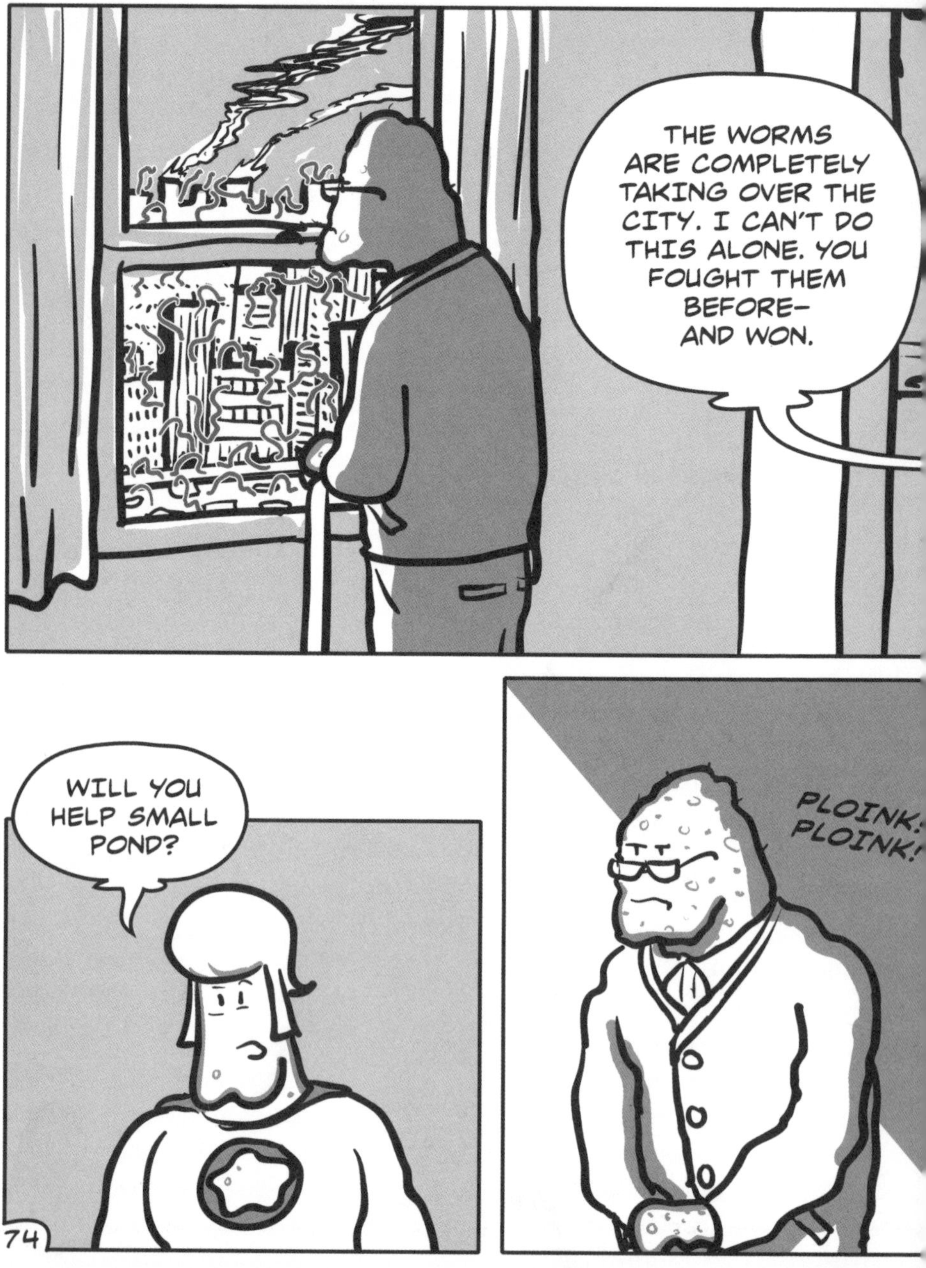
THE WORMS ARE COMPLETELY TAKING OVER THE CITY. I CAN'T DO THIS ALONE. YOU FOUGHT THEM BEFORE— AND WON.
WILL YOU HELP SMALL POND?
PLOINK! PLOINK!

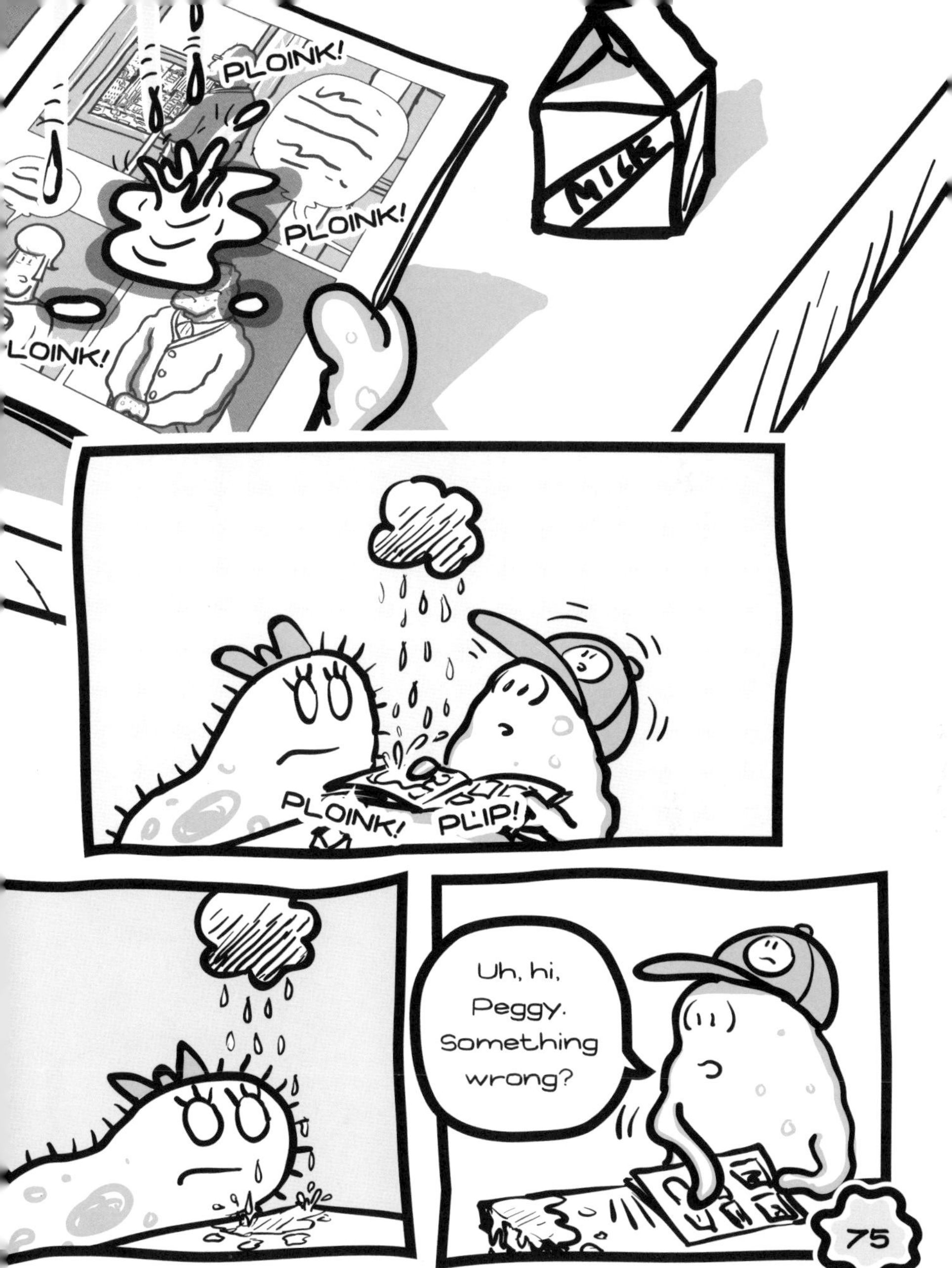
PLOINK!
PLOINK!
LOINK!
MILK
PLOINK!
PLIP!
Uh, hi, Peggy. Something wrong?

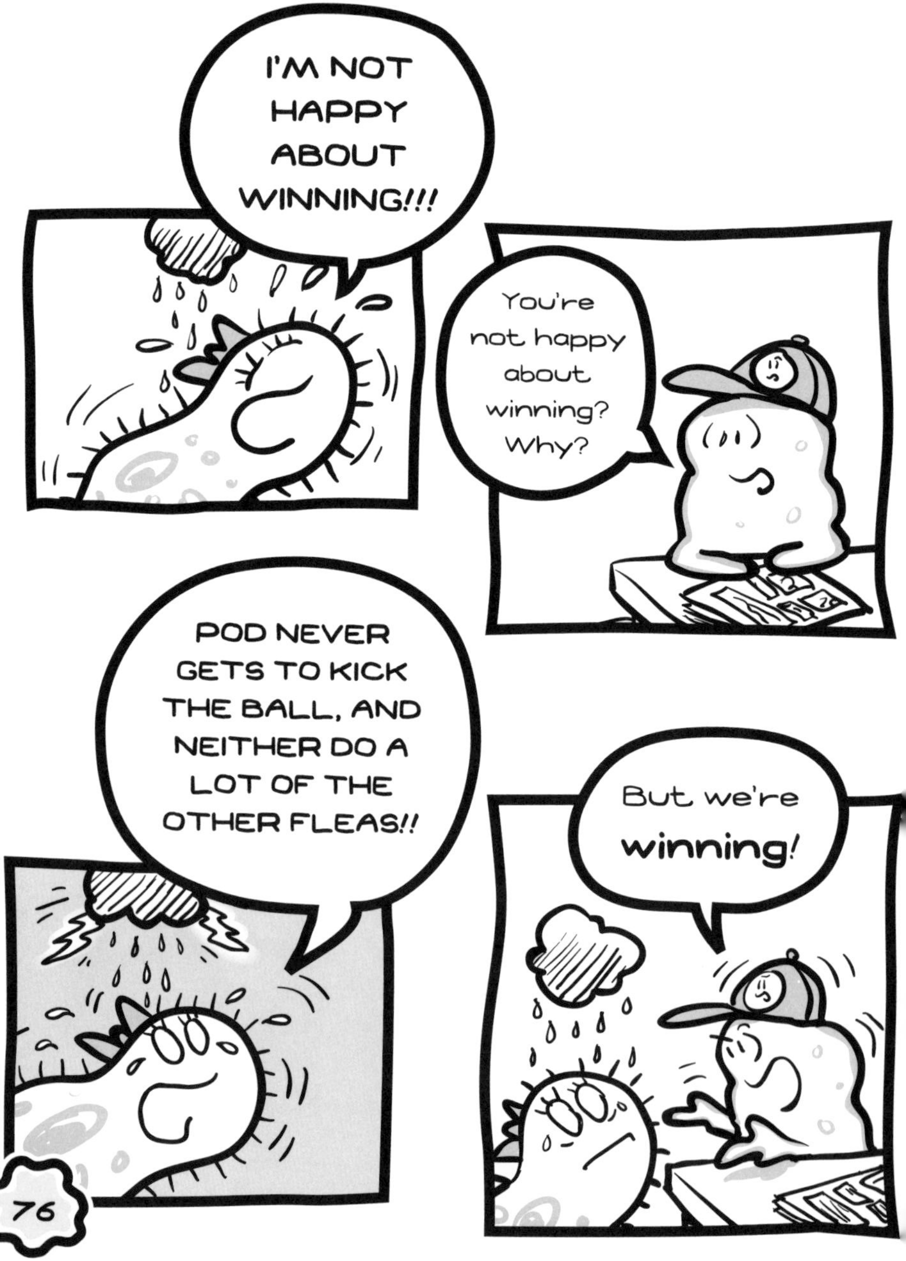
I'M NOT HAPPY ABOUT WINNING!!!
You're not happy about winning? Why?
POD NEVER GETS TO KICK THE BALL, AND NEITHER DO A LOT OF THE OTHER FLEAS!!
But we're **winning**!

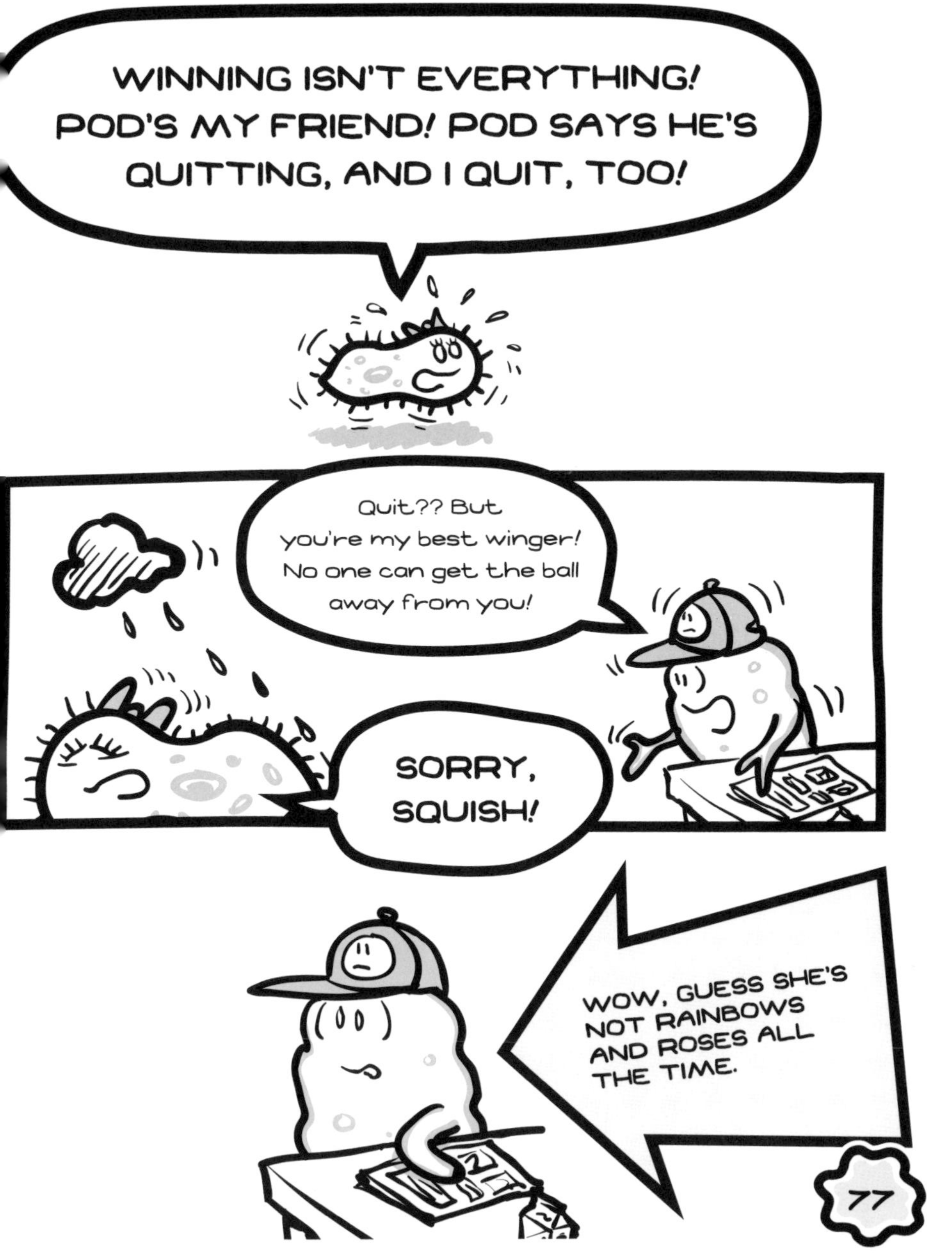

WINNING ISN'T EVERYTHING! POD'S MY FRIEND! POD SAYS HE'S QUITTING, AND I QUIT, TOO!
Quit?? But you're my best winger! No one can get the ball away from you!
SORRY, SQUISH!
WOW, GUESS SHE'S NOT RAINBOWS AND ROSES ALL THE TIME.

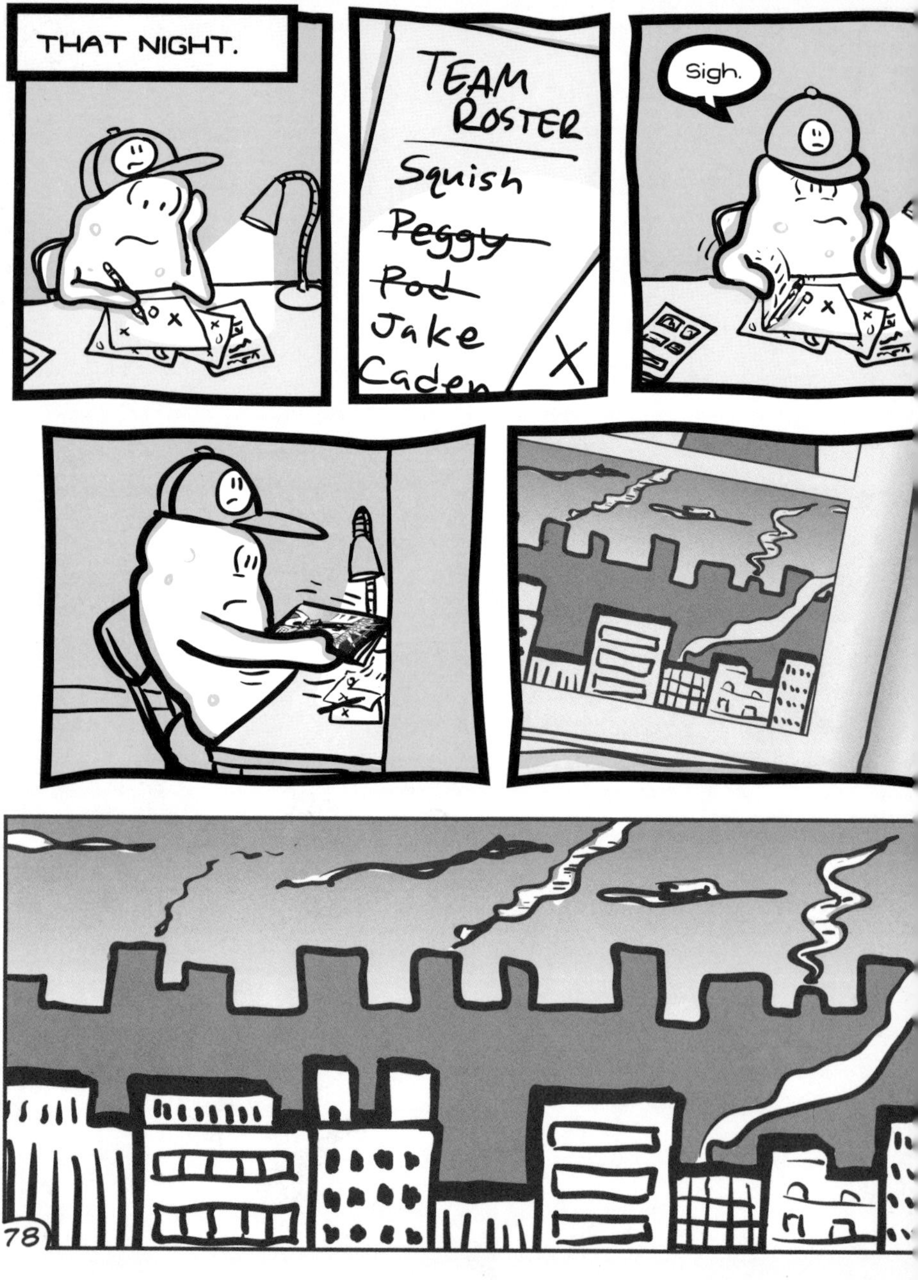
THAT NIGHT.
TEAM ROSTER
Squish
Peggy
Pod
Jake
Caden
Sigh.

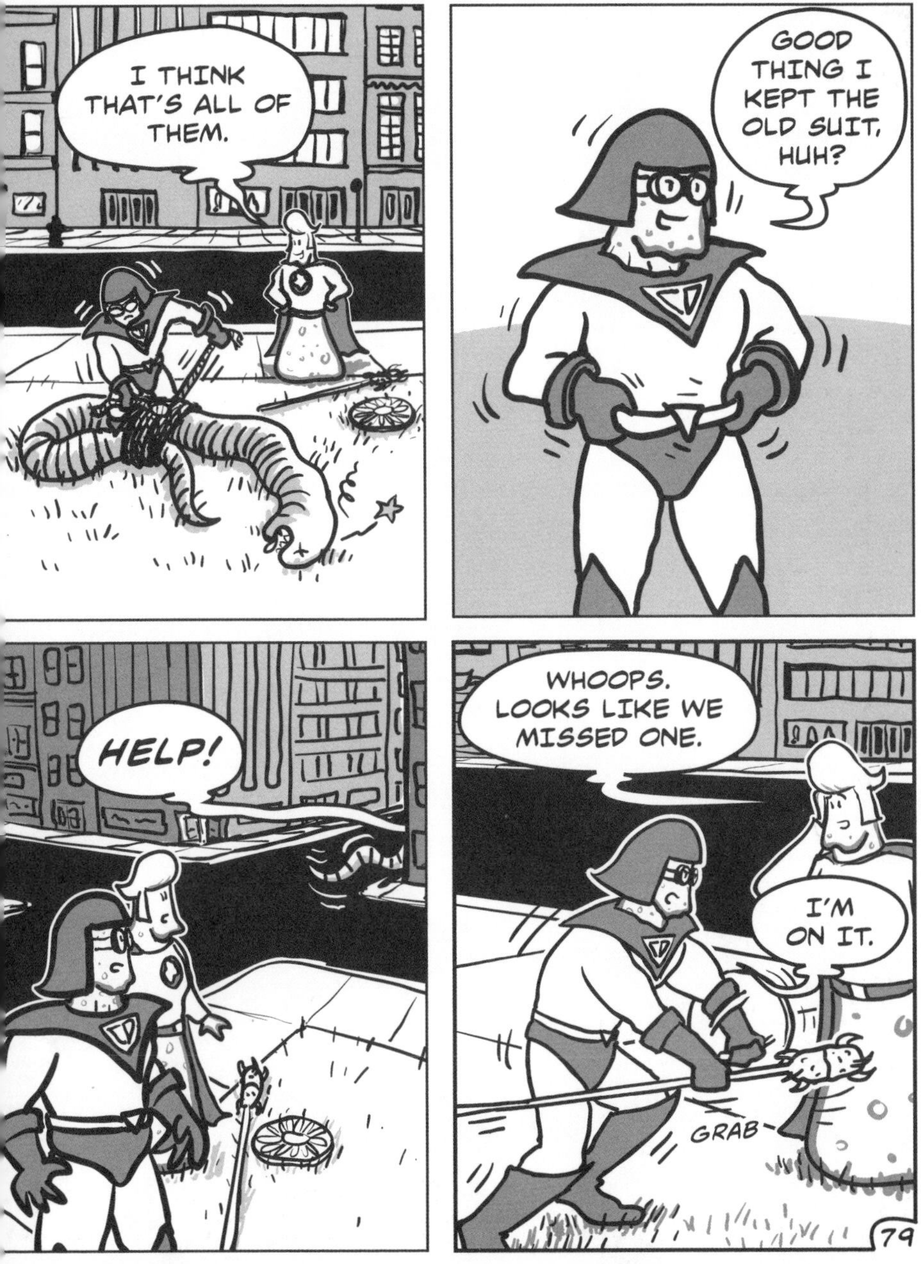
I THINK THAT'S ALL OF THEM.
GOOD THING I KEPT THE OLD SUIT, HUH?
HELP!
WHOOPS. LOOKS LIKE WE MISSED ONE.
I'M ON IT.
GRAB

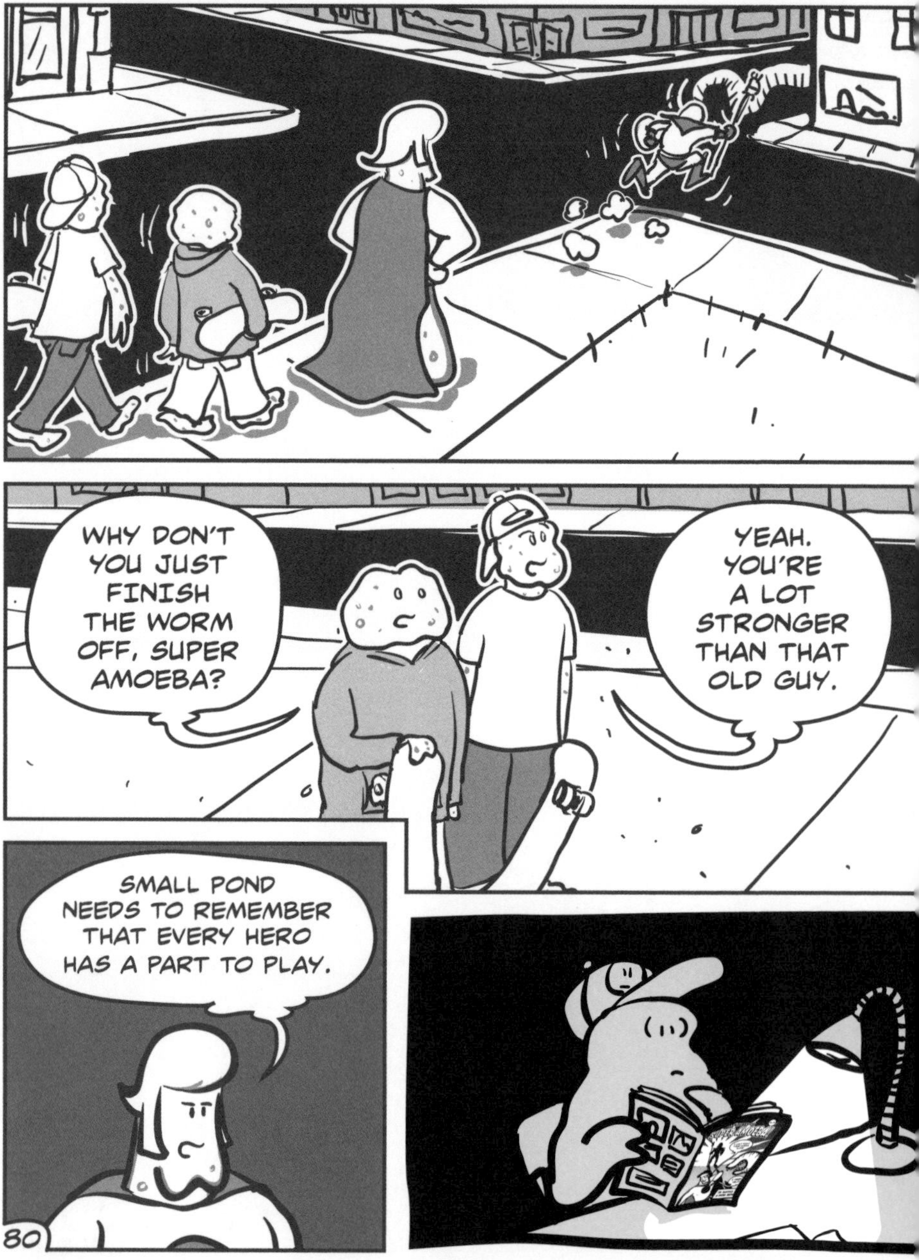
WHY DON'T YOU JUST FINISH THE WORM OFF, SUPER AMOEBA?
YEAH. YOU'RE A LOT STRONGER THAN THAT OLD GUY.
SMALL POND NEEDS TO REMEMBER THAT EVERY HERO HAS A PART TO PLAY.

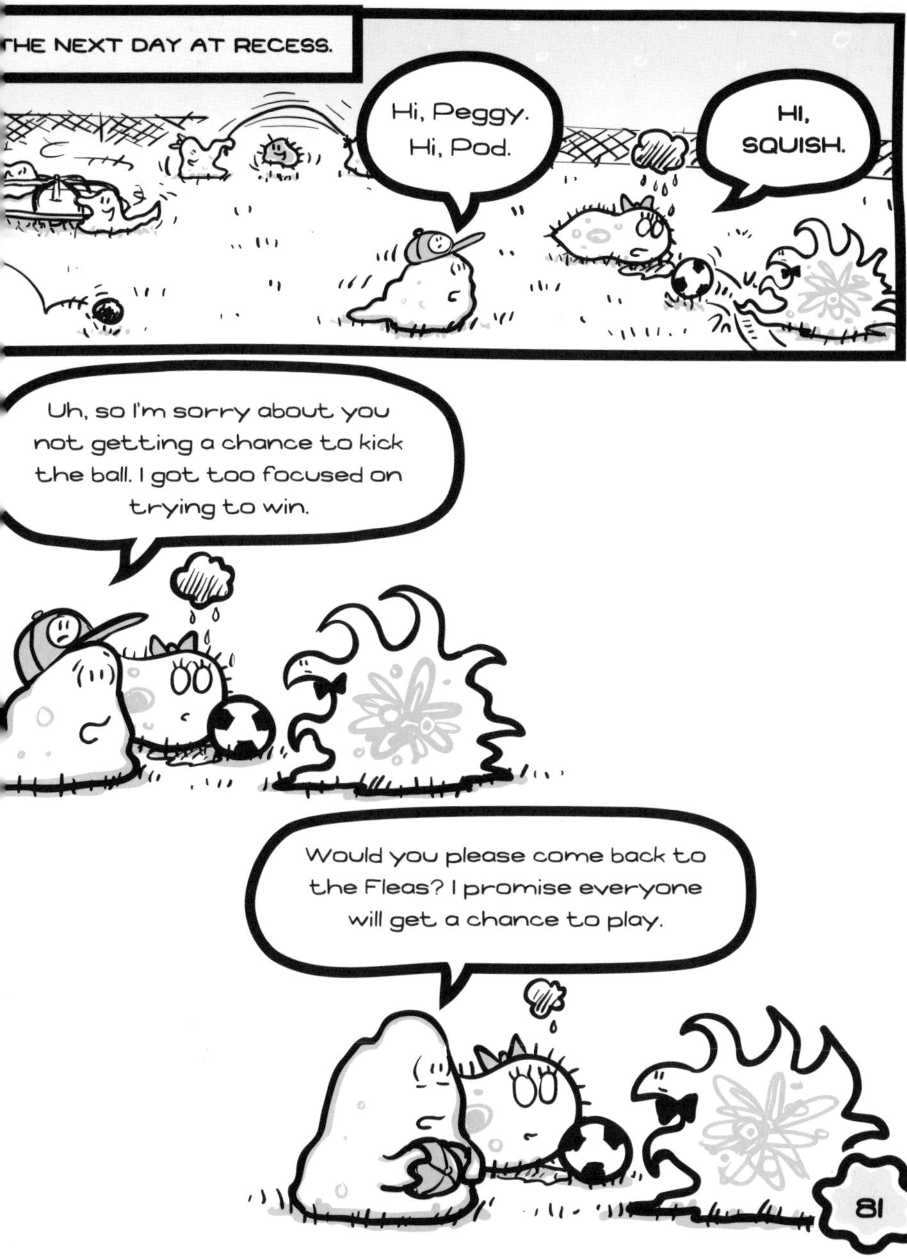

THE NEXT DAY AT RECESS.
Hi, Peggy. Hi, Pod.
HI, SQUISH.
Uh, so I'm sorry about you not getting a chance to kick the ball. I got too focused on trying to win.
Would you please come back to the Fleas? I promise everyone will get a chance to play.

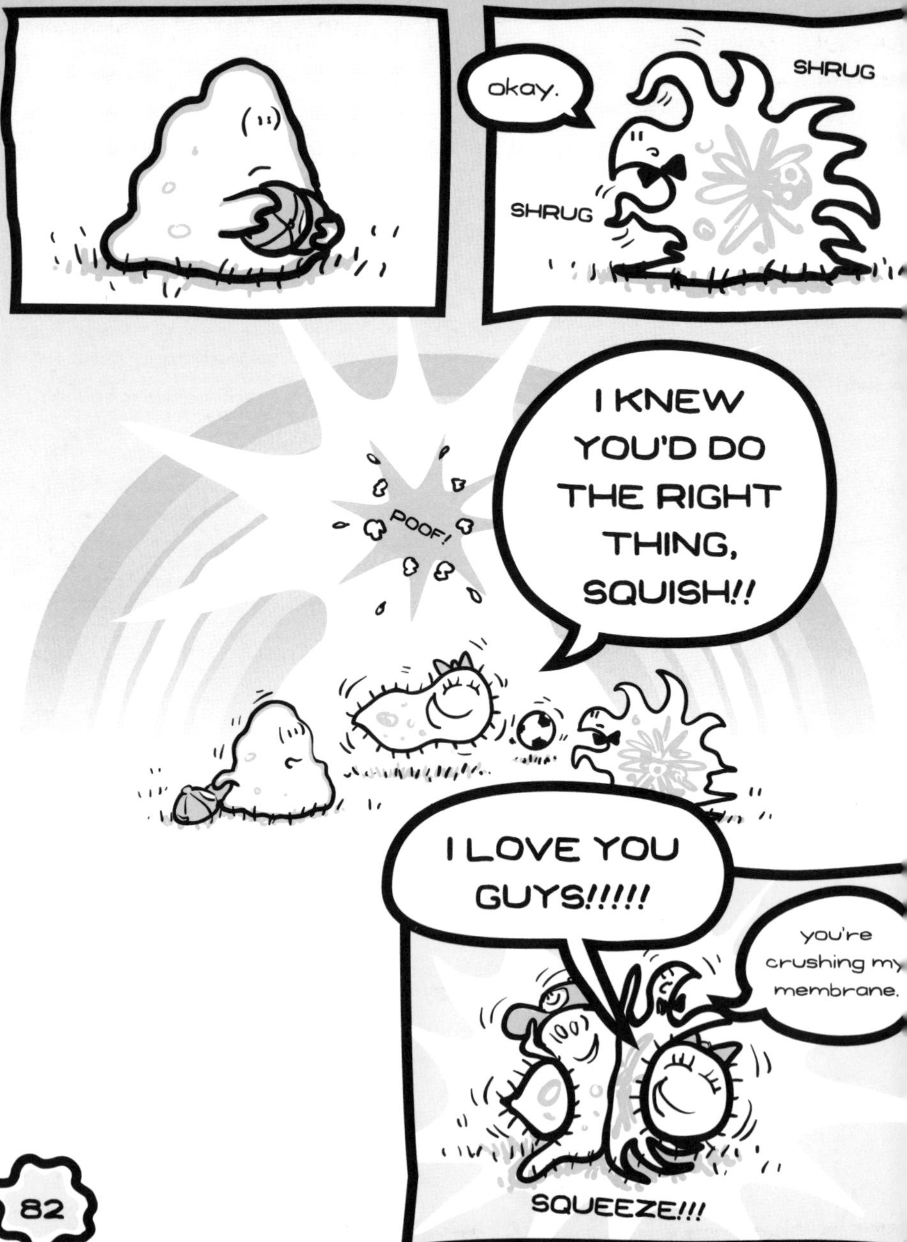
okay.
SHRUG
SHRUG
POOF!
I KNEW YOU'D DO THE RIGHT THING, SQUISH!!
I LOVE YOU GUYS!!!!!
you're crushing my membrane.
SQUEEZE!!!

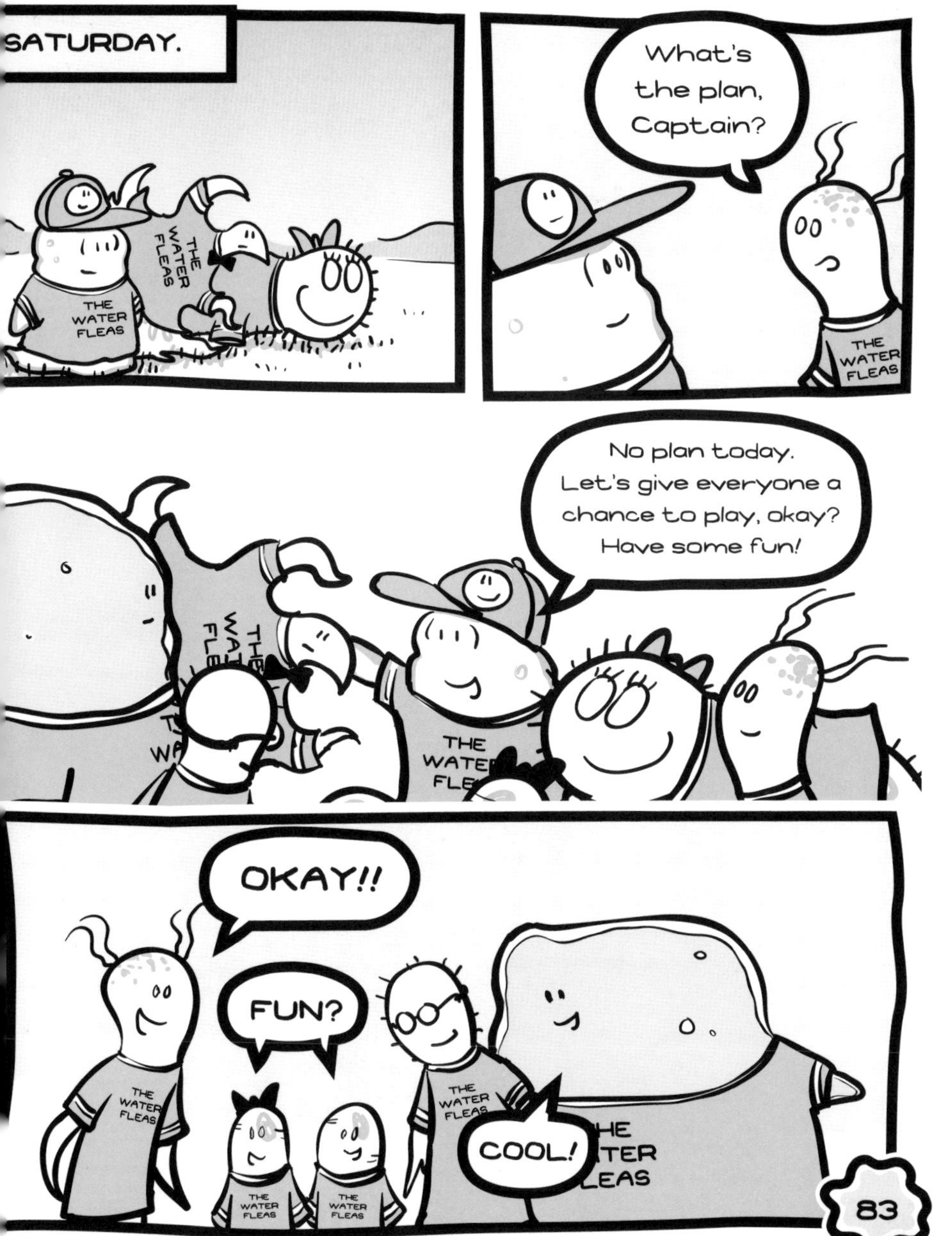

SATURDAY.
THE WATER FLEAS
What's the plan, Captain?
No plan today. Let's give everyone a chance to play, okay? Have some fun!
OKAY!!
FUN?
COOL!

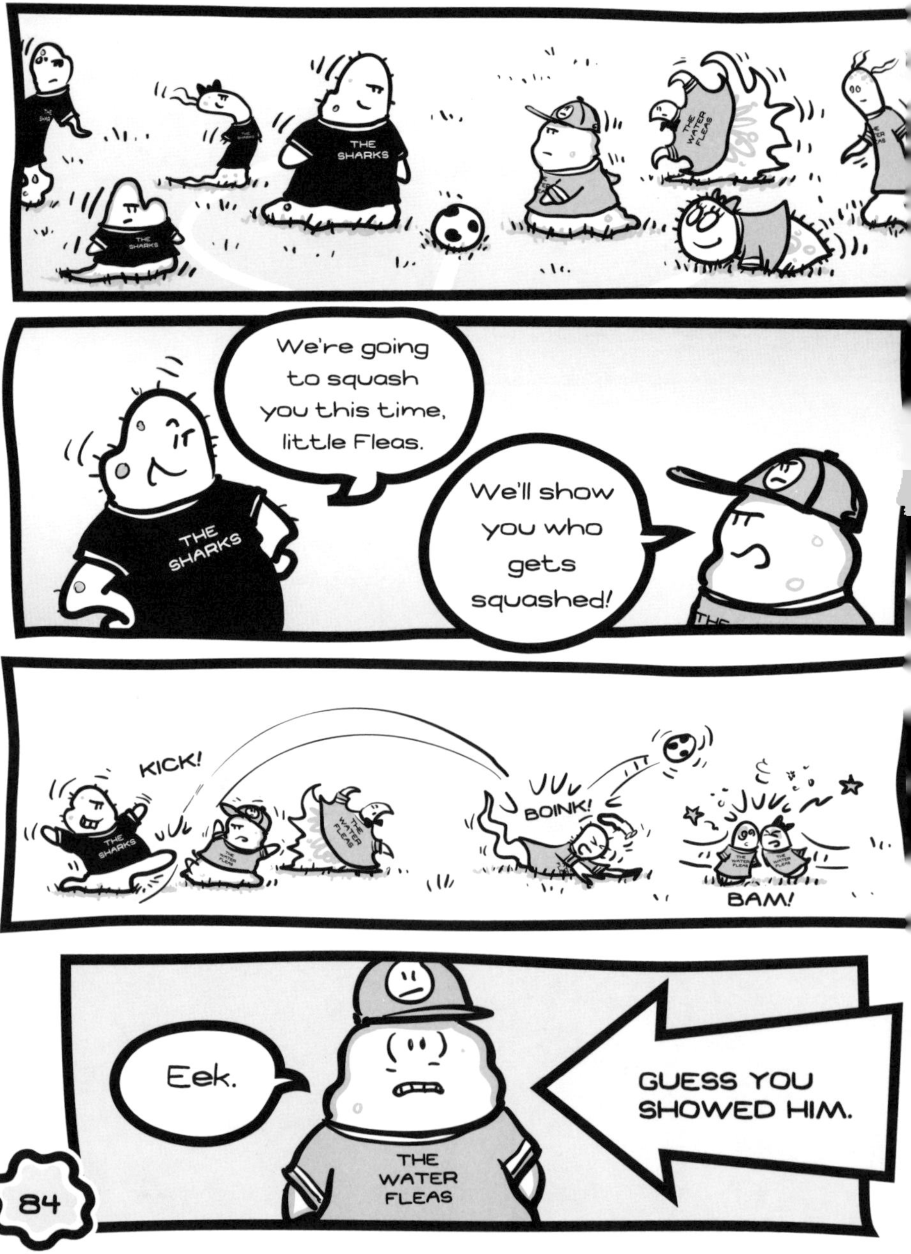
THE SHARKS
THE WATER FLEAS
We're going to squash you this time, little Fleas.
We'll show you who gets squashed!
KICK!
BOINK!
BAM!
Eek.
GUESS YOU SHOWED HIM.

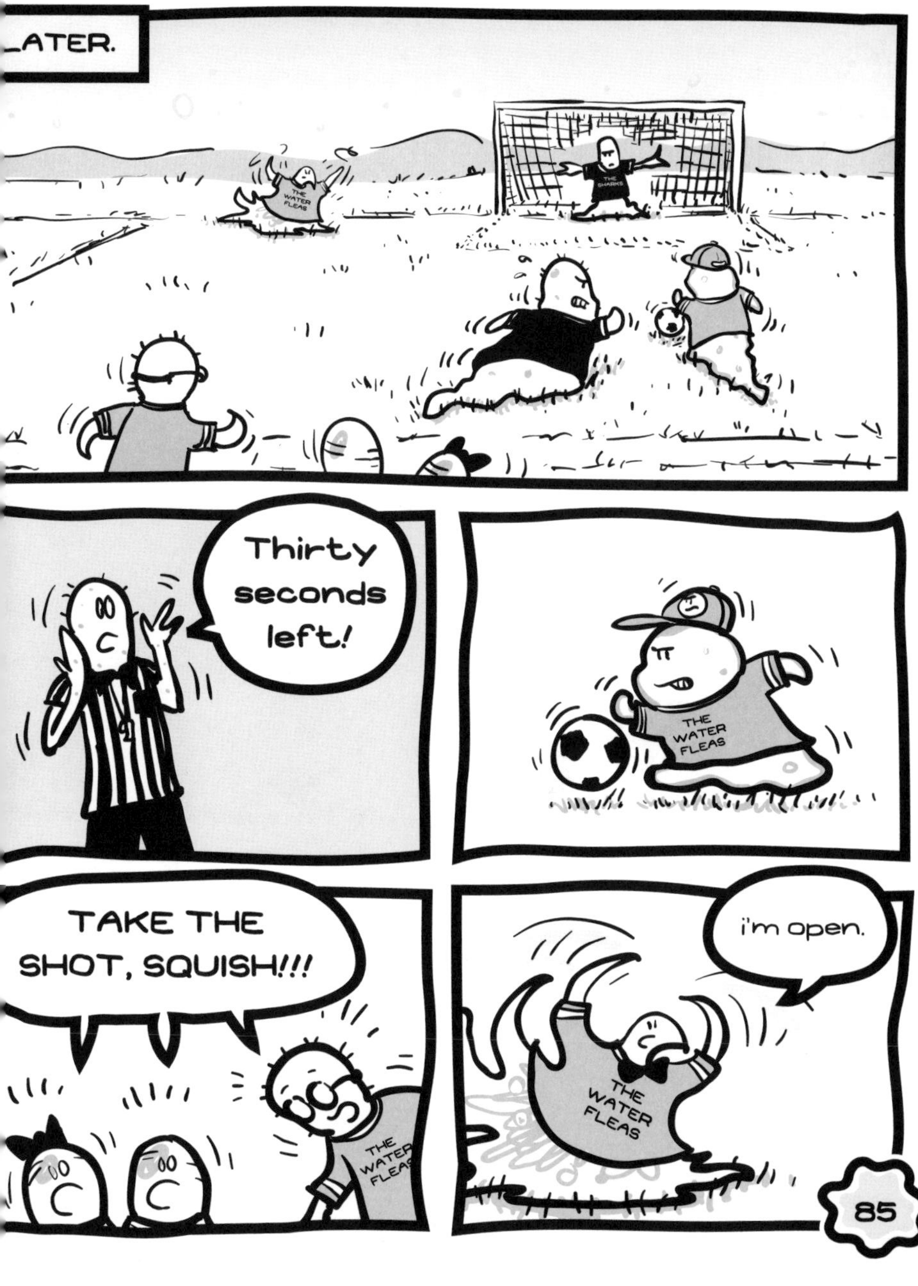
LATER.
THE WATER FLEAS
THE SHARKS
Thirty seconds left!
THE WATER FLEAS
TAKE THE SHOT, SQUISH!!!
THE WATER FLEAS
i'm open.
THE WATER FLEAS

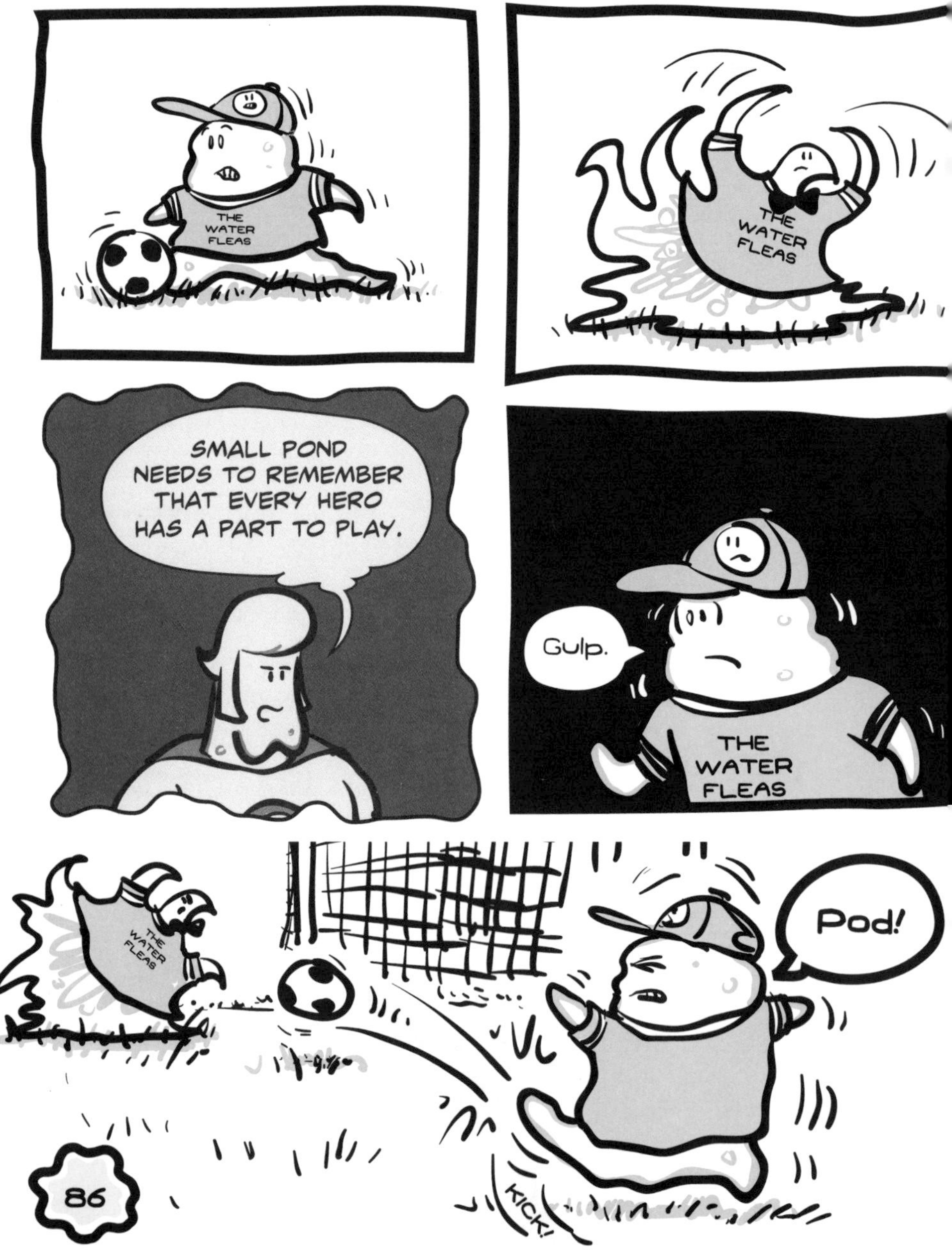
THE WATER FLEAS
THE WATER FLEAS
SMALL POND NEEDS TO REMEMBER THAT EVERY HERO HAS A PART TO PLAY.
Gulp.
THE WATER FLEAS
THE WATER FLEAS
Pod!
KICK!

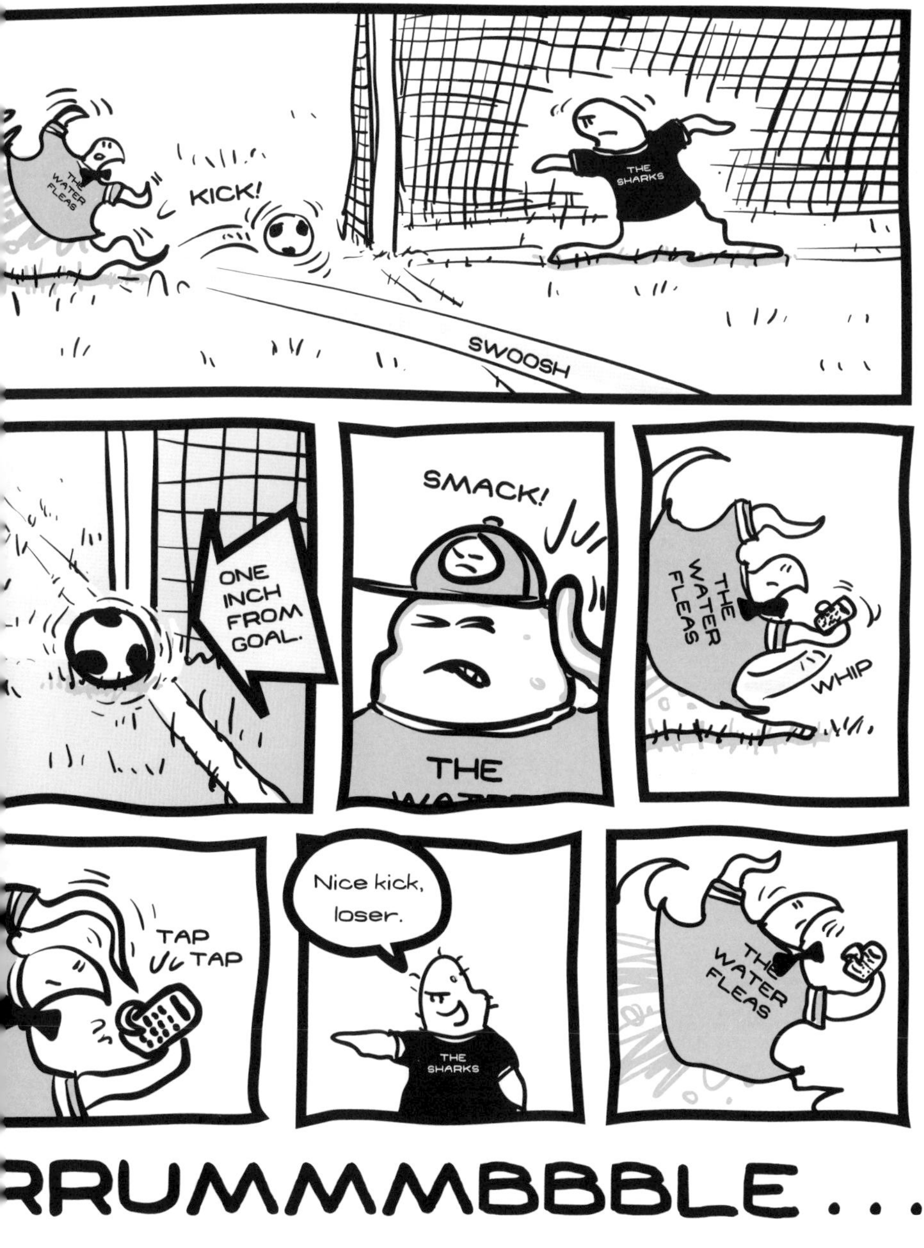
THE WATER FLEAS
KICK!
THE SHARKS
SWOOSH
ONE INCH FROM GOAL.
SMACK!
THE
THE WATER FLEAS
WHIP
TAP TAP
Nice kick, loser.
THE SHARKS
THE WATER FLEAS
RRUMMMBBBLE . . .

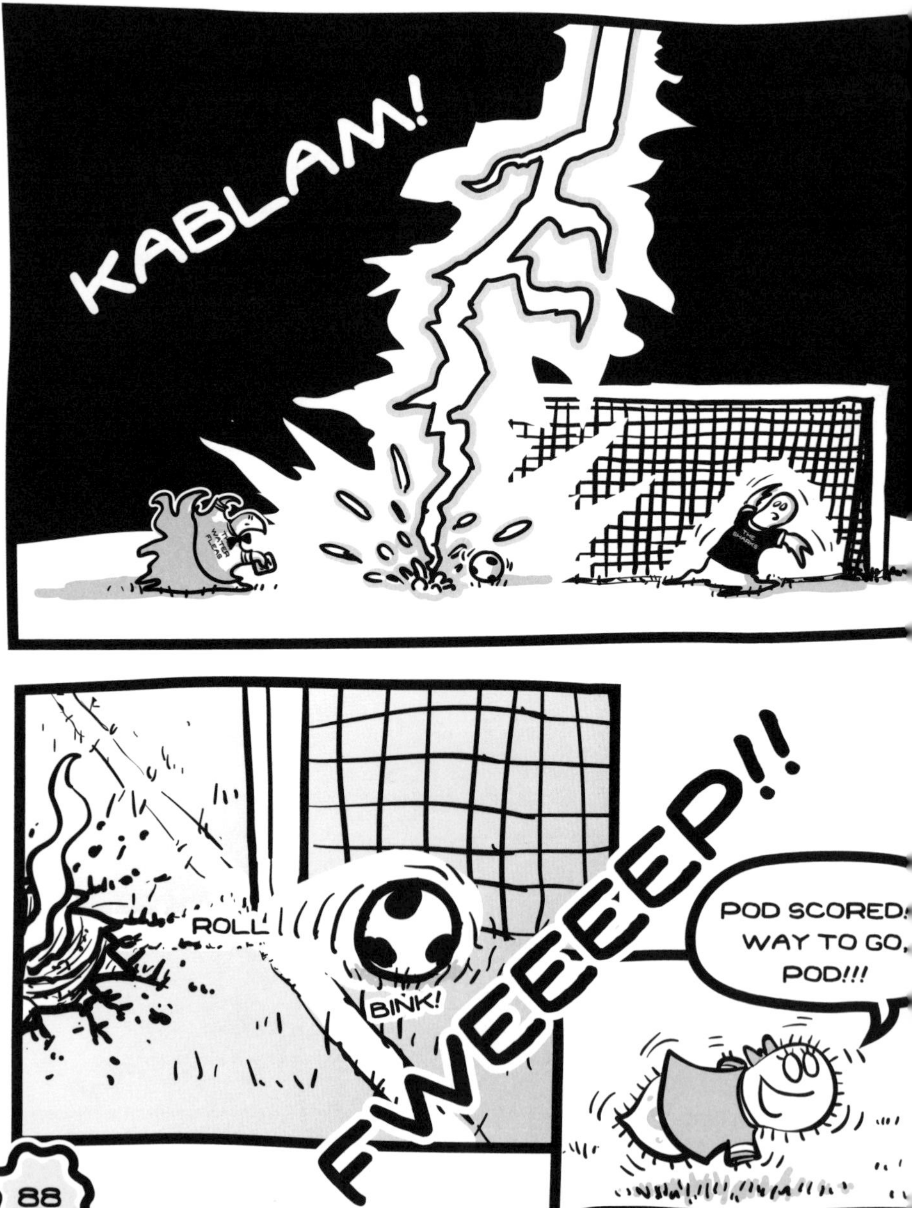

KABLAM!
ROLL
BINK!
FWEEEEEP!!
POD SCORED
WAY TO GO,
POD!!!

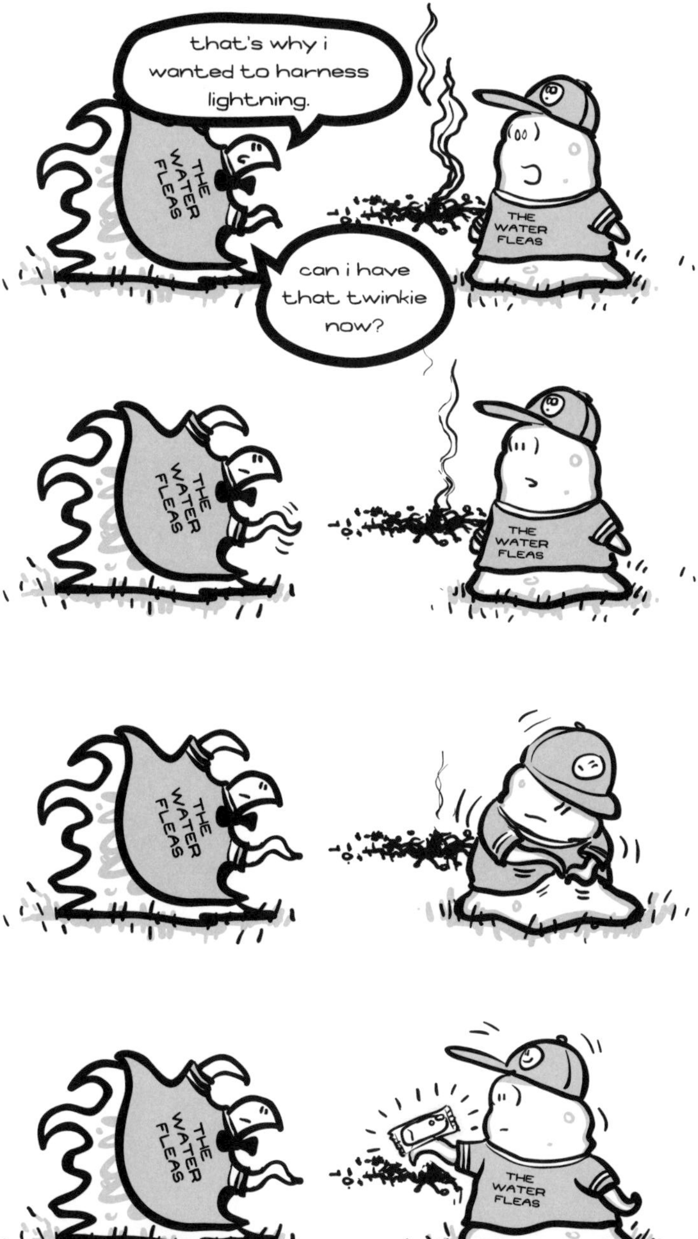
that's why i wanted to harness lightning.
THE WATER FLEAS
THE WATER FLEAS
can i have that twinkie now?
THE WATER FLEAS
THE WATER FLEAS
THE WATER FLEAS
THE WATER FLEAS
THE WATER FLEAS
THE WATER FLEAS

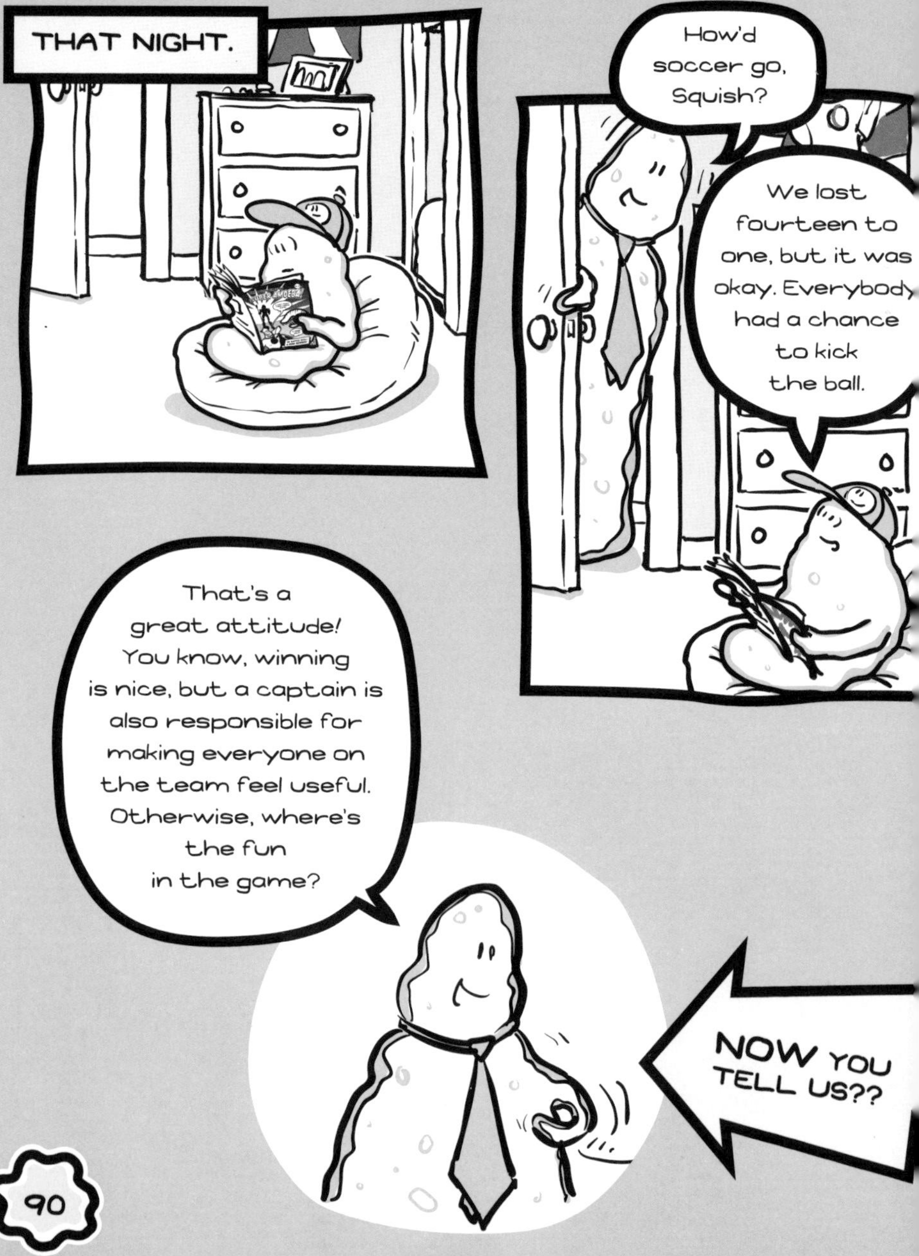
THAT NIGHT.
How'd soccer go, Squish?
We lost fourteen to one, but it was okay. Everybody had a chance to kick the ball.
That's a great attitude! You know, winning is nice, but a captain is also responsible for making everyone on the team feel useful. Otherwise, where's the fun in the game?
NOW YOU TELL US??

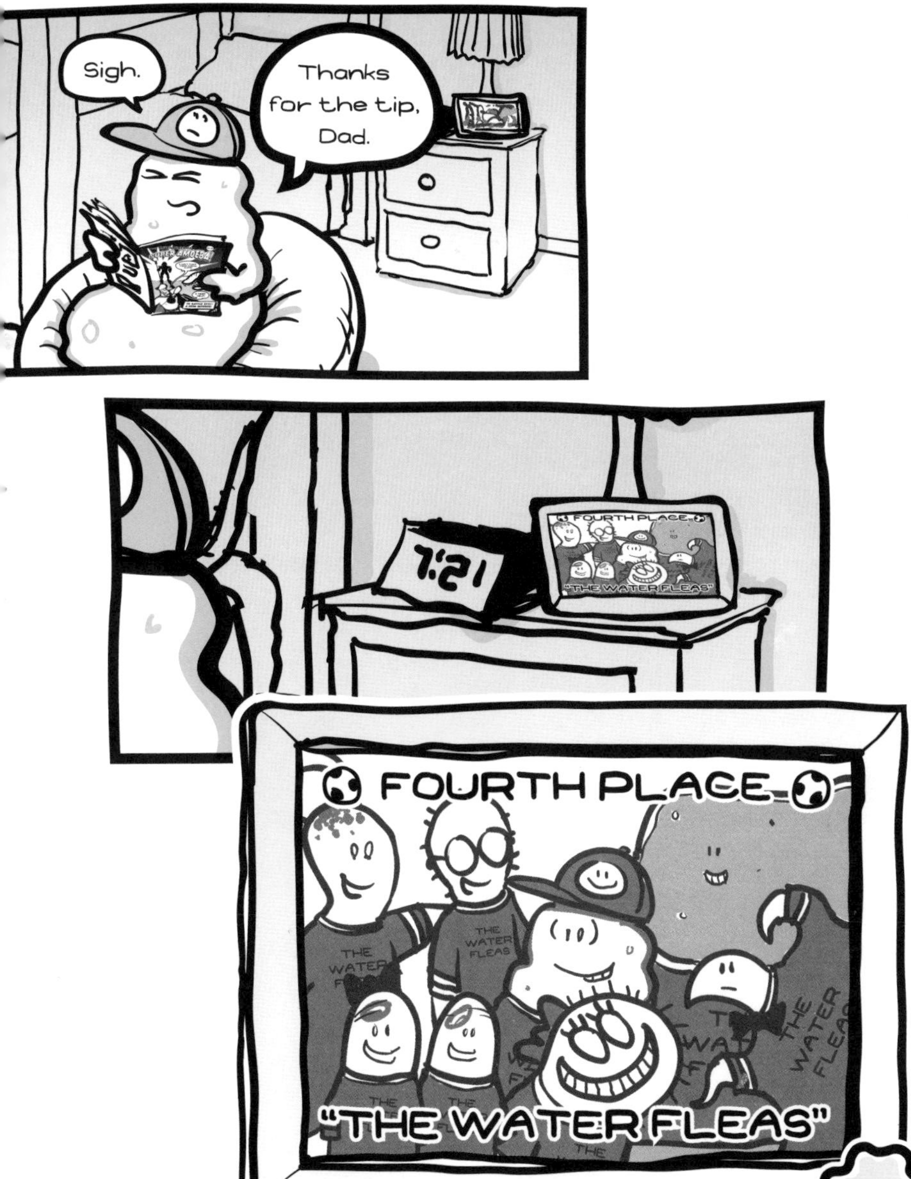
Sigh.
Thanks for the tip, Dad.
SUPER AMOEBA!
7:21
FOURTH PLACE
"THE WATER FLEAS"
FOURTH PLACE
"THE WATER FLEAS"

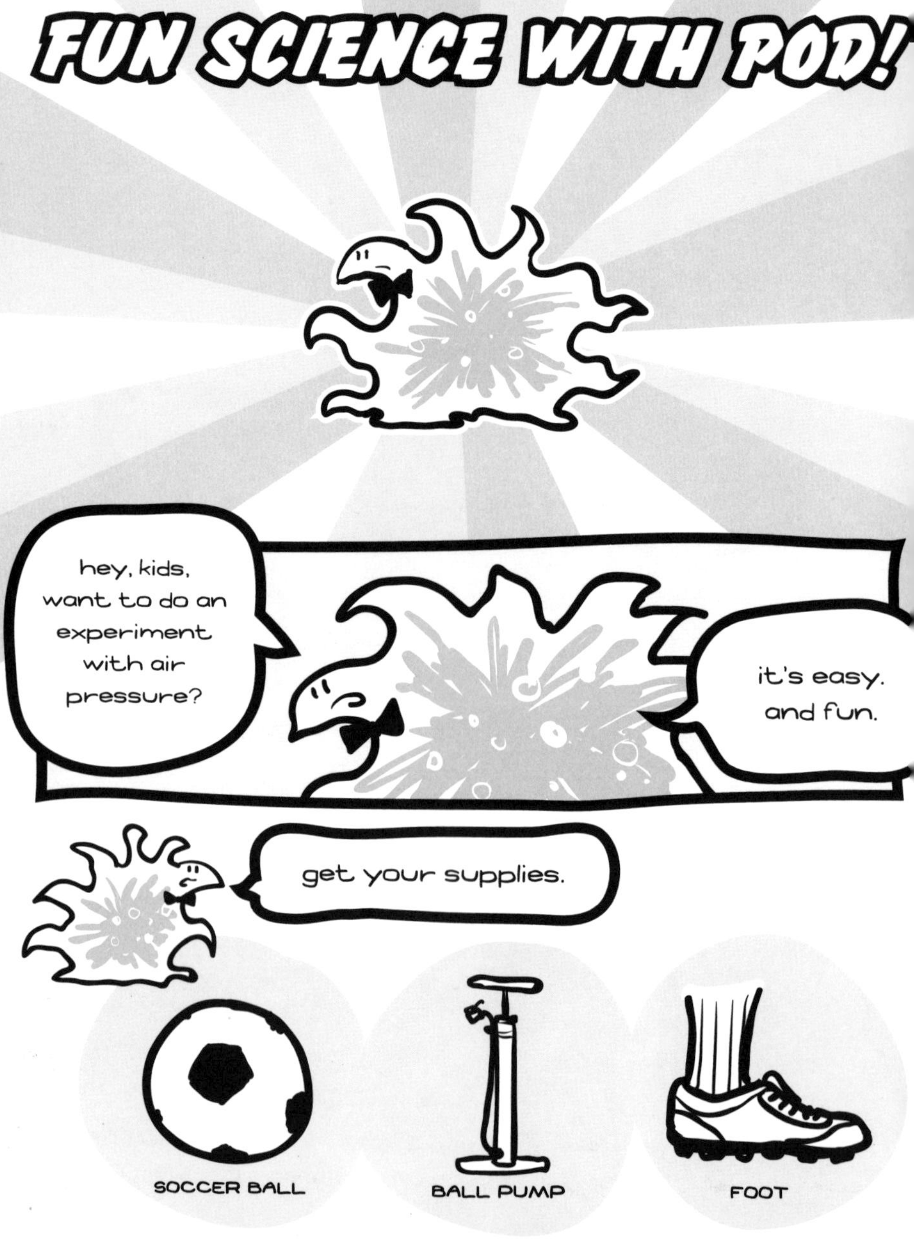
FUN SCIENCE WITH POD!
hey, kids, want to do an experiment with air pressure?
it's easy. and fun.
get your supplies.
SOCCER BALL
BALL PUMP
FOOT

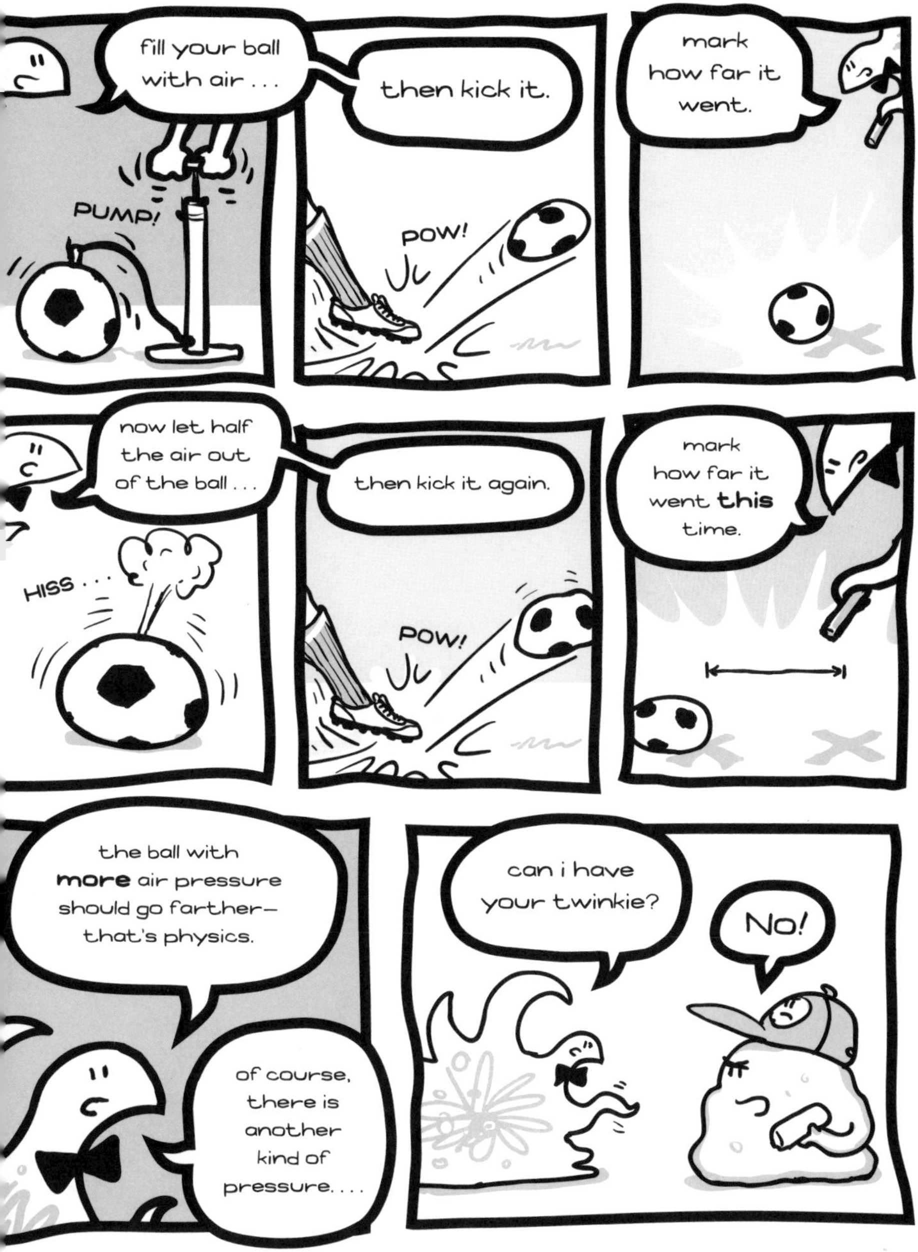

fill your ball with air . . .
PUMP!
then kick it.
POW!
mark how far it went.
now let half the air out of the ball . . .
HISS . . .
then kick it again.
POW!
mark how far it went **this** time.
the ball with **more** air pressure should go farther—that's physics.
of course, there is another kind of pressure. . . .
can i have your twinkie?
No!

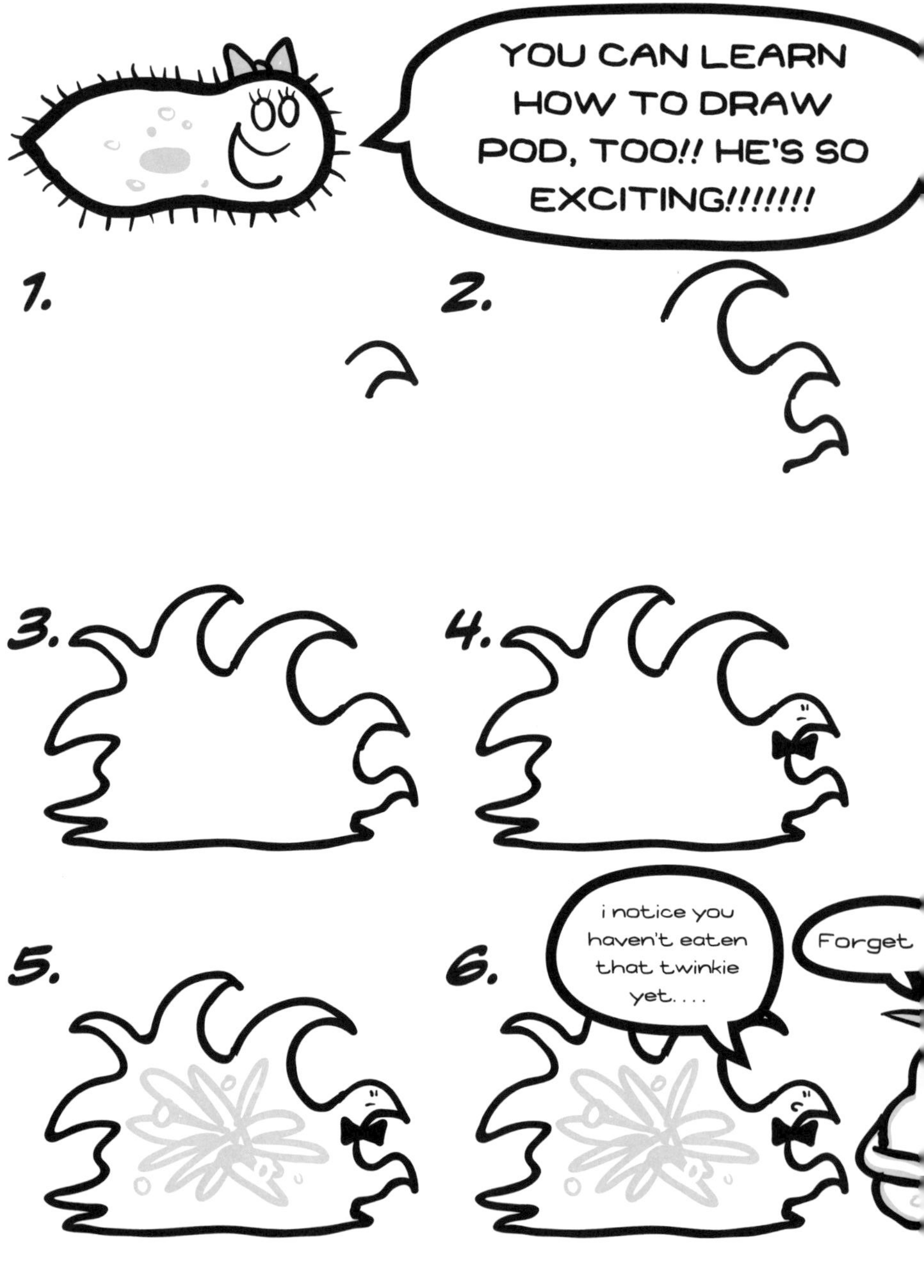
YOU CAN LEARN HOW TO DRAW POD, TOO!! HE'S SO EXCITING!!!!!!!!
1.
2.
3.
4.
5.
6.
i notice you haven't eaten that twinkie yet....
Forget

IT'S GREEN . . .
IT'S BLOBBY . . .
IT'S GROSS . . .

ʼs squish!

DON'T MISS SQUISH'S NEXT *AMAZING, ACTION-PACKED ADVENTURE!*

COMING IN MAY 2013!

squish
GAME ON!
NO. 5

FROM THE DARING DUO WHO BROUGHT YOU BABYMOUSE!
JENNIFER L. HOLM & MATTHEW HOLM

I am **NOT** a blob!

IF YOU LIKE SQUISH, YOU'LL LOVE BABYMOUSE

#1 BABYMOUSE: Queen of the World!

#2 BABYMOUSE: Our Hero

#3 BABYMOUSE: Beach Babe

#4 BABYMOUSE: Rock Star

#5 BABYMOUSE: Heartbreaker

#6 CAMP BABYMOUSE

#7 BABYMOUSE: Skater Girl

#8 BABYMOUSE: Puppy Love

#9 BABYMOUSE: Monster Mash

#10 BABYMOUSE: The Musical

#11 BABYMOUSE: Dragonslayer

#12 BABYMOUSE: Burns Rubber

#13 BABYMOUSE: Cupcake Tycoon

#14 BABYMOUSE: Mad Scientist

#15 A Very BABYMOUSE Christmas

#16 BABYMOUSE for President

And available in January 2013:

#17 EXTREME BABYMOUSE

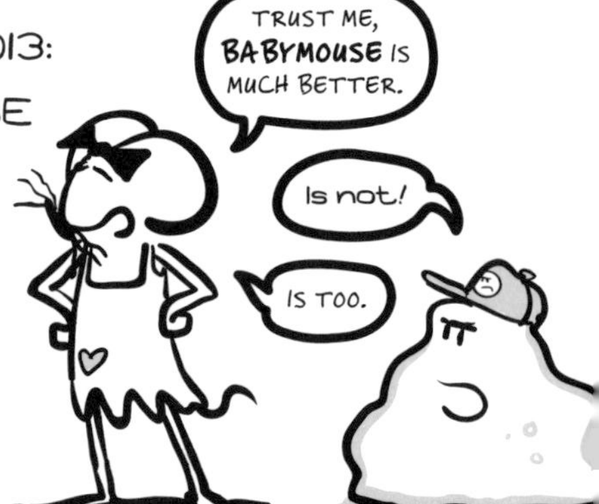
TRUST ME, BABYMOUSE IS MUCH BETTER.
Is not!
IS TOO.